C000186655

A Quiet Rebellion: Restitution

M. H. Thaung

Copyright © 2018 by Caroline May Hla Thaung

All rights reserved. This book or any portion thereof may not be reproduced or used in any manner whatsoever without the express written permission of the publisher except for the use of brief quotations in a book review.

This is a work of fiction. Any similarity to real persons, living or dead, is coincidental and not intended by the author.

Cover image by **Creative Covers**

ISBN-13: 978-1-912819-02-7 (ebook)
ISBN-13: 978-1-912819-03-4 (print)

mhthaung.com

A backwards glance

...We do know their society was conditioned to view those with psychic powers as unstable and dangerous, even referring to them as "cursed". Rather than being openly acknowledged and valued, enhanced recipients were secretly deployed by the governing Council, with severe penalties for revealing their abilities. Even worse, the officially mandated method for controlling such powers focussed on pain as a trigger. They had no idea of hygienic transfer of the agent, and powers were gained randomly, under uncontrolled circumstances, when infected feral carnivores happened to bite unprepared victims. It's no wonder recipients found the whole process so traumatic. I suppose we can't be too surprised at this descent into superstition. They had already lost much of the technology and knowledge their forebears brought with them. Even domestic animal power was out of the question, with all the taboos around "beasts".
Returning to the situation with Shelley...

From *Queen Eleanor: The Early Years* by D. Brigham

Chapter 1

ESCAPED PRISONER ON THE RAMPAGE
*Jonathan Shelley (56), a former captain of the guard, has
been concealing unnatural curse-bestowed powers. This
shocking discovery was made by the respected Scientist Jed
Silvers, who described Shelley's behaviour as "a shameful
breach of trust."*
*Shelley was apprehended and imprisoned, but subsequently
broke free from his cell. During his escape, he murdered the
prison guard Colin Bookman (27), who was married with
two young children. Shelley is extremely dangerous and
should not be approached. It is believed he is lethal from a
distance.*
He should be killed on sight.

Ascar Daily Informer

"Killed on sight!" Susanna gaped at the young captain
who'd barged into her barracks quarters and thrust the paper into her hand.

Lester nodded and started to pace, running his hands
through unkempt dark hair. The lamp flame flickered with
his movements and sent up a plume of greasy smoke. He
waved it away. "Yeah, I couldn't believe it. I'd no idea he
was even back in Ascar. What's going on?"

Halting, he grimaced at the misaligned buttons on his
brown jacket and undid them. One of them popped off, and
he scooped it up from the floor.

Prison. Murder. Should be killed on sight. Susanna took a deep breath to stave off dizziness. "Sit down. I can't think with you fidgeting like that."

"What's Silvers playing at?" Lester's voice rose. "Will he come after the rest of us? Are the other scientists in on it? What's the Council saying—"

"Lester!" The last thing she needed was neighbourly curiosity over a pre-dawn visitor. She grabbed his shoulder and pushed him towards the chair by her utility table. "Stop panicking, sit down and be quiet. Let me wake up properly. I need to think. *We* need to think."

A muscle in his unshaven jaw twitched, but he subsided onto the chair. Head bowed, he refastened his buttons with trembling fingers. Only his ragged breathing broke the silence while Susanna strove for calm. *Breathe in... breathe out...* She eased herself into an upright position on her battered chaise longue and smoothed out the news sheet beside her, face down.

Lester rubbed his hands over his face before straightening. "Sorry. I've been a bit jumpy lately. Using my power too much. He won't believe I can't influence—"

"You're not the only one with problems," she snapped. *Just tell Silvers where to shove his blackmail!* At his reproachful look, she sighed. "Sorry, I shouldn't take things out on you, just because you're the bearer of bad news."

"This is a setup, isn't it? I mean, Jonathan wouldn't kill someone, would he? Surely you'd know that sort of thing." His kale-green eyes pleaded with her.

"No, of course not." *But he did, once before.* A chill ran down her spine, but she shook her head. That was different, demanded by his duty. Jonathan never shirked his duty, no matter what it cost him. However, she'd do Lester no favours by shielding him from the unpleasant aspects of being a captain. "Well, any of us might be forced into it, to protect civilians. But not like this. Not Jonathan."

"Like if someone attacked me, or threatened someone else's safety? I suppose even you might..."

Susanna pursed her lips. Had she been so naïve at his age? "We have more important things to address. Such as, why was Jonathan imprisoned? The Council must have approved it. It can't be due to 'concealing unnatural powers'." At Lester's blank look, she added, "That's just their usual cover story for the ignorant. What happened between his departure for Maldon and now?"

"He let something slip? Got into a fight?" His brow wrinkled. "Or maybe Silvers planted some evidence against him?"

"I can certainly believe your last suggestion—" She gasped, a hand to her lips. Of course. Jonathan had even told her he'd used his power to give the odious scientist a nosebleed. That was the day before he left Ascar. It would take a mind reader to prove he'd done it deliberately, but Silvers wasn't stupid. "Silvers bears him particular animosity. I'm sure he had a hand in this. And that article credits him for the investigation."

"So, now what? Are we in danger as well?" He drummed his fingers on the waxed tabletop that Isabel had bled on earlier. At Susanna's frown, his hand stilled.

"I suppose it's a good thing Jonathan didn't spend much time in the city. Silvers is unlikely to know we're his friends. It's probably safe to investigate, if we're prudent."

Lester's eyebrows rose. "I'm one of Jonathan's friends? He didn't seem to—"

"Allies, then. The point is, Silvers won't target us."

Hopefully. "He can't possibly imprison all captains and other workers with powers. Even if the Council have let Jonathan's arrest slip by, they'll only allow the scientists so much authority over us before stepping in." The scientists might demand complete power over the afflicted for their research schemes, but the Council didn't claim such lofty motivations. They'd rather use those with powers to bolster their governance. And thank the Settlers for that. Susanna would work until she dropped rather than spending middle age and beyond as an experimental subject in the Keep.

"What about Jonathan's theory, that Silvers is trying to curse more people?" Lester picked a loose thread from his buttonhole. "Maybe Jonathan found something out and was imprisoned to stop him from sharing it. Maybe whatever he discovered was so important that he thought it worth, er, killing someone over it."

Her chest tightened. Lester could be right. Jonathan's duty had required a killing: to maintain the secrecy of powers. If he'd uncovered a scheme to produce and abuse more people with powers, how desperate might he have become? If a prison guard stood between him and some necessary—

"What happens now?"

She scowled. "Don't rush me. We have to plan carefully, not run around like headless fowl."

He flinched. "No, of course not. I mean, what will the Council and scientists do? And the guards?"

Oh. She glanced past her laden bookshelves towards the window with its shabby chintz curtains. "Now that it's getting light, squads of guards will go out to search." She swallowed. "With orders to eliminate him, it seems. There must be a cover-up if they're not even attempting a capture."

Lester raised a finger. "Why not send captains too? We

know about powers, after all."

"If they *really* think he's a dangerous murderer, we're too valuable to risk. Silvers' plans aside, our numbers don't increase quickly, and most of us don't have powers useful in a fight. And... they might be concerned we'd sympathise with him. Because we have powers of our own."

"They think we might help him instead? But as the regular guards are no wiser, they'll see him more like..." He regarded Susanna's face.

"Yes, like a monster." Her voice wobbled on the last word.

Lester studied his hands while Susanna pulled a handkerchief from her dressing gown pocket and wiped her eyes. Decades of responsible service might not be enough to protect a captain if those under his command believed him a danger. And Jonathan had never cultivated friends.

When she could trust her voice to remain steady, she spoke again. "Genuinely rogue captains are almost unheard of, and best dealt with by other captains acting together."

"Like Denton? The guy whose rooms I moved into? Jonathan told me the story."

She shuddered. They'd only recalled her to the city after that incident, but the lurid details still permeated the captains' lounge. The man's abuse of his mind control ability, murder of his colleague and gruesome execution were a cautionary tale to all.

"Jonathan's nothing like Denton." And neither was Lester, even though he had the same power. Susanna wouldn't let the young man follow the same destructive path. She folded her hands, took a breath, picked a mundane point to focus on. "Though, as with Denton, they'll impound his assets. If he's deemed guilty, proceeds from the sale of possessions are passed on as compensation to victims or their families."

"I see." Lester slumped. "Sounds like someone could make a nice little racket out of it, picking us off one by one."

She regarded the crystal flowers glinting on her shelves. They probably weren't worth much to a collector. Her bank account, on the other hand... "You're right, especially if nobody examines the system too closely. If someone's finding laws to exploit, this is definitely a bigger matter than Jonathan. In addition to finding out what's happening, we need to sound out the other captains. Keep your ears open, see if you can chat with some of the regular guards."

He brightened. "I can do that, maybe at mealtimes in the mess. I also play cards with them a couple of times a week."

"You would. I hope you don't cheat."

He reddened. "Of course not. You're the mind reader in this room. Anyway, I don't play as much as I used to. Having them call me 'Sir' is kind of awkward."

"You'll get used to it. We'd better keep up with our practice sessions. Strengthening your power could give us an edge." She rubbed her eyes, suppressing a yawn. Isabel's visit had already robbed her of sleep. "There's something odd about Staunton too. I should look into him. He more or less told Jonathan that Silvers was blackmailing him, driving him to drink. But Isabel mentioned seeing Staunton in good shape at some palace reception." No need to mention patching her up from a beast injury, or wiping bloodstains off the table.

Lester's eyes widened. "Isabel? I know you said they wouldn't send any captains after him, but if she went..."

Susanna's mouth dried up. Jonathan would have no

chance. She ordered her shoulders to relax. "Isabel keeps her own counsel. She wouldn't burn anyone without thinking. If it came to a confrontation between them, they would at least talk first." *Though she didn't talk to Denton.*

"I hope so." Lester sighed and stood. "I wish I was back in the regular guard and didn't know any of this. But I can't turn the clock back, can I? I'll head over to the mess now, try to catch some breakfast gossip. See you in the practice room."

"Before you go..." After rummaging in her sewing box, she handed him needle and thread, almost smiling at his stunned expression. Then she checked the corridor was empty and ushered him out.

Jonathan's muscles burned as he slogged through the tunnel, patches of glowing mushrooms on its walls the only marker of his progress away from the city. The silence was broken by his laboured breathing and the uneven *scuff, scuff* of his stolen city guard shoes. There was an occasional *thunk* as he kicked a stray stone, and it bounced off the rails on the floor. It felt like he'd been walking forever along this escape route. But he couldn't have been walking long enough if he hadn't arrived on the other side of the Cleon Mountains and emerged into the northern fields. It should take two hours. What time was it? He had no timepiece.

Willing strength into his trembling legs, he increased his pace. But after a few steps he stumbled, catching himself with a hand on the tunnel's wall. His hand squashed a mushroom, slipped on the smooth surface and left a luminous smear. Great, confirmation for anyone coming after him.

He stopped, leaned forwards with his hands on his

knees and took a few deep breaths. If he chanced sitting down for a rest, he might not get up again. He touched the sabre at his side for reassurance. It wasn't much use against a flechette gun, but one way or other, he'd make sure he wasn't recaptured. Not just for his own sake, but for Tabitha's. All he could do now for that poor cursed girl detained in the Keep was to stay away, so she wouldn't be drawn further into his troubles. If he were gone, in whatever meaning of the word, Silvers would have no reason to mistreat her. At least, not to use her as a hold over Jonathan. Maybe Susanna could look after Tabitha, train her and help her achieve a better life. His vision blurred. He might not see either of them again.

How much of a head start had he managed? Once they discovered his escape, they'd send guards after him, who would follow him in a pedalcart. He'd hear the rails humming. He cocked an ear. Nothing so far. A fit young man could easily outpace a pedalcart. But he was neither young nor fit. *I'm unfit. These shoes don't fit. How fitting.* A harsh laugh escaped his dry throat. He choked it off and staggered on.

He certainly couldn't outrun anyone, so his only option was to hide. And for that, well, he'd need to reach the end of the tunnel. *You know how to walk, Shelley. Just keep going.*

How could everything have gone so wrong? After leaving that cursed young boy in Maldon instead of hauling him back to Ascar, he'd expected resistance from the Council. But he'd not even got as far as their meeting room. There'd been no chance to make his case before Silvers snatched him away from what should have been a routine post-mission interview. *Some routine.* Had he been waiting for Jonathan to make a slip? The audacity of the man!

As Jonathan moved further along the tunnel, an ache manifested in his right thigh, underneath the bandage. His breathing quickened. The drug was wearing off: the painkiller they'd administered after removing a sample of his flesh. Not that Silvers cared whether prisoners were suffering. However, no pain meant no power, and therefore no way to escape. Someone would have been in to give another dose by now, and they would have found him gone.

And they'd have discovered the dead guard, whose clothes he was now wearing. How had he died? Settlers' sakes, Jonathan certainly hadn't killed him.

Silvers... *scuff*... drug... *scuff*... He'd seen Silvers give the guard a drink. Had he poisoned the man? But why? It made no sense. If he wanted Jonathan to escape, why imprison him in the first place?

Think, Shelley. What if Silvers hadn't meant for him to escape? The result of that poisoning would be a dead guard and no obvious signs of violence. Jonathan would still be in his cell, unable to use his power without the stimulus of pain. Or so Silvers must have thought, not knowing Jonathan had found another way to activate his power. He'd claim Jonathan had killed the guard somehow and would never be safe for release. The bamboozled authorities would ask no questions. That would guarantee Silvers a source of "cursed flesh" for as long as Jonathan survived.

Dammit, when Jonathan visited Staunton just a few weeks ago, the retired scientist had even suggested an extract of cursed flesh might transmit the curse to others. If Staunton could think of the idea, so could Silvers. Did Silvers plan to deliberately curse large numbers of people and exploit their powers? That fitted with what Jonathan knew of his arguments, so at odds with those of his colleagues.

The other scientists might be stick in the muds, but at least they weren't abusing victims. *I should have trusted Lady Nelson.* If mass cursing was Silvers' plan, he had to be stopped.

But what could Jonathan do? He was a fugitive. With no clear plan or destination, he stumbled onwards.

Chapter 2

Relieved of Lester's presence, Susanna locked the door and pulled a bottle of brandy from a cabinet. Hands shaking, she poured a shot and gulped it down. A risky indulgence, but she could get away with it. If her control slipped, and her mind-reading power manifested, she could let people's thoughts wash over her without anyone noticing. That was one advantage she had over Jonathan since his power had more obvious physical effects. Her gaze dropped to the tabletop where he'd moved her ornaments around while she assessed how he did it. That had been the last time they'd met: naïvely, she'd looked forward to his return.

While the brandy slipped down to her empty stomach, giving her the illusion of warmth, she picked up her flower press and opened it. Inside were two pink roses she'd kept from the bouquet he'd brought that night. How ironic that she'd pressed them flat, like his affection had been for so many years. *What have you done, Jonathan?*

... murdered the prison guard...

No. She wouldn't believe it. There had to be more to it than that. Even for those who didn't know him, his care for Tabitha after sending her to the Keep should show he had a conscience. He was innocent of murder, and Susanna would prove it.

Approaching the problem from another angle, what was

the real reason behind his imprisonment? Surely Jonathan wouldn't be foolhardy enough to bait Silvers without considering the consequences? She closed the flower press and pursed her lips. He might, at that, like he had done with the nosebleed. But even if he had, Silvers could only retaliate by due process: he wasn't the monarch, who was above all laws. If his actions were criminal, she'd find out and make him regret it. There had to be a reason, and one bigger than Silvers and Jonathan.

After donning a uniform, she inspected herself in the mirror. Although the captains' dark brown garb commanded respect from regular guards—and wariness from civilians—creased clothing would detract from her authority. She peered at her face. No more wrinkles than usual for a middle-aged woman, and her eyes weren't particularly reddened. Lifting her chin, she summoned a veneer of composure which would have to carry her through the day. Time for breakfast.

The route to the captains' lounge took her along the corridor that led to Jonathan's rooms. Her steps faltered. A handful of guards clustered around his doorway, loading crates onto trolleys. Low-pitched conversation sounded from inside, and a woman's voice rose above them.

Susanna stopped and peeked into the room she'd never entered. With half the contents gone, its austereness contrasted even more starkly with the cluttered cosiness of her own quarters. Despite ten years on a captain's salary, he'd not even bothered replacing the rudimentary furniture with items more to his taste.

Emily, neat in her housekeepers' dress, stood with hands on hips. She glared at a guard who held a pair of dark grey trousers. "I don't care what Scientist Silvers says about it. Uniforms are Crown property. If you disagree with me, young man, feel free to do your own laundry from now on!"

"What's happening?" murmured Susanna to the nearest guard in the hallway.

The lad straightened up and saluted, bringing a clenched right fist to his chest. "I'm not sure, ma'am. We were told to empty Shelley's rooms and deliver everything to Scientist Silvers. But Emily—we all know Emily, of course, wonderful woman—is saying we can't take the uniforms." He held a paper out. "See? This Council document gives Scientist Silvers authority to remove all of Shelley's assets. Doesn't it?"

Sighing, she read the document. City brown or convoy grey, what did uniforms matter when Jonathan's whole life was being torn apart? *Hmm.* At least the wording gave her an opportunity to strike a blow against Silvers, no matter how insignificant. Susanna raised her voice to address the guards in the room. "Emily is correct. You may not take the uniforms. They belong to the Crown and not to Captain Shelley. The same applies to the furniture." The next words stuck in her craw. "But you may remove everything else."

Head high, back straight, she walked away. *I'm sorry, Jonathan. I'm failing you already.*

She arrived in the captains' lounge to find two colleagues sitting opposite each other at the dining table. David usually worked on convoy, his burly frame backing up Crown authority over recalcitrant rural officials. Richard was based in the city, where his ability to sense the location of an item was valued in crime investigations. A quick glance confirmed the overstuffed armchairs and writing desks to be unoccupied, and this early in the day nobody was playing billiards or darts.

David raised an eyebrow as she approached the table, but he didn't pause from shovelling lumps of porridge into his mouth. Susanna's stomach spasmed. How could he eat that stuff? And so much of it? Though as one of the few captains with no power of his own, he relied more on physical prowess than the others did. It would certainly take a lot of food to maintain that physique.

"I'd never have believed it of him," said Richard, inclining his fine-boned head towards Susanna. He placed his fork on the plate, which held the remains of a mushroom omelette, and dabbed his lips with a napkin. He frowned at his empty glass then tapped the service bell with a manicured finger.

Susanna winced at the sound. She really hadn't had much sleep. "You're talking about Jonathan?"

They paused while a waiter entered the room. Richard ordered rhubarb juice, and Susanna requested a pot of tea and some toast. David, still eating, waved a hand at his empty toast rack.

After the waiter departed, Richard continued. "Yes, of course Jonathan. Shocking news. Some of the story is a cover up, of course..."

Thank the Settlers. It seemed not everyone was against Jonathan. Perhaps she could mention—

"... though I wonder what made him unstable."

Unstable? The waiter returned with their orders, and she focussed on her teacup until he left the room.

She spread jam on her toast in an uneven layer and took a bite. She chewed and forced it down. "Jonathan's perfectly stable. What are you talking about?"

Richard sipped his juice and wrinkled his nose. "From what I heard, Silvers approached the Council about some incidents. Seems Jonathan hadn't been controlling his powers too well, even admitting it himself. They agreed he should be detained if it happened again. So I presume that's what happened. Surely you would know more than me about him, given the nature of your, ah, association."

Association? She drew in a sharp breath, then coughed. Richard must have meant her mind reading, which was a theoretical advantage when interacting with people. However, in addition to the usual trigger of pain, physical contact was best if she wanted more than simple lie detection. That wasn't something mind readers bruited about. "There's nothing wrong with his control." Seeing David pause mid-bite to stare at her, she moderated her voice. "I observed him using his power, the day before he left Ascar on a mission. He was absolutely fine."

David pushed his empty bowl away and reached for the toast. "I've always got on well with him. Means well. Straight talking. Practical. So why not take his medicine, put up with his detention until they let him out again? Did something push him over the edge?"

Susanna's teacup rattled on the saucer as she set it down. "Are you suggesting he went *mad?*"

"Just a thought." David bit into his toast. "Seems to me those of you with powers don't have an easy time of it. I mean, we're all answerable to the Council, but you're pushed around by the scientists too... I can see a temptation to throw it all in and go rogue."

Go rogue? For what? To spend one's life on the run in the wilderness somewhere? She shook her head.

With a glance at the clock, Richard dropped his napkin on the table. "Jonathan's never been what you might call forthcoming. Sometimes we wonder what makes him tick."

He stood, flicked a crumb off his sleeve and left the room.

She picked at her toast. She hadn't expected everyone to march out in support of Jonathan, but they weren't questioning the matter as much as she had hoped. Well, he didn't mingle much. They didn't know him like... like she did. In fact, many of the other captains would only have met him at the time they came together to kill—execute—Denton. After such a horrific experience, they'd all have gathered in this lounge for mutual support. No doubt Jonathan would have been the exception, quietly returning to his modest room to deal with the trauma in private. Did he have to be so independent?

"You still hanging around with Lester?"

Jarred out of her thoughts, Susanna met David's enquiring gaze. "Yes, we're working together. Your point?"

He shrugged. "Just wondering. I wouldn't have thought him the easiest person to get on with. We all admire your aplomb, but Lester seems rather... excitable? Opposites attract, I guess."

The crockery clattered as her hand slammed down on the tabletop, and she glared. "We're not *a couple*, David. We have complementary powers, that's all. Settlers' sakes, man, he's young enough to be my son!"

"Hey." He held up a placating hand. "Take it easy."

"Sorry." She rubbed her stinging palm. Admittedly, she'd found Jonathan's jealousy rather touching. "I'm just worried. I'm sure there's an explanation."

"I'm sure there is." David lowered his voice. "Look, it might not be so bad. They were a bit premature with that news announcement. The later editions have been amended to call for Jonathan's capture, rather than... They'd rather take him alive. Earlier on, Silvers sent guards out to search the Royal Compound. And some went through the Armstrong Tunnel. He's pretty confident Jonathan wouldn't have headed into the main city."

Susanna nodded. The route between the Royal Compound and the inner city was closely monitored.

He continued. "If they catch up with Jonathan and he doesn't offer any violence, if he cooperates, he'll be treated fairly. They value him alive more than dead. If he acts sensibly, I'm sure he'll be fine."

She relaxed a little. They wouldn't kill him out of hand. Though since he must have had a reason to escape, giving himself up wouldn't be part of his plan, whatever it was.

David stood, his chair scraping on the wooden floor. "Anyway, I need to move. Got some new recruits to whip into shape. Catch you later." With quick stride, he departed.

Alone again, Susanna choked down the rest of her toast and the cold tea. The Council had approved his detention; she couldn't fight against that. But the mystery of why he chose to escape remained. What had been so important, or terrifying, that he fled? And maybe killed someone on the way. As she left the lounge, she mulled over David's words. Did he think she was in touch with Jonathan? If only she were.

Chapter 3

Jonathan's breath caught in his chest as he staggered out of the Armstrong Tunnel and took a gulp of the biting air. A dim gleam of sunlight peeked over the eastern horizon, glittering on the frosty ground. So, he must have escaped during the night. At least that meant the fields were empty of workers, especially this late in the year.

Ahead of him lay the stubble of the northern fields, the neatly tended agricultural area that provided a third of Ascar's food supply. Had it only been yesterday he'd led his guards past that ploughed soil and those bare-branched apple trees? His plan then had been an argument with the Council, not a prison breakout. Now what?

He squinted at the cluster of handcarts standing to one side of the tunnel's entrance. A pile of spades and pitchforks lay on the other side, partly covered by waxed fabric sheets.

A bout of coughing overtook him, and his vision darkened. While recovering, he leaned on a handcart, keeping an ear out for any pursuit from the tunnel. The only sound was his rasping breath and a faint twitter of birdsong. Well, maybe his escape wasn't a high priority. Maybe he attached too much importance to himself.

All he had were his stolen clothes, a sabre and a pocketful of surgical instruments and dressings. His legs ached, his mouth was parched, and his empty stomach complained. The wound on his right leg throbbed, and a blister on his left heel smarted. *Useless city guard shoes.* His jaw clenched at the thought of his sturdy custom-made boots, which Silvers had no doubt discarded. The city scientist wouldn't appreciate their practical value: even if he did, he'd likely smile at their destruction.

Think, Shelley. Walking unprepared into the wilderness would leave him dead of thirst or exposure within a day or two. Though maybe that wouldn't be such a bad way to go. *Ha, no "maybe" about it.* At least he'd die a free man rather than a victim of Silvers' experiments.

But he didn't want to die. Not unless he had to. Not until he'd done what he could to ensure Tabitha's safety and prevent Silvers from doing further damage. Well, there was always that letter in his barracks quarters, tucked into a jacket pocket. But it wouldn't suffice: it would be a miracle if anyone other than Silvers discovered or believed it.

Nobody with an ounce of decency should support vivisection experiments. If Jonathan's reasoning were right, Silvers was working alone. Could Jonathan warn the Council or Lady Nelson? His lip curled at the irony of appealing to those in power. When he'd arrived back from Maldon yesterday, he'd been determined to challenge them over their handling of the afflicted. Here he was now, wishing he could run to them for support. If that wasn't possible... he'd deal with Silvers himself and take the consequences. Somehow.

Of course, all his plans required him to avoid recapture. Dawn was breaking. Time to move. He eased himself upright and moved away from the handcart. Beside the tunnel's entrance stood a first aid cabinet, the one he'd pillaged when treating Franka's injuries only last month. That would be a good place to start.

He limped over to it, lifted the lid and stared.

Other than a small jar of antiseptic salve and a rubberised waterskin, it was empty. Where were all the bandages and dressings? Had nobody restocked it? Bastards. Just as well he'd grabbed the ones near his prison cell: likely left there by Silvers to taunt him. He pocketed the jar and affixed the waterskin to his belt.

Four buildings stood between him and the fields. He dismissed the one with the windmill—he'd no use for the processing *techne* and tools inside. The three others might hold harvested and processed foods. Could he afford to spend time pilfering supplies? Could he afford not to?

Approaching the first barn, Jonathan peered at the padlock on its door. A quick grope above the doorframe yielded a splinter in his finger, but no key. He scowled then pulled one of his two scalpels from a pocket. Maybe someone could teach him lock picking if he survived this.

He eased the blade into the keyhole and wiggled it around, pushing against some resistance. There was a sharp click, and the resistance disappeared. He grunted. *Ha, natural talent.* But the padlock held firm, and when he withdrew the scalpel, he found the blade snapped off. He cursed and shook the blade fragment out of the keyhole.

Now what? Hacking through the door with the sabre would take too long. He clenched his fist, and his punctured finger twinged. Of course. His wits must have been addled by Silvers' drugs. Concentrating, he placed a hand over his wounded thigh and squeezed. The throbbing in his thigh became piercing, and his breath hissed as he channelled the pain. His power awakened, heavy and expectant. Focussing on the innards of the padlock, he *let go*, easing the mechanism around.

The padlock clicked. He yanked it off then swung the

door wide open.

The close darkness within the building was redolent with the smell of apples. He barked his shin on a barrel, but his groping hand found a couple of sacks atop it. He fumbled with the barrel's lid, levering it off with his sabre. His mouth watered as the sweet scent intensified, and he stuffed handfuls of dried apples into one sack. He thrust his arm into another barrel, his fingers sinking into coarse grain. Scooping out big handfuls, he filled the second sack.

Leaving the barn, he growled at his sabre, now bent. Removing that lid must have damaged it. *Stupid city guard sabres.*

A flutter on the ground caught his eye. He bent and picked up a waxed paper wrapper, a few matches still inside. Was someone cooking at work? He cast his gaze around. There! A rusty billycan lay discarded beside some broken barrels and other rubbish. He even found an old pair of field workers' boots: nearly worn through at the sole, but a better fit than the shoes he was wearing. His lips twisted at the difference between his habitual convoy preparations and the indignity of this scavenging. Things were looking up.

Now he knew the trick of the padlocks, he approached the second barn, which bore a "CAUTION: FLAMMABLE" notice on the door. Inside, rather than the accelerant and fuel he'd hoped for, he found sacks and barrels of flour. He shook his head as he imagined the guards tracking him by a trail of flour. *Useless.* He turned away.

On his way to the third barn, a distant metallic screech drew his attention to the tunnel's mouth. *A pedalcart.* His head swung round to the expanse of fields, now lit by the morning sun, and his chest tightened. There was no concealment. He couldn't outrun them, not in his condition. He'd spent too long and trapped himself.

Could he hide in a building? They weren't idiots.

He drew his bent sabre. His tongue passed over cracked lips, tasting blood. *I nearly made it.* "You're not taking me back."

Limping to the tunnel entrance to make a last stand, his gaze was drawn to the handcarts. What if...

With an idea only half-formed, Jonathan shoved his sabre into its scabbard, cursing as it stuck partway. He forced his limbs into action, grabbed a handcart and propelled it to the second barn. He snatched up several sacks and a barrel of flour and threw them into the handcart. Leg aching, muscles burning, chest wheezing, he heaved the laden handcart into the tunnel. The wheels clunked over the track of the turning circle, and he let the handcart halt where the rock walls narrowed.

The rails hummed gently.

He pushed more handcarts beside the first as a makeshift barrier. Pathetic, but it would delay them by a few seconds as they climbed over it.

Faint voices now overlaid the soft note from the rails.

With his sabre he slashed the flour sacks open, and their contents spilled onto the floor. He snatched the wax fabric that covered the tools and tossed it on to the pile.

The rising dust caught in his throat, and his cough echoed up the tunnel.

Brakes screeched in reply, followed by shouts. "We've got him!"

Jonathan positioned himself just inside the tunnel's mouth.

A sunbeam pierced the dust cloud, revealing figures approaching his flimsy handcart barrier. Someone laughed. "Ha, stupid as well as cursed. Does he think that'll slow us down?"

He struck the match and held it up. "Stop!"

A gasp. A cough. The figures paused. A few of them backed away.

A rough voice penetrated the cloud of dust. "Give up, Shelley. Come back peacefully, and you'll get a fair trial."

Not if Silvers got to him first. What had the scientist told them? "For what? Being cursed?"

"As if you don't know." The voice grew cold. "For murder. And a guard, at that."

The match's flickering brought to mind a campfire when travelling on convoy. In the flame he saw the face of the elderly man he had killed some three months previously. *That* had been murder, even if Council sanctioned. But he hadn't murdered the prison guard.

Harsh speech broke into Jonathan's memories as the city guard stepped forwards, the others crowding behind him. "You'll run out of matches soon, and you can't fight us all off. Even if you have some weird cursed power, we're too many for you, and armed. The reward's higher if we take you alive, but don't count on that to protect you."

Jonathan pulled a dressing out of his pocket and lit it with the remains of his match. He held up the dressing and licked his singed finger. "Believe me or not, I didn't kill him. True, I can't fight you all and win. But if you come any closer, I'll blow you up instead."

The guard laughed. "And yourself with us? If you're cowardly enough to run away, you wouldn't blow yourself up."

"No." The time for concealing his secrets was past.

Jonathan raised his voice as he backed out of the tunnel. "You don't know what being cursed means. It's time for you to learn."

He focussed on the burning dressing and *let go*. It floated into the tunnel, towards the cloud of flour. *Slowly...*

"It's moving by itself! Get back!" shouted the guard.

Jonathan's pursuers fled back up the tunnel with cries of alarm, and he allowed his flame to touch the dust cloud.

The flour ignited, followed by the waxed cloth. With a dull *whump* that reverberated round his head, the barrel exploded. A plume of dirty grey smoke crawled out of the tunnel into the morning sky, accompanied by the odour of burning bread. That should keep them occupied for a while.

Coughing and grinning in equal measure, Jonathan waved smoke away from his face. Let them fear to come after him. He picked up his two sacks and hobbled into the wilderness.

Chapter 4

Annetta frowned in concentration as she spooned medicinal paste into her new pill-maker. She wasn't just Maldon's herbalist, but an apothecary now. After fastening the lid tightly, she positioned the device on her workshop bench. Counting under her breath, she turned the handle at an even pace. Neat little pellets fell onto the tray below with a satisfying patter, and she breathed deeply of the rich grassy scent.

The tricky part done, she moved on to more familiar tasks. The machine had saved her so much time, she wouldn't need to rush across to Giselle's. Batch production was such a boon. She'd learned something about it from Opal, the guard who'd remained in Maldon to help with Samuel. That had been at Captain Shelley's request: he certainly wasn't taking chances over the boy's care.

Opal said handmade items were a sign of status in Ascar, and nobles looked down on factory-produced goods. How could they? Annetta scratched under the collar of her smock with a work-roughened finger. Why anyone would prefer homespun garments to soft, smooth city fabric and regular machine-sewn seams was beyond her. And as for this new way to produce pills... More consistent dosage, faster to prepare, and they would last longer. The pill-maker had been her best gift ever. Adrian claimed Ascar's *techne* folk had provided the plan, but he was just being modest. Even though it wasn't his invention, he'd still built it for her.

Her smile broadened. *And he charged in to rescue you from Captain Shelley.* Admittedly, the captain would have won if it had come to a real fight, but Annetta appreciated the attempt. Before that incident, her biggest concerns had been settling into somewhere as large as Maldon, ensuring her clinic ran smoothly and developing good relationships with her neighbours. But after she'd been attacked—an attack she'd provoked, even though accidentally—her eyes had been opened to a new world.

She nudged a pill with a spatula, spacing it evenly from the others.

An unwelcome world, but one that made more sense than what was publicly claimed. Annetta had grown up pitying curse victims as if they had a terminal disease, accepting their incarceration to protect everyone from their violent unnatural powers. But that wasn't the real story. Captain Shelley's revelations had shattered her illusions the way he'd shattered her teapot. He'd told her victims sometimes developed controllable powers—powers the Council exploited. In addition, Samuel had been cursed, and just when the poor orphan had found a new family in Adrian and his daughter. Not to mention Giselle, although the logistician bossed everyone in Maldon around, not just Samuel. *Goes with the job, I guess.*

If anyone else had told her such a tale, she'd have laughed at them or wondered if they were deluded. But Opal's words after Captain Shelley left had tallied with his claims. There was also the evidence of Annetta's own eyes, when his power had slipped out of control. *After you drugged him.* At least the teapot had been the only casualty: it could have been much worse. He'd assured her afterwards it hadn't been her fault, though even now she cringed at the memory. She brushed away the thought. Best not to think too much about that incident or speculate over future surprises.

Had Captain Shelley spoken with the Council yet? If he succeeded in his talks, Samuel would be permitted to remain here rather than being locked up in Ascar's Keep. The boy was so harmless with his drawings, the only odd aspect being glimpses of far-off people and places. Just like a powerful spyglass or something, nothing worse. In fact, his curse had nearly gone unnoticed, and no wonder after such a tiny beast bite. Surely the Council would agree? Their members had the authority of years and wisdom gleaned from the whole realm. *Settlers help Captain Shelley persuade them.*

With the pills neatly lined up, she placed the tray on her workbench where a shaft of sunlight would speed their drying.

She glanced at the clock on her shelf. Just in time. Adrian and Opal would be at Giselle's house as well, to discuss Samuel. Captain Shelley had sworn them to secrecy, and they'd taken care not to let anyone else suspect. Last week's meeting had been uneventful, and Annetta hoped today's would be the same. Once things settled down... maybe she'd finally have time to see a bit more of Adrian. Although Giselle was Adrian's ex-wife, she'd seemed amused rather than disapproving. *Yikes, I'd hate to get on her wrong side.* And their daughter didn't seem to mind. However, Lisa was unaware of Samuel's secret ability, which made things awkward. At least at the age of fourteen, she wasn't jealous of Samuel the way a younger child might have been.

As Annetta was tying her sandals, a knock sounded at

the door. She straightened, and smoothed her hair back. Maybe Adrian had come to walk over with her. Her house was on his route to Giselle's, after all.

She opened the door and blinked at the plump girl who stood on the doorstep, twirling a lock of blonde hair round her finger.

Argh, of all the people! Annetta licked her lips. "Oh, hello. Do you need something?"

Lisa glanced back over her shoulder. "Can I come in for a minute?"

"Well... alright." Annetta stepped back, and Lisa entered. "I was just on my way out, but I can spare a few minutes. What's up?"

Lisa wandered over to the workbench and peered at the tray of pills. "I'm worried about Pa."

"What?" Her stomach lurched. Had his accidental poisoning several weeks ago caused unexpected long-term effects? He'd seemed mostly recovered, but liver damage could be unpredictable. If Samuel's actions had caused Adrian permanent damage... *Don't think about it.*

"He's behaving oddly. I mean, like he's distracted. Barely even acknowledges me some days." Lisa's voice sharpened. "Though he pays Samuel plenty of attention. I've asked him if there's a problem, and he just brushes me off."

Annetta's chest eased. Secrets were less dangerous than illnesses. But maybe not if Ascar was involved. Her chest tightened again. "Samuel can be quite a handful, and remember your Pa's not fully recovered."

"I guess. But the other day, I went into the workshop while they were talking. As soon as I opened the door, I heard Pa telling Samuel to 'hush'. Like they're keeping something from me. Do you know if something's going on?"

Why did she have to ask that right now? "Um... I couldn't say I noticed. Maybe they're planning a surprise for you?"

"It must be some surprise. Pa got pretty grumpy when I pushed him."

"Maybe don't push him too hard? I mean, nothing good ever comes from confrontation." *Phew, I'm such a coward.*

"Ha, you always say that. Doesn't mean you're right." Lisa's chin jutted towards Annetta.

"Er..."

Lisa snorted. "Anyway, I guess there's nothing you can do, but thanks for listening." She headed towards the door. "Samuel's over at Pascal's, and Pa went off somewhere for the afternoon. I'll go and see Ma now, see if she can talk some sense into him."

"Wait!" She couldn't let Lisa go to Giselle's, not when they were meeting there. Words tumbled out of Annetta's mouth. "I mean, can I ask you a favour?"

"Sure, what do you need?"

"Can you just wait here for half an hour? Um, I'm going out for a bit, but someone needs to turn these pills so they dry evenly." She winced at the feeble excuse.

Lisa frowned. "Well, I suppose so, but seems like an odd way to—"

"Thanks. I'll be back soon. Just... stay here." She thrust the spatula into Lisa's hand and fled.

Annetta hurried towards Giselle's house, catching up with Opal on the way. Although the guard still wore her grey uniform, she'd left her jacket unfastened and rolled the sleeves up. A turquoise scarf of the local weave was draped casually over one shoulder, setting off her short brown hair.

Opal gave her a nod. "How're things?"

"Good. Busy." Annetta fanned her face and tried not to sound too out of breath. "I see you're settled in, starting to dress like a native."

"Sure, I like it. Reminds me of where I grew up." She ambled on. "I'd forgotten how peaceful it is here, compared to Ascar. And it's great having a house to myself rather than being stuck in the barracks. Maybe I'll hand in my notice, go back to being a civilian."

Annetta grinned as she knocked on Giselle's door. She'd been a bit nervous around Opal at first, but the guard had proved friendly for an Ascarite. Likely it was because she'd been born in the country.

When they entered the living room, Adrian was sitting at the table, tinkering with a clock. He set his work down, nodded to Opal and gave Annetta a smile. Annetta returned the smile and sat by the window while Opal took the padded bench opposite.

After closing the door, Giselle also sat on the bench, retying her black headscarf over her auburn hair. "No messages from Ascar, which is good. I'm sure if they disagreed with Captain Shelley's actions, they'd let us know quickly. Adrian, how's Samuel getting on?"

Adrian returned a screwdriver to the tool belt that encircled his paunch. "Pretty well, actually. I've been pleasantly surprised by how restrained he's been."

"Any more drawings?"

He waved a callused hand. "Nothing out of the ordinary. I've been making excuses to visit the posthouse, but he's been behaving himself there too. The only drawings he's produced have been to Pascal's instructions."

Annetta's breathing slowed. Samuel was kept busy

drawing training images for Pascal's messenger birds. At the age of ten, he was too young—and too scatterbrained—to work on the roof or to trust with bird care. Every day without a disaster was a success. Though knowing Samuel, it was only a matter of time.

Giselle nodded. "Opal?"

The young guard shook her head. "I've been wandering around 'to keep an eye on things', as per Captain Shelley's official instructions. Nobody's talking about him, I mean Samuel. I guess that's a good thing." A slight flush crept up her neck. "Well, Marcus asked after him a couple of times, but I don't think it was because he noticed anything odd."

Annetta smirked, remembering the farmer's persistent attention after she and Samuel arrived in Maldon. It seemed he'd changed his focus. And why not? Opal's rural beginnings stood her in good stead when helping around the town, and she also had the cachet of spending time in Ascar, not to mention her status as a guard.

"Annetta?" asked Giselle.

"Nothing from me about Samuel." Glad of the breeze cooling her back, she shifted in her chair. "But Lisa's not happy, thinks Adrian's hiding something from her." She nodded at Giselle. "She's planning to talk to you about it, so we'll need to come up with a story."

"I know." Adrian's lips curved downwards. "On the one hand I have to deal with Samuel, and on the other to keep everything secret from Lisa... It would be so much easier if I could just tell her—"

"No." Opal's hair flew around her face as she shook her head. "If you're sworn to secrecy, it's a seriously bad idea to break it. They have... penalties."

Adrian's brow wrinkled. "Captain Shelley told us how

seriously the Council take secrecy, which I understand. If they removed the town from the convoy's route, it would be catastrophic. But could we negotiate with them, maybe offer to pay compensation? If it's not too much, it might be worth scraping together enough to—"

"No!" Opal shuddered. "It might be different for civilians. But really, don't push it."

Annetta's gut churned while her mind supplied ideas about what Opal wasn't saying. Maybe the Council weren't so reasonable. Captain Shelley hadn't given much detail, but his frightening—almost violent—attack on her previously made more sense if the Council were pressuring him from above. She swallowed. "Ascar sounds like a terrible place, if they're so heavy-handed."

"The regular civilians get on with their lives just fine, in happy ignorance. As do people in the settlements. Even I did, until..." Opal's lips twisted. "Anyway, Ascar's not so bad, as long as you play by the rules. I didn't, and I paid for it."

"Paid for what?" came a trenchant voice from outside.

With a gasp, Annetta jumped up from her seat and stuck her head out of the window, but nobody was there.

The front door opened and closed, and footsteps thudded in the hallway. Lisa entered the room, and leaned against the wall, arms folded. She still held the spatula.

Annetta's heart dropped into her sandals. She should have thought up a better distraction.

Giselle pursed her lips. "How long have you been there?"

"Long enough to know there's something going on about Samuel, and you want to fob me off with a story." Lisa's wavering voice firmed, and she scowled at Giselle.

"I'm not going to let you make stupid excuses or say I'm too young. I'm old enough to help you run the guesthouse, so I'm old enough to be told. What's going on?"

Opal chewed on a fingernail. "Well... Lisa did happen to overhear us. Like, by accident, nobody's fault."

Lisa waved the spatula towards Opal. "And that's better than just telling me up front?"

"Maybe. They have *techne* to tell whether someone is lying. And they'd not punish anyone for an honest mistake. They're harsh on"—she reddened—"deliberate insubordination."

"*Techne* to detect lies?" Adrian's eyebrows crept upwards. "How would that work? Do they measure people's reac—"

"Best not to ask." Opal's voice was flat. "The point is... we might as well tell Lisa what we know. Captain Shelley won't like it, but I think he'd appreciate the problems of her living under the same roof. It's better she knows the consequences." After a glance at Adrian and Giselle, she cleared her throat and briefly summarised the arrangement they'd agreed with Captain Shelley.

Lisa blinked at the news of Samuel's curse, but she didn't faint or panic or any of the other things Annetta might have feared. Well, anyone who knew him could tell he meant no harm. And it wasn't as if his "power" was physically dangerous. Not like Captain Shelley's, although Opal didn't mention that.

"... so Captain Shelley's going to ask the Council if it's permissible for Samuel to stay here, and be looked after by, well, his family." Opal coughed. "I think, maybe, he'll suggest it's possible to relax the requirements for sending the afflicted to Ascar. I know this goes against current Council guidelines, but they do modify them on occasion. This might be a chance to make life easier for everyone."

"What if they don't agree?" asked Lisa, eyes wide.

"A group of guards will take Samuel away to Ascar."

"And what would happen to Captain Shelley?"

"I don't know. Maybe nothing." Opal's jaw clenched.

"He's making a big gamble?"

"Yes. He's sticking his neck out for us, taking full responsibility. We owe it to him not to misuse his intentions. So if they overturn his decision and tell us to give Samuel up, we must obey. No trying to cheat the system."

Lisa tugged at her hair. "I see... it's a big deal, isn't it? We don't dare do anything other than cooperate. For Samuel's sake, and for our own. And for Captain Shelley's."

Seated in the monitoring room, Susanna wrinkled her nose as she set the water glass on the shelf. The energy bun's greasiness lingered on her tongue, but fainting would be worse. She reattached the clip to her ear and checked the lead was plugged in. Her foot tapped the floor until she crossed her ankles. *Patience.* She'd rather have been elsewhere seeking evidence on Silvers, but shirking her assigned duties would attract attention.

A knock on the partition indicated her partner on the other side was ready, and she responded with a knock of her own. Working in pairs was supposed to improve reliability and reduce bias, or so the scientists claimed. It also meant a longer queue. If their next interviewee—Scientist Fellows—didn't like it, he had only himself and his colleagues to blame. *Serves him right, being the last one of the day.*

A creaking door announced Fellows' arrival in the interview room. Through the observation slit, she glimpsed his dark hair as he sank into the seat, ignoring the restraint column. Being a scientist and in charge of those with powers, he knew about the concealed mind readers. He needed no fiction about the column being lie-detecting *techne*. Additionally, because he had no cursed power, he didn't need to be restrained for the mind readers' safety. Susanna's lips pursed. He might be the least bad of the bunch. Certainly more benign than Silvers, and not as opinionated as Lady Nelson.

"I'd appreciate a speedy read, please," Fellows called. "Queen Eleanor's asked me to copy a map in a hurry."

Did he think they were dawdling on purpose? The scientist didn't appreciate how draining monitoring could be for participants on both sides of the wall. Most ordinary interviewees found the clasp of the column stressful even if they weren't conscious of being restrained. And as for Susanna's side of the wall... *It's your duty*, they'd say. *For the safety of all*, they'd claim. But it was the mind readers' effort and pain.

She sighed. It was her partner's turn to present the prescribed questions. If Susanna had been leading this session, she might have nudged the interview towards something useful: some discretion being permitted. An extra question about colleagues' behaviour wouldn't have been out of place. As it was, she could only try to pick up stray thoughts. But the chances of that through a wall, in addition to the distance, were minimal. And assuming the man had a clear conscience, guilty thoughts wouldn't be floating on the surface of his mind.

Impatient rapping on the partition had Susanna scrambling for the knob on her calibrated stimulus generator. She turned it up too quickly, and her eyes watered when the pain hit her ear. Focussing on Fellows, she channelled the pain into her sense of his veracity: wispy strands that would quiver if he lied.

"Scientist Fellows," asked her partner, "are you aware of the penalties for inappropriately divulging classified information?"

"I am," replied Fellows.

Penalties. Her gaze flicked to the labelled buttons within arm's reach. Such a sanitised word, considering the range of gases that could be pumped into the interview room. They had short-term effects and were non-lethal—bar one— but might make the victim wish they were dead. *Gases.* Had Jonathan been rendered unconscious in a room like this one, helpless in the restraint column's grasp? Presumably he'd come back with his team of guards and passed through an interview room on the way. What might he have said? Had he really admitted to more problems with his power? Or maybe he'd finished the interview without incident and been seized afterwards?

"Have you, at any point during your duties, intimated, suggested or implied to individuals without the appropriate clearance level, verbally, by gestures..."

Duties. Susanna's eyes stung while she attempted to concentrate on Fellows' truth strands. Jonathan had been dutiful. The last time she'd tested his veracity, he'd admitted killing that poor traveller he was escorting. It had been to protect the Council's secrets, to conceal their use of people like him. *And me.* Even through the wall, the distress in his thoughts had been overwhelming. She blinked back tears. *And I couldn't even offer a word of comfort.* Even if he didn't recognise it himself, his guilt over that killing had prompted his protectiveness towards Tabitha.

"... classified information pertaining to the existence of any individuals with cursed powers, either confined within the Keep, or unconfined."

Well, he was unconfined now, she hoped. Was he safely hidden? Fed and warmly clothed? An experienced convoy captain like Jonathan—*he was always more at home in the wilderness than I was*—should have a good chance of achieving his objectives. Whatever they were. Meanwhile, she would attempt to aid him as best she could. If only it had been Silvers next door, rather than—

"You may leave," her partner told Fellows.

Susanna jerked upright. Had they finished already? She removed her earclip and flicked off the calibrated stimulus generator. Picking up a pen, she initialled the "No Concerns" box on Fellows' monitoring sheet, trusting that her partner hadn't picked up a lie. If he had, she'd apologise and explain she'd been distracted, which had the major advantage of being true. Plus, her power was weaker than her partner's. She could even point out the usefulness of having them working in pairs.

After packing away the equipment and saying farewell to her partner—it would be someone else next time—she headed back towards the barracks. Tomorrow would be a recovery day: a chance to visit Staunton. The retired scientist seemed no friend to Silvers and might be willing to talk. And if not, she might still pick up on something. It would be a fine line to tread, however, to avoid accusations of misusing her power.

Chapter 5

"More tea, my dear?" Lady Nelson's blue-veined hand hovered over the teapot as she aimed a bright smile at Eleanor.

Ugh, no. "Thank you, Catherine, but I am quite replete." Eleanor shifted in her chair, its ornate carved back digging into her shoulder, a splinter catching her chiffon tea gown. She'd take modern comfort over heirloom furniture any day. Still, duty was duty, as she told herself every week. Sometimes these social calls were fruitful, and at least this hostess didn't insist on calling her "Your Majesty", unlike the other, non-noble scientists.

Lady Nelson poured herself some of the watery brew. "It was a dreadful business, that guard's murder. I can't fathom why Shelley didn't cooperate with his detention until he regained proper control of his power. And I thought him one of the more dependable captains." She pursed her lips. "This supports what I've always said. The afflicted are dangerous and can't be trusted among normal people. They can break at any point. Your dear cousin Isabel is an exception, of course. Her noble character shines through."

"Indeed." Eleanor raised her half-full cup, so it briefly touched her lips. *Noble character? You have no idea.*

"I don't care for the Council's stance, that the benefits from cursed powers outweigh the risks. In my opinion, the best place for the afflicted is the Keep where we can isolate them from normal people. I've said so multiple times. Though that's something your father and I didn't always see eye to eye on."

I bet. Eleanor sighed. Always the same argument, like a broken phonograph. What happened to innocent until proven guilty? The afflicted weren't criminals. Her ancestors' journals had been clear on that. But somehow life had changed over the generations until pragmatism prevailed over humanity. How could she improve things? She didn't know where to start.

The old woman sniffed. "We received the report about the murdered guard. Apparently there wasn't a mark on him..."

Her lips continued moving, but further words were lost in echoes from Eleanor's memory. The gold and purple wallpaper of Lady Nelson's parlour blurred in front of Eleanor's eyes.

... there wasn't a mark on him...

That's what they'd said when investigating her father's death last year, wasn't it? They'd come up with no explanation. How could he have died so suddenly, if not by foul play? Yet nobody had found anything. And now she was head of state, unprepared, with almost nobody she could trust.

A faintly bitter taste filled her mouth, and she found she'd taken a sip of tea. She swallowed. "Did they have any suggestions how the guard died, if there was no mark on him? Maybe poison?"

"There was no poison in the guard's canteen though I don't know why they bothered testing it. Shelley's used his power before to stop someone's heart, undetectably. Clearly, he did it again."

Eleanor set her teacup down, pushing away visions of

her father trying to defend himself from Shelley. Knowing about powers was one thing, but hearing of their effects another. She'd never even witnessed cousin Isabel in action. "Are there many afflicted who have that power?"

"Manipulating items from afar? No, my dear, and a good thing too." Lady Nelson placed her fingertips together and gazed up at the ceiling. "In addition to Shelley, there's one working in the Keep's infirmary. I concede he's very helpful with delicate procedures. Lastly, there's a girl who's still in detention. Tamara... no, Tabitha. I agreed to supervise her training, but her ruralite uncouthness is proving quite a burden."

So, not many could kill like that. *Shelley.* What did she know of him? She'd met him in the blimp workshop a few weeks ago. A convoy captain. He'd looked familiar... she'd previously noticed him in her rooftop garden one day when she went up to take some air. He'd been with a young girl. What was he doing? Spying? Checking the palace entrance? Taking the girl with him as camouflage? Her shoulders tensed. Did she need to see conspiracies everywhere? Maybe she did. Maybe her father hadn't. Perhaps his usual perceptiveness had failed him. She'd better add Shelley to her list of concerns.

"Jed—my new junior colleague, Jed Silvers—was furious about the escape." Lady Nelson chuckled. "The Council gave him such a dressing down earlier, especially as he'd insisted on overseeing the prisoner himself. Obviously he didn't plan properly. Then he overreacted when he heard of the escape. Ordered that Shelley be killed, so the Council had to countermand his orders and tell him to issue a retraction in the *Informer*. Still, he claims to know where Shelley was heading. Says he has a way of tracking him."

Another power she'd not come across? Tracking sounded useful, though dangerous in the wrong hands. "Do you know how he does it?"

"What? The tracking? No, I wasn't interested. Sounds like he's getting distracted from his job, trying to invent new methodology rather than studying people with the curse."

Eleanor's eyebrows rose. "But if we had a way to find people, whether through *techne* or powers, mightn't that be beneficial?"

Ignoring the question, Lady Nelson waved a hand. "Anyway, Shelley's headed north. He set a fire in the tunnel, or else the guards might have caught up with him. Now he's disappeared into the wilds. We've sent messenger birds to warn the settlements, but I expect that's the last we'll see of him, unless someone happens across his bones in a few years' time."

"As you say." Eleanor wasn't so convinced. After their brief encounter in the blimp workshop, she might have described Shelley as "durable". Not someone to dismiss as a threat.

"At least he didn't damage the tunnel or run amuck in one of the settlements. He'd just returned from one. It was during that post-mission interview he admitted to losing control. If Jed hadn't been so impatient as to detain him immediately, we might have got more details. I suppose Jed thought he could interrogate him further at leisure. Well, too late."

"An important mission, I take it?" Eleanor reached for a scone.

"A ruralite was bitten in a beast attack, so we sent him out to check the victim. Since he didn't bring the victim back, either no curse was passed on, or the victim didn't survive. The guards who returned didn't detect any beasts, so I hope that's the end of that. Anyway, my dear, what of your own news?"

Eleanor swallowed a mouthful of scone. *Stale again.* "I've been looking at maps. Your colleague, that is, Karsten Fellows, kindly provided records of beast sightings and attacks over the last ten years. I think there are some promising patterns."

"How very interesting." Lady Nelson poured herself more tea. "But you should focus more on your duties as queen. It's been nearly a year since your dear father passed on. If you're not careful, the Council will go on their way without you. You've not attended any of our meetings, and the others are forgetting you exist."

"I know." She gazed at the part-eaten scone on her plate. If her father were still alive, he'd be so much better at all of this. *And I'd be free to work on my research.* "Just that..."

"We're all old fogeys? It's boring?"

Eleanor hadn't quite regarded meetings as *boring*, the few times she'd attended with her father. But a room full of old men who wanted confirmation of their prejudices? "Ah..."

"You can't always do as you please, you know, absolute power or not." The woman's lips flattened. "The trust invested in the royal line demands a sense of—"

"Oh, of course, but I think I'm on to something useful. I plotted locations of beast incidents with known cursed mounds and—"

"Dreadful things! You—" Lady Nelson's shoulders shook as she coughed. "You shouldn't spend too long pondering them. At least, get the Council to take you seriously first. Some of the members need to be reminded of their place, Hastings especially. He thinks that chair has his name on it, not yours."

Eleanor bowed her head. "I shall consider your words. Thank you for the tea. Delicious, as always. But I should be going now. I have an appointment this evening."

"With a man?" A hopeful smile touched Lady Nelson's lips.

She had to laugh. "Yes, actually." Even if not for the reason the woman assumed, there was always a possibility...

"Good girl. I do hope he's suitable. And don't leave it too late, like I did."

When Eleanor stepped out of Lady Nelson's mansion, the four guards escorting her today saluted.

"Where to now, Your Majesty?" asked the chief guard, squinting at her with his single eye.

"Palace, Paton. I have arrangements to make." *And you're not going to like them.*

Strolling back towards the palace with her guards, she thought over Lady Nelson's words. *Shelley.* She remembered another detail about the man. He'd asked for permission, via Isabel, to access the royal library. Eleanor had granted it, not knowing what she did now. She tripped on a cobblestone and waved away Paton's extended arm. Shelley might have been seeking another way to get close to her. She shivered at the thought of her narrow escape. *Murder.* If they caught him alive, she might find out what really happened to her father. After this evening's outing, she'd better ask Isabel what she knew of Shelley. If he were truly mad, even if he were a murderer, she should pity him. Though that wouldn't save him from the noose. Not if he had killed a king.

With the afternoon sun still in the sky, Jonathan rested with his back against a tree. He watched the billycan over his tiny smokeless fire. His hunger had waned an hour or two ago, but years of hard lessons had taught him the value of nourishment.

He'd hastened due north from Ascar's fields, unsure how much of a head start the tunnel fire had given him. He hoped the guards had turned back once they searched the buildings and scanned the fields. Venturing into the wilderness was risky for the ill-equipped and unprepared. *Like me.*

Convoys travelled too infrequently for there to be established trails. Nevertheless, Jonathan had played it safe and cut away from the usual routes: neither the low hills in the north towards Maldon, nor the woodland towards Burnley in the east. He instead aimed for the virgin lands in between, which offered concealment by trees and bushes. His experience in the wilds would help him evade pursuit. Surely he'd hear other travellers blundering around before they detected his presence.

But what if they sent a blimp? He shot an anxious glance at the sky then chuckled at his paranoia. Those contraptions were being commandeered for the queen's entertainment, not to track fugitives. Anyway, he could always hide among the trees.

Now he was safely out of reach, he could maybe find somewhere to eke out the rest of his life, away from other people and responsibility. Build himself a shelter, carve out a piece of the land, make a quiet place all of his own. Pretend he was an ordinary person rather than a murder suspect, a fugitive with unnatural powers. Someone else could deal with Silvers and his schemes.

And where would that leave Susanna when she caught

wind of his troubles? She might consider helping, but opposing Silvers would risk her career and unblemished reputation. Jonathan could hardly expect that of her: she might not even think he was still alive. He clenched a fist, remembering Silvers' smiling face as the man taunted him in his cell. No. Running away wasn't the answer. Better that he solve his own problems.

Murderer. If the odds of clearing his name were too unfavourable, he'd settle for neutralising Silvers. Might as well live up to the way he'd been labelled. With Silvers out of the way, the Council wouldn't let things go too far. Tabitha's future might be more secure. Jonathan's actions had placed her in the Keep, and his attempts to help had only made things worse. He owed her a chance at something better.

Susanna would condemn his deeds—she could hardly approve of murder—but removing Silvers as a threat would be worth the price. Jonathan snorted. Even Lester would benefit. The young captain might be a simpering twit—not to mention annoyingly flirtatious with the ladies—but he didn't deserve to be blackmailed. He'd been present when Jonathan discussed Silvers with Susanna, although expecting help from such a shallow personality was optimistic.

But this wasn't the time for Jonathan to think of those he had left behind. He tucked away the memory of Susanna's dimpled smile before turning his attention to medium-term planning.

Attempting to return to Ascar through the tunnel was madness. Could he circle around the Cleon Mountains and re-enter the city through its southern gate? He grunted as he glanced at his brown uniform, already smoke-stained and ripped. A dark wet patch on his right thigh signalled where the wound had leaked through his bandage before he stopped to apply a new dressing. Even those dim-witted gate guards might suspect something amiss with such an appearance.

If he couldn't travel to Ascar, he should at least visit a settlement and re-provision. The obvious one would be Maldon. He'd left Opal there, and she might be willing to help, although they hadn't always been in accord. Not only did she know about Jonathan's power, she had experienced how the Council treated those who broke rules. She might not condemn him out of hand.

He closed his eyes and considered. Attention would turn to Maldon since he'd just returned from there when he was imprisoned. The townsfolk should cooperate with Ascar's enquiries as he'd told them to when he visited. The Council wouldn't punish them for following a captain's instructions, even if the captain were later discredited. So, Jonathan would have to hole up for a while, then approach the town with care, checking no guards were visiting.

"Well," he muttered, "you've spent enough time outdoors that you can survive on your own for a week or two. Just find a flint for fire-starting, and stick close to water. Easy."

Of course, he'd survived on his travels with access to more equipment than a stolen billycan and waterskin. And a dead man's uniform and sabre.

A man dead for no apparent reason. His brows drew together, and he stared into the flames. *Murder.* He had once before used his power to kill. Had that damaged his control? Had he killed the guard unintentionally, just by hoping the man wouldn't notice his escape attempt? Was he blaming Silvers for something he, Jonathan, had done? *Admit it, Shelley, you* have *lost control recently.* There was that time in the blimp—even now, the memory of his terrified reaction made him sweat—and then after Annetta's herbs. But each time he'd known about it. Was he losing awareness of his power as well as losing the ability to suppress it?

Focussing on the flames, he directed his attention to his core, to that place where his power resided. Despite the ache in his leg, it lay quiescent. He eased out a breath of relief. If his power rose accidentally, overcoming his years of conditioning, he'd have a chance to direct it away from the innocent. It might even become useful to call it at will, without the stimulus of pain: a secret weapon against Silvers.

Silvers. He scowled at the fire, recalling the man's callousness, especially his threats against Tabitha. His breathing deepened and his anger grew at the thought of Franka and Terry, the guards injured because of Silvers' manipulations. How much more suffering would the man cause before he was stopped? Jonathan's power uncoiled and started to rise. He grinned, waiting for it to prime.

A twig snapped in the fire.

His concentration slipped, his power retreating into dormancy. *Damn.*

Still, it was a start. He'd stay away from people until the hunt for him died down. Meanwhile, he could tighten up his control. He could try out different ways of calling his power and see what worked best for him...

Jonathan opened his eyes and blinked up at the stars in the cloudless sky. The odour of burnt gruel lingered in the cold air. He groaned, eased out a kink in his neck and reached for the billycan and its congealed contents. He scooped out what he could from the tin with a finger, choking it down with sips from his waterskin. A piece of dried apple completed his repast. *Enjoying the taste of freedom, are we?*

He stood and stamped his feet, swinging his arms to restore some warmth. No point in attempting further travel tonight. Not that he had a destination, anyway. He paced around the clearing and gathered armfuls of leaves. Once he had a sizeable pile, he crawled into his makeshift bed and shivered. He'd better get used to this.

Once the sun rose, he would dredge up what he could remember about foraging and make some proper plans. But he'd do it after a night's sleep. Tomorrow.

Chapter 6

Artur rang the bell pull at the servants' entrance to the palace then squeezed himself into the shadow of the doorway. Although it was unlikely someone would pass by and see him, his presence might raise some eyebrows. Clutched in his sweating hand, his overnight bag weighed him down further every second. In accordance with the *other* instructions on the queen's missive, he wore work overalls. In deference to her elevated position, he had donned his newest set.

What was the queen planning? Surely this wasn't a joke at his expense. She hadn't struck him as the frivolous type, no matter what the gossips said. Might she have a workshop in addition to her library? Maybe she wanted help with some new *techne*. His breathing quickened. Maybe she even wanted him to—

The door creaked open with a waft of mushroom and garlic smells. A plump woman in the pink uniform of the palace staff looked down her nose at him. "Yes?"

Despite the chill in the early evening air, sweat prickled his back. "I'm Artur. Uh, Blimp Engineer Granville, ma'am. I was requested to report here by Queen Eleanor." Was that as odd as it sounded?

For a moment she frowned. Was she going to send him away? Maybe the queen had changed her mind, despite her enthusiasm during that first visit. That might be a relief, although a disappointment too.

But no, the woman's frown transformed into a beam. She stepped back and beckoned him in. "Of course. You're just not quite what I expected. I'm Martha, the head housekeeper."

Hunching his shoulders, Artur stepped inside. Maybe he'd misunderstood the message. Should he have hired a formal suit again? Overalls of surplus blimp fabric—constructed by his frugal mother—might not be suitable attire.

"I thought you'd be more bookish. Like a clerk or librarian." She looked him up and down. "Not quite so sturdy."

His face heated.

Martha led him through the kitchen and up four flights of service stairs, their footsteps echoing in tandem. A pair of red-clad royal guards stood at each landing. The older ones scowled at Artur while the younger ones grinned. One even gave him a thumbs-up. Artur winced. *Hey, it's not what it looks like.* Though he wasn't even sure of that. *Maybe she wants*—He yanked his thoughts away.

On the residential floor, he tiptoed down a hallway behind Martha, his heavy work boots creaking. What if he trod grease into the plush carpet?

The housekeeper opened a door. "Go on in, lad. This is your room while you're here. Someone will collect you shortly."

When he paused in the doorway and blinked, she pushed him inside and shut the door behind him. Her footsteps scuffed softly as she moved off.

He dropped his bag in the middle of the room, which was lit by free-standing oil lamps. So, they'd only installed electrical lighting downstairs. A padded couch with silk cushions stood against the wall, underneath a portrait of

King Frederick. He gave the king a cautious nod. A carved oak writing desk and chair occupied one corner. Through an open door he could spy the edge of a bed with an embroidered coverlet. Craning his neck, he took a step towards the doorway—

At a rap from the hallway door, he jumped. He ran his hands through his hair and opened the door, fumbling with the handle.

A woman in the brown uniform of a city captain swept past him into the room. She was taller than he, with a braid of rich chestnut hair. A sabre hung from her belt.

She pivoted and faced him. "I'm Captain Hanlon." She grinned. "You can call me Isabel. I'm accompanying you and Eleanor tonight. But first, I need to set you straight on something."

He gulped. "Yes, ma'am. Isabel." This was the queen's chaperone? He'd expected someone more delicate.

Her gaze bored into him. "I take Eleanor's reputation and privacy very seriously. Whatever happens tonight, you are not to speak of it to anyone. Anyone at all. If you do, I'll make sure you regret it. Got that?"

Mouth dry, he nodded.

"Good to see you're quick on the uptake." Her smile returned, and she smacked him on the arm, making him flinch. "Have you mentioned visiting here to anyone already?"

"I told my parents I was working on a special project tonight, which they assume is blimp-related." He licked his lips. "And Captain Shelley was in the blimp workshop when Queen Eleanor first invited me here. Last month, I mean. He asked me about it afterwards."

Isabel frowned.

Crap, did I do something wrong already?

She sighed. "I don't think that will matter. Not now." She gave him a sidelong glance. "You don't pay much attention to the news, do you?"

News? "I've been a bit busy." He'd been thinking about tonight rather than any news. What had he missed?

"Never mind. Let's go."

Two picnic hampers stood in the hallway. They each carried one towards the stairwell. Artur's brow creased at the sight of her mud-spattered boots ascending. Wasn't the queen's drawing room on the floor below?

He caught up with Isabel as she opened a door. After following her through, he found himself on the rooftop, a stray sunbeam making him squint. Just past a raised flower bed, four red-clad figures stood, straight and tall, their backs to him.

"Your Majesty, won't you reconsider?" asked a gruff male voice.

Queen Eleanor's voice responded. "No guards on the rooftop until dawn. I shall be perfectly safe in Captain Hanlon's company. You may leave."

"As the queen commands."

After saluting, the four guards marched towards the doorway. The grizzled one-eyed man in the lead nodded at Isabel but glared as he passed Artur. *Just great.*

Isabel returned the guard's nod then touched Artur's arm. "I've a few things to sort before we go. You go speak with Eleanor. Take your time." She strode away, waved at the queen on the way past and continued towards the connecting bridge to the Keep.

Artur approached the queen, his eyes widening, the faint scent of lavender tickling his nose. "Uh... Your

Majesty?"

The petite figure before him wore dark green overalls, and her hair was tucked under a matching headscarf. She looked like someone he wouldn't mind working with. Someone he'd quite like to work with, in fact. An intelligent expression, graceful posture and—*Cut that out, dummy.*

She smiled. "I think you can call me Eleanor."

He swallowed. "Certainly... Eleanor. May I ask what we're doing?"

"We're going on a blimp ride. I think you'll find it interesting."

That somewhat explained why she'd invited him. Though it remained a mystery why she wanted to do it this way rather than her regular requests via Haslett.

She led him across the bridge to the rooftop of the Keep. A familiar blimp balloon was inflating. Artur had serviced that balloon a couple of weeks before: fortunately, the fabric and his overalls didn't match. His nose twitched at the bracing tang of levium gas as some escaped the valve. Some found the odour unpleasant, but it signalled an improvement over the flammable gases they'd used previously. He'd take smells over explosions every time.

His eye was drawn to the gondola, one of the older models. Just the right size for three. His pulse increased. As an engineer, he'd not been up as much as he'd have liked, even though he was no heavier than the regular operators. Things looked promising.

They found Isabel by the gas controls, talking to Artur's chief. "... private business. I'm sure we can rely on the discretion of Chief Blimp Engineer Haslett, can't we?"

Haslett spluttered then paled when Isabel grinned at him. "Yes, ma'am."

His gaze shot between Artur and Eleanor, then back to Isabel. He bowed to Isabel, then to Eleanor. "It's ready to go now, ma'am. Your Majesty. And Artur. Do you need me to wait, in case the boy can't manage?"

Artur stiffened. The old fogey hadn't got his hands dirty for years, but now it was royalty... He cleared his throat. "As with Chief Engineer Haslett, I'm no operator. But I'm well acquainted with this blimp."

Eleanor inclined her head to him, pulling a pair of gloves from a pocket. "In that case, I'm sure you can help with anything we need, Engineer Granville." She addressed Haslett as she drew the gloves on. "Once we take off, you are free to leave. We will send word to you on our return, should we have need of your skills. Thank you for your co-operation."

Haslett bowed, beads of sweat on his forehead. "A pleasure, Your Majesty."

Eleanor and Artur climbed aboard, and Isabel handed him the baskets. One clinked when he set it down. After a few final words with Haslett, she clambered in herself, treading on Artur's foot. He bit his tongue. At least she hadn't prodded him with that sabre.

"Sorry." She grinned at Artur and Eleanor. "You small people have it easy."

Eleanor snorted and turned to the controls. She ran her hands over them, muttering, "... wind speed... correct with Armstrong coefficient..."

The queen's mumblings were lost in the whirring of the propeller units attached to the gondola's sides. The angle of their blades shifted in readiness to boost their ascent.

Isabel waved at Haslett. "Off we go!"

Haslett untied the tether and tossed it to Isabel, who

caught it and stowed it away. Then they were off.

Artur's legs adjusted to the gondola's swaying, and he watched the Keep's recognition symbol shrink while the blimp rose. Not that people used that symbol painted on the rooftop: it was just for messenger birds to find their way. Hmm. Perhaps in future, if blimps became more common, people could navigate by similar markings, or even written signs?

The inner city's blocky layout and outer city's winding roads shrank beneath them. Pinpoints of light began to twinkle as the lamplighters went about their early evening business, although it would be a couple of hours until the sun fully set.

The wind rushing past his face gave him something familiar to hold on to, in such exalted company. Although he'd previously taken test rides, he'd never been far from the city. Even on foot, he'd only ventured into the southern farming area as far as his parents' greenhouses. It would be a new experience to see what lay further afield.

But he wasn't here to stand idle while the ladies did all the work. His attention drifted to Eleanor, whose hands caressed the controls. *Come on, I'm not here to enjoy the scenery.* His gaze flicked to Isabel, crouching on the floor. Was she airsick or afraid? That might make things tricky. No, she was rummaging in a basket.

He coughed. "Can I help?" Surely they'd brought him for a reason.

Isabel stood, clutching a sheaf of papers. "How's your map reading?"

He held out a hand. "I can do that."

She passed him the map and pointed. "We're aiming for this spot here. Should take us... Eleanor?"

Eleanor replied over her shoulder. "Based on our earlier discussions, a bit less than an hour. We should get there before sundown."

Where was "there"? The location meant nothing to him, just an area of hills about ten miles east of the city. Why would royalty make an evening trip to the middle of nowhere? Did she have a secret residence? Somewhere that she... He started to sweat.

Concentrate. He relaxed his grip on the map. "Where are we going?"

"We'll see when we get there," said Isabel. "Or, if we don't see, no point in raising your expectations."

"Thanks for the clarification," muttered Artur as she smirked.

He leaned over Eleanor's shoulder—squashing himself against the gondola's side so as not to touch her—and checked the compass on the control panel. He peered through a spyglass, orientating himself by landmarks indicated on the map. It held far more detail than he'd previously seen, including some unfamiliar symbols. The river was easy to spot, as were clumps of tall, mature trees. Satisfied he knew their position, he provided Eleanor with directions. She nodded at his words, adjusting the propeller units with seasoned precision and alacrity, and he allowed himself to relax. At least he needn't worry about having to wrest control from her. Would that be treason? He didn't want to find out.

They arrived at the indicated spot with the sun low in the sky. He scanned the ground with the spyglass, squinting in the reduced light. Below them lay hilly terrain with clumps of trees, but not the silhouettes of buildings he'd half-expected.

"Just about there." Eleanor pointed. "Flashlight."

She cranked the blimp control wheels back and forth, releasing a little of the levium, before angling the propeller units to push against their residual buoyancy. The blimp settled into a stationary hover some dozen feet in the air. Artur's eyebrows rose. Who would have imagined the queen a natural blimp pilot?

Isabel switched on a flashlight and clamped it to the side of the gondola. A strong beam of light hit the ground below, and Artur aimed his spyglass at the illuminated area. His grip tightened.

Unnatural, twisted shapes reached up towards them, glinting and unmoving in the flashlight's beam. He jerked the spyglass away from his eye and sucked in a breath, the back of his neck prickling. The pile of shapes could only be described as a mound. A *cursed* mound.

But that wasn't all.

Eyes. A dozen pairs of yellow-green eyes flickered up at them. Their owners stalked around, fur bristling, fangs bared and tails lashing. *Beasts.* He moaned. Was that why he was here? To be sacrificed in some ritu—

"You were right!" crowed Isabel. She jumped up and down, then clung to the side of the gondola as it wobbled. "Whoops. But this is great. We've had rumours and ideas and suggestions and folk tales. But this is direct observational proof that beasts *do* congregate at cursed mounds."

Artur shuddered then shook his head. What had he been thinking? Of course they hadn't brought him here to kill him.

Isabel opened the hamper. "We should have tried this as soon as the first blimp was functional. Would have saved a lot of time."

"*You* might not mind trusting your life to experimental equipment." Eleanor's voice held a note of exasperation. "Some of us prefer a little more certainty." She glanced at Artur. "And support. How about making some pictures rather than gabbing?"

Isabel pulled out a hand-sized box and unfolded it. A glass lens glinted as she turned a handle, and Artur gaped.

His fingers twitched. "Is that an actual *camera*?" He'd heard about those from a craftsman friend.

"It's a prototype. I'm assured it works in the dark." She aimed the box downwards, twisted a lever and pressed some buttons. She paused to wind a handle before repeating the process. After a few more shots she stowed the camera away. "They won't be able to argue with *that*. What shall we do now?"

Eleanor joined Artur in looking over the side. His grip on the handrail tightened, and his stomach churned. He couldn't have said whether it was Eleanor's proximity or the spectacle of the glowing eyes moving to and fro that was the cause.

"One might postulate," she murmured, her breath brushing his cheek, "that if beasts cluster here, there's something about the mound that curses them. So if we destroy the mounds, or make them inaccessible, we might eliminate the curse. It would take time, of course, and it's only a hypothesis."

Artur caught himself leaning towards Eleanor, and he clenched his jaw. *Behave, idiot! Let her do any leaning.*

"Sounds more convincing than most of the garbage the scientists spew." Isabel looked up from scribbling some notes. "You go, girl! In a few years, you'll be renowned as the queen who cured the curse."

"Ever the optimist, Isabel. I wish it was that straightforward." Eleanor peered into the distance. "We should decide what to do now. It's too dark to take further pictures, and I don't fancy hunting for more mounds tonight. This proof should be enough to support daytime expeditions."

He blinked. "Can't you just order surveys of mounds? Whether in blimps or on foot?" He'd thought the monarch had absolute authority.

She squeezed his arm, and he bit his lip. "Well, I could. But then they'd do it grudgingly. I want to convince the Council and the scientists that this is the right approach, not just a fancy of mine. Once we return from this trip with evidence of beasts at mounds, it'll be easier to justify sending out exploration teams. The more information they have in advance, the better they can prepare, and the safer they'll be."

"As long as they're not too scared to go," muttered Isabel.

Artur regarded Eleanor's indistinct profile. "Sounds like a good reason for more royal blimp rides."

She laughed.

"Are you done here?" Isabel put her notes in the hamper.

"I suppose." Eleanor released Artur's arm. "Back to Ascar, then."

Isabel pulled out two bottles. "Wait, I have an idea."

"No, it's too dangerous." Eleanor clutched her arm but let go when Isabel winced. "Sorry, I forgot."

"Bah, I've had worse. It only needed a few stitches. But since I've spilled blood over it—î

"That's not the point!"

Artur tensed. Surely Eleanor's chaperone should defer—

"You're the one who thought it up in the first place. This might be our only chance to try." Isabel pushed Eleanor away, shoved one bottle in a pocket and uncorked the other.

Artur steadied Eleanor with a hand on her back, but she advanced on Isabel before he could apologise. The rich aroma of brandy hit his nose. Premium quality, not something his parents' tavern would stock. Still, why was Eleanor worried? What did it matter if Isabel wanted a drink? She wasn't piloting the blimp, although if she got sick it might make things awkward.

Isabel put the bottle to her lips and took a swig, keeping the approaching Eleanor at bay with her other arm. "Ha, no chance, cousin! That's what you get for not learning grappling."

"Artur, grab the bottles!" Eleanor's shaky voice rose high over Isabel's laughter.

Were they mad? The blimp's floor tilted while Artur shuffled towards Isabel, wishing he were on the ground. Despite the cramped surroundings, she managed a couple more gulps while keeping the bottle out of his and Eleanor's reach.

Changing tack, he snatched the other bottle from her pocket, backed away a couple of steps and held it safely away from her by dangling it over the side. "Uh, Captain Hanlon, perhaps this isn't a good time—"

"Wait—" Eleanor lurched towards him, jostling his arm.

The bottle slipped out of Artur's hand, and he winced. That brandy wasn't cheap. Though at least it was away from Isabel.

The splintering of breaking glass was followed by a chorus of snarls from below. He sniffed. Not brandy. A scent that reminded him of his uncle's funeral. *Accelerant.* What was this insanity?

"No!" Eleanor's voice rose in a shout that scattered birds from the trees and drew howls from the beasts. The flashlight's beam showed them running around and jumping up towards the blimp.

Isabel, still laughing, leaned out of the blimp and dropped her bottle, the one that really contained brandy. Why throw it away deliberately?

She pointed at the mound. "Here we go!"

Under Artur's horrified gaze, she dropped a flame from her fingertips. If only he'd noticed her striking the match, he could have prevent—

The mound blew up.

When Artur came to his senses, he was standing with his hands clamped on the side of the gondola, which rocked as Eleanor and Isabel shouted at each other. It wasn't a dream, then. But maybe a nightmare. His stomach roiled at the odour of accelerant and burning flesh.

The ringing in his ears gave way to high-pitched squawks, then to voices over the hum of the propeller units.

"You idiot!" shrieked Eleanor, jabbing a finger in Isabel's face. "We talked of incineration, not explosion, and now it's spread everywhere."

"How was I supposed to know it would explode? The mound looked like it had been sitting there for decades." Isabel wasn't laughing anymore. In the flickering glow from the fire below, her face resembled a demon's mask from an old tale.

The burning mound heated his face, which stung. After touching his cheek, he stared at the blood on his gloved fingertip. He must have been hit by a fragment from the explosion.

Flames crawled over the mound and blackening corpses. No live beasts remained, and no wonder. After an explosion of that size, anything with sense would make tracks.

The light cast by the dying flames was enough to show the damage, with scattered chunks of rock and metal covering the area. The flashlight's dancing glare picked out details he'd rather not have seen: shapes reminiscent of distorted *techne* components and unmistakable charred body parts.

He frowned. The mound hadn't seemed so close before. He scanned his surroundings and cleared his throat. "Ladies?"

Their argument had progressed to recriminations about Eleanor's sheltered upbringing versus Isabel's adventurous life experience.

Taking a deep breath, Artur stepped between them. "Ladies, save your squabble for later! We're losing height." He flinched at their matching glares then picked up the flashlight and aimed it upwards. "Um, see? There's a puncture near the bottom of the balloon. Leaking gas, so we're descending."

Eleanor leaped to the controls. "He's right."

"Shit," said Isabel. "Sorry."

"Artur, we might need an emergency landing." With Eleanor spinning the wheels, the propeller units whined and shifted their angle as she strove for elevation. Despite her efforts, the blimp continued to drift downwards, although away from the still-hot mound.

Artur knelt and fumbled behind Isabel's legs, his hands patting the storage area within the gondola frame. "Repair kit's here, but we need to land to use it. You might as well touch down. Somewhere as flat as possible."

"Isabel, can you manage to watch for obstacles without getting distracted?" asked Eleanor.

"Gotcha. I'll handle safety when we land." Isabel patted her sabre hilt and placed one hand on the side of the gondola.

"Knees bent for impact! Hang on!" called Artur.

He was still unstrapping the repair bag when the gondola hit the ground. His face hit Eleanor's back. The scent of apple blossom filled his nostrils, and he twisted his head away so quickly his neck protested.

Isabel vaulted over the side before he could stand. She drew her sabre and paced round the blimp, head swinging from side to side. "Seems clear, but you'd better get a move on. We're still too close to the mound."

Artur clambered over the side while lugging the repair bag, and Eleanor followed. The balloon sagged on the ground, part-deflated, and they hastened towards the tear.

A howl arose in the distance.

Some part of his mind gibbered. He ripped open the repair bag and tipped out its contents, scrabbling for the standard-issue patch. Eleanor crouched by him with the flashlight. Seizing the patch with relief, he placed it over the tear, nodding as he assessed its size. Easily big enough. Now they just needed to apply the adhesive.

At a gasp from Eleanor, he followed her gaze to where the flashlight illuminated a second hole. Crap. They had only the one patch. Now what? Hoping against hope to find something useful, he patted his pockets. *Empty, dammit!* His head pounded, and he yanked the material with frustration. Why hadn't he thought to bring more—*Fabric!*

Sweat running down his face, he unbuttoned his over-alls.

Eleanor's head jerked round. "What the—Oh." She swung the light round to the pile of repair tools and ran her hand over them while Artur squirmed out of the top half of his clothing.

The howl was answered by another, from the opposite direction.

"Save your games for later," called Isabel from her sentry position.

Absolutely, completely mad.

"Scissors," snapped Artur, holding out a hand.

Eleanor shook her head, kneeling on a sleeve and grabbing another edge of the fabric to keep it taut. "I'll do it— guess those sewing lessons were useful after all."

With a ripping noise, she cut a square of fabric from Artur's overalls. He shivered as the cold metal slid across his buttock. What if she saw his—*Worry about that later, stupid!* She laid the pot of adhesive between them, and they scooped out the glue with their gloved fingers to apply to each patch. He part-folded his, slipping it through the hole and running his hand around the outer edge so the glue would stick. A glance at Eleanor showed her copying his movements.

"How long till it sets?" Her voice was breathless.

He gulped, shrugging back into the remains of his clothing. "Instructions say an hour—"

"But you don't have that long," broke in Isabel. "They're coming back, and I can't protect you both."

And we know where that leaves me. "The instructions assume the patch is on the outside of the balloon." Artur wiped his brow with a sleeve. "But we've put them on the inside—"

"So the gas pressure will help keep them in place, and it probably doesn't need an hour." Eleanor stood. "I don't know why that's not your usual procedure."

"I don't know either." None of the engineers or operators followed the official instructions, but nobody saw fit to rewrite them. "We should start re-inflating now."

Isabel pulled the emergency canister of levium and its tubing from the gondola. Artur attached the inflation valve and emptied its contents, leaning on the balloon to keep it in place as it expanded. Eleanor climbed into the gondola and arranged herself at the controls.

A few bays and yips drew closer.

His gut roiled. It was time to be brave. "What I do know, however, is that this repaired blimp can't lift three people. I'll stay here, and it can carry the two of you back to Ascar." His voice cracked. "Can you please send word to my parents? I wouldn't want to leave them wondering..."

Isabel gripped his shoulder, making him wince. "Don't be silly. She'll need your help. I'll remain. I'm the heaviest. I've no clue how to repair or handle a blimp. And, well, this was all my fault. Eleanor, this one's a keeper."

Artur gaped. "But you're her cousin! I can't let you—"

She kissed him, and he tasted brandy.

"Now, go." Isabel pushed him towards the gondola.

Even as he climbed in, the gondola's floor shifted, marking the blimp's imminent ascent. He clung to the side, eyes on Isabel, as they limped into the air.

His last view showed Isabel loping away from the mound. She held her sabre in one hand, a flaming torch in the other. He blinked. Where had she magicked that from?

Eleanor's voice interrupted his thoughts. "Can you direct us back to Ascar?"

"Yes? Yes. Yes, I can." His voice shook and his breathing shortened. He picked up the map and attempted to unfold it.

"Artur, what we've done tonight is important."

His trembling hands crushed the map. "More important than Isabel?" He clamped his mouth shut.

"Maybe. She..." Eleanor shuddered. "She knows what she's doing. I'll explain when we get back."

Chapter 7

Artur's hands were still shaking when he and Eleanor neared Ascar. Even without Isabel's daunting presence, the gondola's confines pressed in on him as he huddled against the side. *Madness.* The city's lights had never been such a welcoming sight. He'd never before seen them from above, and he hoped to never again. What had she dragged him into?

Despite the damaged balloon, Eleanor maintained the blimp at a safe altitude as they approached the rooftop of the Keep. With the tethering rope clutched in his hand, Artur peered towards the landing pad. If he hit some unsuspecting guard with the rope, well, wouldn't that just round off the evening? But dim lamplight from the walls supplemented moonlight's faint glimmer to reveal an unoccupied rooftop. Of course. She'd dismissed the guards before they set out. Had she wanted to avoid witnesses to this mad venture?

After dropping the rope, he slid down it so fast he shredded his gloves and landed sprawled on the rooftop's surface. *Thank the Settlers!* He kissed the unmoving solidity beneath him, savoured the coolness of the stone slab against his cheek. But there was work to be done. Regaining his feet, he attached the rope to the winch. Ignoring his smarting palms and the draught from the gap in his overalls, he cranked the levers. The machinery drew the blimp in until the gondola touched the ground.

Eleanor flicked a switch, and the remaining gas hissed out, allowing the balloon to deflate. She swung herself over the side and landed with a soft scuff. "Artur, can you help me with the hampers? I don't want the pictures and maps falling into the wrong hands."

His jaw clenched at her poise, such a contrast with his shaking hands and churning gut. Didn't she care what had happened? Had she no heart? But she was the queen. "Of course." He bowed. "I am yours to command, Your Majesty."

They removed the hampers from the blimp in silence.

He licked his lips, remembering the taste of brandy. Isabel was Eleanor's cousin, wasn't she? "Your Majesty?"

She sighed and rubbed her face. "Yes, Engineer Granville?"

"About Isabel... are you going to send someone out? To help her?"

She stiffened, then shook her head. "No. It's best all round if she makes her way back herself. She'll be fine. I'm sure of it."

He sneaked a look at Eleanor's face, at the shadows under her eyes. Maybe she wasn't so offhand. "I'm sorry."

"This wasn't a pleasure trip, you know." Her voice wavered.

His lips twitched. "You can say that again. Should I notify someone about the damaged blimp?"

"Please. There's a runner station one floor down. I'd hoped to keep this trip quiet, but it'll need more hands than Haslett's to repair."

"Yes." Artur regarded his scraped hands. "I'd offer to help, but..."

He walked downstairs and sent a messenger to fetch

Haslett.

A short while later, Haslett arrived, sleepy creases adorning his face. His jaw dropped open at the damage. "What? But... how?"

Eleanor drew herself up straight. "Your young colleague here is to be commended. His quick thinking prevented a disaster."

Haslett bobbed his head and murmured, "Of course. I ensure all my staff are well trained."

She nodded. "His composure as he handled the blimp following such an unexpected bird strike was truly impressive."

Artur stared, wondering how plausible the story would be.

"I think," she continued, "that it would be worth exploring modifications to make the balloons more bird-proof. Just as a suggestion, maybe mounting permanent lights on the gondola? I think most birds would avoid lights."

Haslett bowed. "I shall see that it is done, Your Majesty. It may take a little—"

"I would like Engineer Granville to oversee the work. I can see he has a bright future. Of course, such developments cost money. I will ensure his project is funded."

Artur gaped. Then he clenched his fists, his palms stinging. Was she bribing him?

Haslett murmured his agreement and assured Eleanor the damage to the blimp would be repaired quickly.

"Good," said Eleanor. "I have full faith in you."

"Er," said Haslett, "didn't Captain Hanlon depart on the blimp with you?"

She drew in a sharp breath. "Indeed she did, but I have sent her on another errand." She smiled, her face waxy in the lamplight. "Shall I let her know you were asking after her?"

"No, no, that's fine!" Haslett's hands fluttered. "But thank you for the offer, Your Majesty. I'll go and send the messages right away. As soon as it's light, the team will get to work."

Eleanor inclined her head and took a few steps towards the palace. She called over her shoulder, "Engineer Granville, could you please bring those two hampers?"

Artur ground his teeth but picked up the hampers and stomped after her.

Once they were on the bridge, Eleanor glanced over her shoulder and stopped. "Sorry. He's gone. You can put them down now."

He dropped the hampers. While he was flexing his fingers, she picked them up and strode on, leaning to one side with the uneven weight. He followed her in scowling silence across the bridge, back into the palace and down the stairs to the royal apartments on the third floor. The guards on the stairwell saluted, and one of them frowned at Artur. He dropped his gaze. *I guess I should have carried the hampers back.*

Eleanor led him along a hallway with threadbare carpeting, past the drawing room where they had met on his previous visit. When he'd thought she only wanted a chat, fool that he was. Further along the hallway, the housekeeper snoozed in a comfy chair, her stockinged feet on a footstool.

"Martha," called Eleanor as they approached. "We're back."

The woman's eyes popped open, and she beamed at them. "I do hope you had a nice time with your young man." She stood and pushed her feet into slippers. "What would you like first? Bath? Supper?"

Eleanor patted her shoulder. "You're a marvel. Bath first, please."

Artur found himself led into a bathing room, disrobed, and whisked into a hot bath, though thankfully Eleanor had disappeared in some other direction. His skin reddened as the elderly housekeeper poured jugs of water over his head. Was this how royalty lived? Always attended, even while performing ablutions? Not to mention during more intimate—

When she advanced on him with a sponge, he grabbed her hand. "I can manage that myself. Thank you. Could you wait outside, please?"

After he'd scrubbed his grazed hands clean and finished his bath, he pulled on the cosy dressing gown left out for him. Martha led him into a snug sitting room.

Wrapped in a shabby bathrobe, Eleanor was curled up in a cushioned armchair beside the crackling fireplace, gazing into the flames. Her hands cradled a mug of mulled wine, and a plate of sandwiches lay on a table beside her. On the other side of the fireplace was a second chair with its own table bearing a similar repast. The two hampers stood by the wall.

Martha pushed him into the chair and shoved the plate into his hand. His mouth watered at the scent of smoked turkey and pickle. So much for the quails' eggs and larks' tongues he'd imagined as standard palace fare. Maybe royalty didn't have such refined tastes.

"Thank you, Martha." Eleanor set her mug down and picked up her plate. "Off you go and get some sleep. You shouldn't be up so late."

"And who else would you want looking after you? But if you don't need anything else, I'll seek my bed now." She nodded at Artur. "I've placed your bag in the second bedroom. Saves you from wandering around."

Artur blushed as the housekeeper left.

"Please, eat," said Eleanor. "It's been a long evening."

He took a mouthful. Soft, fresh bread, delicate slivers of meat, and pickle with just the right amount of bite. *The best part of this damn evening.* But he'd have to spoil supper by asking questions. He swallowed. "You did say you'd explain when we got back. Please."

"Yes. What would you like to know about first?"

He gathered his thoughts. Despite his naïve conjectures earlier, the evening's trip hadn't been for entertainment. She obviously hadn't *planned* the explosion and damaged blimp, even though that's what stuck in his mind the most. And the beasts, of course. "It seems like you're trying to examine the cursed mounds, see how they're related to beasts. And I can see the value in doing it from the air. Yes?"

She nodded.

"But why do it in the dark? Wouldn't it be easier and safer during the day? Any of us could have been attacked after the accident—even cursed—and Isabel's still at risk out there."

"I know." She squeezed her eyes shut for a moment and sighed. "She's... experienced in travelling outside the city. When she returns, she'll probably laugh at us for worrying about her."

"I see." He could almost believe that. If anyone could survive in the wilds, fighting off hordes of beasts, it would be Isabel. "But the dark?"

She gazed into her mug. "We know not all animals are beasts, but we can't always tell the difference just by looking at them. One of the scientists, name of Fellows, had an idea that beasts' eyes glow a different colour in the dark to other animals, green rather than red. I think he was right. Certainly our domestic fowl have eyes that reflect red in torchlight."

Artur shuddered, remembering the eerie green glow of the beasts' eyes at the cursed mound earlier. "That makes sense." He gulped his mulled wine then sucked in air as it scalded his tongue.

"Another scientist, Silvers, even managed to capture a live beast—"

He choked, put his mug down and coughed. "What?"

"Yes, I'm not sure how, but it was very helpful. He showed me some daguerreotypes, and the eyes were definitely green. Anyway, that's why we did it in the evening, to identify them more easily."

Setting the plate on his lap, he picked up another sandwich. "No offence, uh, Eleanor, but why are you doing this yourself? Why not get one of the scientists to go out and have a look?"

She frowned. "Don't think I haven't tried. But they're more interested in investigating the afflicted than thinking about the curse's origins. Lady Nelson fobs me off, Fellows isn't exactly practically orientated, and Silvers is quite new. He does seem pretty open to ideas, so maybe I'll try him again. And nobody other than them—and me—would have the clout to commandeer a blimp for the investigation."

"And the secrecy?"

"Until I'm sure of my findings, I don't want people to get the wrong impression. Might cause panic. And I think my father was looking into the curse. When he died." She bit her lip. "Or was murdered."

Artur clapped a hand over his mouth in an attempt to

avoid spitting half-chewed turkey over the carpet. "What?"

Eleanor's knuckles whitened as she clasped her hands together. "It was a shock when he went to Settlers' Rest last year, completely unexpected. Of course I worried it was foul play. They found no evidence, but I've learned recently that some people have access to undetectable ways of killing. So, I'm afraid that whoever got him might come after me. He didn't have the opportunity to implement his plan about the curse."

Oh. Artur nodded, remembering the city's shock over the king's sudden death, followed by the coronation festivities. Eleanor's drawn expression suggested she'd suffered through both events. "So, you don't want people to know you're researching the curse, whatever the reason, just in case you make yourself a new target."

"That's right." She reddened. "It's less noteworthy if people think I'm going on evening blimp rides because I've... taken a lover."

"What?" He leaned forwards, fists clenched. "You were using me! Your interest in me was all pretence." *And like a total idiot, I fell for*–Despite his grab, the sandwiches slid to the floor.

"Sorry." Her lip trembled. "You're right to be angry. I didn't plan this very well."

He sat back and took a deep breath. *She used me.* But then, she hadn't actually harmed him. She'd even tried to compensate him, with payment for a new project. He could understand why she was doing this, even if he didn't like it. She was the queen, after all. She was *supposed* to use people, take the long view, and all those other things. *I suppose I can't really blame her.* "Why are you trusting me with this?"

"Because you offered to stay behind. At the mound. I

mean, even if you didn't know what was going on, it was obviously dangerous. You were concerned about Isabel's safety. And you were prepared to..." Eleanor stood, picked up her plate of sandwiches and placed it beside him. "Here, have mine. I'm not hungry."

Bribing me with food? It could be worse... though she owes me new overalls. "Anyway, why aren't you sending search parties after Isabel? Why do you think she can manage by herself?"

Her head jerked up. "I think that explanation needs to wait for another day." She looked him in the eye. "Artur..."

"Yes?"

"If Isabel doesn't come back—though I fully expect she will do—I'll be on my own, with nobody I can trust. Will you help me?"

Chapter 8

Susanna's temples throbbed as she regarded the stained glass door that had been closed in her face. It seemed Kenneth Staunton was not at home. *That is, not at home to me.*

She hadn't expected an enthusiastic welcome: she'd be a reminder of his truncated career. But such an outright rejection stung. Was it because she'd mentioned Jonathan in her note yesterday? She'd hoped to pique the retired scientist's interest after his suggestions regarding Tabitha's training. Staunton knew her as a captain and knew about powers. He'd not believe any superstition that she'd been contaminated by association with Jonathan.

Seeing no reason to linger, she walked away from the nobles' quarter, through the bustling streets of the outer city and back towards the barracks.

After she'd pinned her hopes on Staunton, the need to find another plan was a blow. Her lips pursed. He'd openly expressed dislike of Silvers to Jonathan. Perhaps there was blackmail involved, going by how Silvers was pressuring Lester. Why talk to Jonathan and not to her? Should she have risked mentioning that she sought information about Silvers?

"Captain Longleaf, ma'am."

"Oh!" Her head jerked up, and she focussed on a city guard with an arm outstretched between her and a procession of handcarts. She'd nearly walked out in front of them. Her face heated. "Sorry, I was deep in thought."

"Not a problem, ma'am. Just some extra deliveries for the blimp chaps. Perhaps you could take the next road along?" He indicated the route and saluted.

She nodded and walked on, cutting through the city square, avoiding street hawkers and nannies with perambulators. Was Silvers influencing Staunton? Maybe forcing him to... to do what? Stop speaking with the captains? But why hadn't Jonathan had a problem? Hmm. Maybe Jonathan *was* the problem, and something he'd done had changed things with Staunton, in addition to landing him in prison.

The scent of paprika-spiced chicken lured her into a cafe. Over a lunch that she ate but didn't taste, she thought further over possible solutions. Isabel? No, she might be motivated by political concerns rather than thoughts of fairness or safety. *It's all very well for her, she can break the rules with impunity.* Confront Silvers? She pulled a face. *He'd find some reason to slap me in prison too, probably.* Lady Nelson? No, she'd side with anyone who detained the afflicted. A direct appeal to the queen? Susanna shook her head. The queen and Isabel were up to something mysterious. Best not to complicate things. Her thoughts circled back to Staunton. Something about him nagged at her...

When Susanna returned to the barracks, Lester was pacing outside her door, folding that day's *Informer* into a bird.

"Sorry." She unlocked the door and let them in. "I lost track of time. What did you find out from the guards?"

He peered out of the window, then at the ornaments on her shelf, then at her book collection. She settled herself on her chaise longue and clasped her hands. Maybe he'd stop fidgeting if she kept still.

At last he took a seat. "They're worried. Shocked about Jonathan's so-called concealed powers and wondering why nobody spotted them earlier. Especially the ones who'd been to Maldon with him. One day he was leading them back into the Keep, and the next morning he was all over the news."

She sighed. "And I suppose they believe he killed that guard."

"They're not rushing to suggest alternatives. At least some of the regular convoy guards are wondering if it might have been an accident." He inspected his nails. "I know you're fond of him and all, but he didn't exactly make an effort to be popular."

"I know." She bowed her head. Jonathan didn't seem to care whether he was liked, as long as he did his job well. The respect, not to mention loyalty, many convoy guards held for him was testament to his abilities. But maybe it wasn't enough.

Lester frowned. "A couple of them shared some stories. I think they were trying to show him in a good light as a captain, but some of the anecdotes may have made things worse."

"Go on." She might as well learn of the damage.

"Well, like how often he patrolled by himself, when it should have been a pair of his guards. At best, that seems overprotective. At worst, an excuse for him to do whatever mad thing they suspect him of, in private. They even commented about his insistence on bathing in full privacy, against regulations, and how he might have been trying to hide scars from when he got cursed. I guess that's actually true."

Despite her worry, Susanna snorted. She explained her

own scars away as a youthful accident, but Jonathan might have baulked even at such an innocuous falsehood. Never mind his awkwardness around communal—or, more precisely, mixed—bathing. She'd pretended not to notice such foibles when he'd been a convoy guard under her command, prior to his beast-inflicted scars and promotion to captain. Poor Jonathan.

Lester continued. "There was reluctance to sign up for the squads that went after him, especially when they decided they wanted him alive rather than, uh, dead. Seems the publicity about how dangerous he was backfired. The Council had to offer a huge bonus before they got enough volunteers. After that tidbit, the guards started complaining about pay, so I left." He flicked a speck of dust off his sleeve. "What are the other captains saying?"

"I saw David and Richard." She summarised the previous morning's conversation and the other captains' speculations about Jonathan's instability. "But I'm sure Silvers is brewing a plot. Everything happened so quickly, it must have been thought out beforehand."

"So, what now?"

How could she persuade Lester to do this? She took a deep breath. "If Silvers is exploiting curses, it's trouble for not just captains, not just guards, but everyone. Serious trouble."

He nodded. "I see."

"So we need the best information we can get. Staunton knows how the scientists work, he has no direct interest in the situation, and he knows Silvers." *He ought to be my best information source, bar Silvers himself.*

"Sure, makes perfect sense."

"I couldn't get in to speak with Staunton. I don't know

why. I think you can do better than me at finding what's going on with him."

He raised an elegant eyebrow. "Me? I don't see why I'd be any—"

"An indirect advance, not to Staunton himself." She licked her lips. "I want you to approach one of his maids."

"What?" He rose from his chair and started to pace, hands clenched. "I don't do that sort of thing. Not anymore. You know that."

Here we go. "It's all I can—"

"You think being pretty is an advantage?" He jabbed a finger towards his face. "Well, it's not. Not for a boy from the slums. An amusement that middle-aged gentility can enjoy for trivial expenditure."

People like me? "I'm not asking you to—"

"I'm not going back to that life. You don't know what it's like."

She stood. "You need to get over it—"

"Six years I played that soul-destroying game, and I don't even know who I am anymore." He drew a shuddering breath.

"Lester!" She grabbed his arms and shook him. Gently. Settling a panic attack would take more effort than she could stomach. "I'm just asking you to chat with her, nothing more. It'll be different from what you used to do. Really. For a start, if you take her somewhere, you should pay, not her. I'll pay you back, of course."

"But why ask me? Get someone else to do it."

"I don't *have* anyone else I can ask!" She released his arms and lowered her voice. "There's no one else I can trust to do this. Listen, you're doing this for yourself as well. Trying to get one up on Silvers, to get him off your back."

He chewed his lip. "You mean, you trust me because he has a hold over me."

"Well, yes." *And because I've read your mind.* Though mentioning that wouldn't be wise. Even when she wasn't using her power, people remained wary in her presence.

"I mean, it's not like the guards who know about my past care. But now I've moved up in rank, and might have other captains sneering at me... Really, I'd rather just go along with what Silvers says for now."

She patted his arm. "Honestly, Lester, they've seen and heard of worse. We all have. And, to put it bluntly, if Jonathan was—*is*—right about Silvers' plans, a seedy past will be the least of your worries."

He slumped on to the seat and stared at the floor.

"I know this is difficult for you, but you're a good man." She tapped her temple. "I can tell."

He gave a strained laugh. "Don't tell anyone else—you'll ruin my reputation. Though... if anyone spotted me out with a girl, they'd assume I was on the pull. Nothing serious."

Poor Lester. Using frivolity as a refuge from responsibility. He couldn't get away with that forever. She eased out a breath. "You'll do the right thing. I'm sure of it."

"Persuasive as ever, Susanna." Sitting up, he straightened his jacket collar. "What do you want me to ask her?"

"See if she's noticed anything odd about Staunton's behaviour since his retirement. Any visitors or messages, that sort of thing."

"It'll take me a few days. But I'll do it."

Off he went, leaving her with her thoughts. She'd have to trust him to do the best he could and hope it would be enough, since *she* couldn't take that line of investigation any further. Meanwhile, she'd try to help the child who'd prompted Jonathan to lower his barriers: Tabitha.

Chapter 9

Annetta frowned at the distant ringing of a handbell. Some kind of signal, obviously, but for what? She had lived in Maldon for a few months now but never heard it before. After labelling the sachet she'd been preparing, she stepped outside her workshop to investigate.

A steady flow of townsfolk drifted in the direction of the town square. She allowed herself to be carried along with them. The fresh crisp air made a nice change from her medicinal workshop odours.

"What's happening?" she asked of a weaver whose arthritis she'd treated.

Small and hunched, the woman twisted her neck to peer up at Annetta. "Oh, that's the mayor's signal. He'll have an announcement to make. He used to do it right regular, but... well, not so much these days. He didn't really need to tell us every time he received a message."

Giselle had a word, I bet. Annetta shrugged and followed the rest, who packed themselves into the square. It was even busier than on market day. She might as well see what was happening.

Between the bobbing heads and shifting bodies, she glimpsed Opal a short distance away. Marcus stood beside the guard, murmuring into her ear. No sign of Adrian, but he might have been in his workshop and not noticed the bell. Perhaps Annetta could drop by later and tell him about the announcement.

A splash of red distinguished Mayor Sutcliff from the rest of the crowd, as did the glint of his chain of office. He waved a hand at the bell ringer, and the clangour ceased.

A hush spread while Sutcliff climbed on one of the benches. He smoothed down his official robes, which were too short to conceal his bony ankles. Annetta suppressed a grin.

"Good citizens of Maldon," he called, "I have dire news."

Only the shuffle of feet and rustle of clothing broke the silence.

He surveyed those around him then nodded. "Dire news indeed. A cursed being has been walking among us!"

A few voices murmured, and Sutcliff patted his hands in the air. "Calm down. There is no need to panic, I assure you. Panicking will get us nowhere."

Annetta's gut twisted. How had he found out about Samuel? She'd better go to Adrian's and warn them. A flash of auburn hair caught her eye: Giselle easing her way out of the square. She relaxed a little. Giselle would keep Samuel away from any approaching trouble, should things get nasty. Annetta had better stay here and find out what was going on.

The other townsfolk looked around with frowns, and those at the edge of the crowd backed away from each other, as if afraid of contamination.

"Who is it?" called someone.

"I should have suspected it from the start..."

"Who?"

"... but appearances can be deceiving..."

"Who!"

"What? Oh." Sutcliff fumbled in a pocket and pulled

out a scrap of paper. "I'll share Ascar's message to me. Obviously, timely dissemination of information in emergencies is a high priority. The bird arrived only this morning, so I'm giving you the news without any delay."

A bead of sweat trickled down Annetta's face. Why had Ascar sent a public announcement rather than dealing with Samuel quietly? Had the Council reacted so badly to Captain Shelley's suggestion? Her vision grew hazy. *Come on, breathe. You need to know the worst.*

"Right." Sutcliff cleared his throat. "Urgent warning to all settlements. Jonathan Shelley, former convoy captain, cursed and roaming at large. Murderer. Imprisoned but escaped. Extremely dangerous. Reward for capture or neutralisation."

There were scattered exclamations. A couple of the younger women shrieked, and Annetta clenched her fists to stop herself from joining them. *Murderer.* What had he done? Who had he killed? Opal, her face white, clutched Marcus' arm. The crowd's clamour rose, then settled.

"But you must not worry. His heinous powers can be resisted." The mayor drew himself up. "I myself withstood his attempts to convince me I was blameworthy for events outside my control..."

Annetta's breathing quickened. Had Captain Shelley been manipulating them? But to what effect?

Sutcliff droned on. "... personal fortitude can overcome the threat..."

"Plus the fact he's not here!" someone shouted.

The mood of the crowd shifted, and Annetta caught a few smirks. Sutcliff continued for a short while in the same vein, but the townsfolk started to drift away. The comments she overheard were along the lines that everyone knew the curse existed, and just because it affected someone they'd met didn't mean they should panic. And anyway, Ascar was nowhere near Maldon.

"Well, I guess Mayor Sutcliff was right to make the announcement," muttered the weaver as they left the square. "Even if it's nothing to do with us."

Annetta frowned. *But it might have plenty to do with us.*

She hurried home to find Opal and Lisa waiting outside her door. A short while later, Giselle, Adrian and Samuel arrived.

"Is Captain Shelley in trouble?" Samuel's lip quivered, and his blue eyes moistened. He huddled into his too-large clothing. "He was nice."

"I'm afraid he might be." Giselle patted his back. "It's going to be a problem teasing out what's actually going on from Henry's announcement."

After a glance outside, Adrian shut the front door. "Yes. I always had good dealings with Captain Shelley. Could he really have mur—"

Giselle coughed and glanced at Samuel.

Adrian reddened. "Could he have... done that to someone?"

Annetta chewed her lip. "I think it's possible, in theory, that he might have done at some point. The official guidance does mention the need for 'neutralisation' in the event of a dangerous curse. For the safety of all. But I don't see what that's got to do with us. I mean, he's not done that to any of *us*, has he?"

There was uneasy laughter. Giselle raised an eyebrow at Adrian, whose shoulders slumped.

"Samuel," he said, "why don't you show me how your sketches of people are coming along? Everyone else can chat in peace next door."

"Sure thing!" Samuel perked up, took a seat at the workbench and pulled out his papers and pencils while the others filed into Annetta's sitting room.

With Giselle and Lisa seated at her tiny table, Annetta perched on the storage chest below the shelf that held her infusions. Opal propped herself against the opposite wall.

Conversation was easier away from Samuel, although they kept their voices low.

Opal shook her head about Sutcliff's mention of the curse. "I think that part's a cover up. I've learned, from someone else, that the Council really do make use of people with cursed powers. Killing? I can sort of understand, if he thought someone was a danger. He's very protective. Once he decides to protect you, you stay protected, like it or not, no matter the consequences. But I can't see him just murdering someone at random." Her lips twisted. "Unless it was one of the Council or scientists. They push the captains more than they do us regulars."

Lisa's eyes widened. "You knew he had a cursed power, and you didn't mention that to me before?"

"Sorry, we all know, but—"

"Yeah, yeah, secrecy." Lisa scowled. "But now everyone knows. Have you seen him using it?"

"Just the once." Opal regarded her hands, wiggling her fingers. "I was on a mission with him, and two guards were injured. One of them seriously. Very seriously. He saved her life with his power."

Annetta blinked. Well, *obviously* his power was more than making teapots explode, but it sounded like he could affect living people too. Such a power might have chirurgical applications.

Giselle sniffed. "Even if we discount the part about him being cursed, they must have had reason to send that warning. If he's really dangerous, he'll need to be dealt with. Though personally, I'd keep an open mind about that claim. Still, the important thing—"

"Is how this affects what we're doing with Samuel," put in Annetta. "Was Captain Shelley lying when he told us he'd negotiate with the Council? Why would he do that?"

"Or maybe he wasn't lying," said Giselle, "but something went wrong when he reported in. I do hope that wasn't why he killed someone, if that's what he did." She waved a hand in dismissal. "Still, if they do investigate us, we can tell them we followed his orders in good faith."

Opal nodded. "And the longer we hold on to Samuel here, the less likely it is they'll take him away. They'd look silly if they detained someone who'd been managing fine for so long without being noticed by anyone else."

Lisa eyed Opal. "Does that mean you might stay here long term? I've noticed Marcus following you around."

The guard smiled, even as her face reddened. "Maybe."

"So," said Giselle, "I don't think this message changes things for us. If Captain Shelley doesn't show up here, no harm done. But if he does, we'll... have to do what's best for Maldon."

Annetta slumped. "We'll have to turn him in."

"Anything else?"

She considered her words, frowning at the replacement teapot on her stove. "Captain Shelley asked me to look into herbal preparations that might affect cursed powers. Sometimes, in emergencies, we herbalists try to treat the afflicted, but the remedies are experimental at best. Information gets shared, and I have a lot of notes from the others to go through. It's difficult to be confident without people to test."

Her gaze dropped to the floor. Her dareth leaf infusion had caused him to lose control of his power. Afraid she might divulge what she'd witnessed to others, he had attacked her before she could use her emergency medicines on him. What if she had damaged him permanently with the dareth leaf, by destabilising his power or making him more prone to violence? But she couldn't turn the timepiece back. All she could do was seek a remedy to reliably suppress powers. If Captain Shelley did return to Maldon and prove to be dangerous... she'd need to have something ready.

The door swung open to admit Adrian and Samuel.

Adrian's face was pale. "Samuel's done a rather... interesting sketch."

Samuel handed his drawing to Annetta. "I'm getting better, see?"

She glanced at it, blinked, and handed it to Opal, whose eyebrows shot up. Giselle peered over Opal's shoulder with a frown.

Annetta swallowed. "You've certainly improved. I can see it's Captain Shelley again."

The boy nodded. "Yeah, I was thinking about him and this picture popped into my head. Then it kinda went through my hand, through my pencil on to the paper. Do you like it?"

"Yes, very nice." She took a deep breath. "But why have you drawn him with no clothes on?"

Too hot.

Jonathan lay shivering where he had fallen, trying to get his breath back. The mud that seeped through his uniform gave him some respite from the heat coming over him in waves. Despite the cool weather and the smell of frost in the air, he was sweating. Was there any point in getting up again? He set his jaw and pushed himself to his feet with a squelch, his wounded leg throbbing with the effort.

The gurgle of running water led him to a brook. He hung his sacks on a tree branch and dropped his broken sabre on the ground.

He knelt and scooped up some water, splashing it over his face. *Still too hot.* He refilled his waterskin then emptied it over his head.

There was something he wanted to do. Something he *needed* to do. What was it? How could he think in this heat?

He regarded the water, clear and inviting, then frowned at his mud-spattered clothing. Maybe that was it. *A bath. Keep my standards up.*

Out of long habit, Jonathan scanned his surroundings for the other convoy guards, to ensure he was unobserved. Then he shook his head. No, he didn't have any with him today. *Of course I don't. I left them... somewhere else, didn't I?* He slipped out of his uniform, tossed it into the water and slid in after it. His teeth chattered. But the chill of the water was a buttress against the heat inside him. He immersed himself fully then resurfaced, grabbed his uniform and scrubbed it.

The cold cleared his head. What was he doing? He scowled down at himself, at his soaked clothing. The red puffy edges of his leg wound stood out against his blue-tinged skin. *Idiot.*

He waded out, shivering as the breeze hit him. Draping the uniform over a bush, he gathered what dry sticks he could find. He retrieved his sabre, pulled a piece of quartz and a handful of tinder from his sack, and coaxed it all into a small fire.

Once he was satisfied with the blaze, he inspected his thigh wound. The skin felt tight and hot. It shouldn't be that red, should it? Not three or four days after surgery. He prodded the edges and frowned at the yellow leakage.

What had Silvers done to him?

... took a sample from you...

Was that all he had done?

Jonathan was neither infirmier nor chirurgeon. But he'd had his share of such wounds, and this should be knitting together by now. If it was red and oozing, there was something going on inside it. Something that needed to come out.

Only a smear of antiseptic salve remained in the glass jar. His brow wrinkled as he inspected his remaining scalpel, stared at the rust blooming over its blade. He weighed up the risks of poisoning himself if he used it. What other options did he have?

He considered the fire, then the jar. Fire first. He could always break the jar later if the scalpel proved too blunt. He laid a couple of rocks by the fire and balanced the scalpel on them, positioning the blade in the flame for a count of one hundred. While the blade cooled, he used his sabre to hack strips of cloth from his too-long trouser legs. The dressings he'd stolen had disintegrated. He'd need to pad and bind this new wound he was about to inflict on himself.

After folding a fabric scrap and gripping it between his teeth, he knelt by the fire. He lifted his scalpel in one hand, a second piece of cloth in the other.

Pain. He bit down on the cloth as he drew the blade along the wound, each stitch giving way with a little tug.

Watery fluid flowed out, with globs of blood and pus. Would this cut be enough?

The twinging as he prodded deeper with the scalpel brought on spots before his eyes. He hissed, and his power awoke, poised to strike in any direction. He wrestled with it, grip tightening on the scalpel. By the time his power lay under control again, sweat dripped down his face.

Blinking to clear his eyes, he dabbed at the wound. Something glinted. Something yellow and metallic. His probing scalpel hit something hard, but without the grating of bone. There was something that didn't belong there.

His hand cramped, and he twitched as the blade moved. Setting it to the side, he stared at his leg, remembering the time he had used his power to treat Franka. He concentrated, telling his power to seek the foreign item. His breathing rasped as he nudged it towards the surface, squeezing it out. It plopped to the ground with a final gush of liquid, and the pressure eased.

After spitting out the cloth, he remained kneeling for a minute, panting for breath. Then he washed the wound, applied the last of the salve and wrapped his thigh. He set his billycan over the fire to heat some gruel while he gathered enough wood to keep the fire going until the morning. The movement helped to warm him, but it promised to freeze overnight. His clothing wouldn't dry quickly, and it would be the height of stupidity for him to die of cold after going through all this.

What had he removed from his leg? He picked it up and wiped off the grime and pus. A golden disc, its diameter the width of his thumb. That made it about the size of a shilling, but shillings weren't gold. Plus, it didn't have the surface patterning of currency. Both surfaces were smooth.

No, *almost* smooth. There was something engraved on one face, barely visible under the setting sun. He squinted.

His heart pounded, and the hairs on the back of his neck rose.

JS

His initials. Someone had marked this disc, and Silvers had planted it in him. Why? Not for Jonathan's good, that was certain. *The bastard labelled me, like a possession.*

Jonathan's jaw clenched, and he hurled the disc into the water. *I'll kill him.* He glared at the blood-red horizon, breathing hard. Shoulders drooping, he shook his head. How, of course, would be the problem. Better concentrate on survival first.

He ate his gruel then cobbled together a lean-to, using some branches and his still-wet clothing. He stacked his extra firewood within easy reach. Between the fire and the shelter at his back, he should survive the night. He'd have to, if he planned to kill Silvers.

After lying down, he closed his eyes. The warmth at his front provided comfort, in contrast to the cold behind him. He concentrated on the warmth, on happier times. He thought of Susanna. She'd kissed him and invited him to stay. That was something to treasure. He was relieved she couldn't see him now: his condition might shake even her unflappable demeanour. *She* wouldn't have incurred Silvers' enmity and be staggering around the wilds. Whatever situation she encountered, she'd have found a sensible solution.

And what of Tabitha? Could she learn to control her power, maybe achieve the respect Jonathan had once commanded?

But what if she didn't?

... a source of cursed flesh...

No. Surely Silvers wouldn't use her like that. He hadn't—as far as Jonathan knew—done this to anyone else. But he'd hardly announce it, would he? Was Jonathan the first victim, or had there been others?

Jonathan's eyes snapped open, and the fire danced before him.

In the darkness beyond the flames, several points of green light caught his attention, moving towards him in pairs.

Eyes.

Chapter 10

"I miss Jonathan." Tabitha tied her unruly black hair away from her face, using a pink ribbon Susanna had brought her. "When's he coming back?"

Susanna's stomach roiled as she regarded the white-clad teenager sitting opposite her in Practice Room D. Of course Tabitha didn't know. There was no reason for anyone to have informed her of Jonathan's troubles. Although detainees in the Keep were permitted newspapers and "reasonable comforts"—Susanna had embroidered several cushions during her time there—Tabitha had made no such requests. It had been Jonathan's decision to take her under his wing and attempt to relieve her isolation. Because of Silvers' threats, he'd then had to negotiate with Lady Nelson for protection. That's how they'd ended up here, under a time limit for Tabitha to master her power.

Susanna dropped her gaze to the weights and pain boxes—Tabitha's term for the calibrated stimulus generators—that lay on the table between them. She swallowed. "He's having problems." No, concealing the truth wasn't fair. "That is, he's in trouble."

"What?" Tabitha's knuckles whitened and she jerked the pink bow tight. "What happened?"

"I don't know for certain. I'll tell you what I can, but some things you're not allowed to know." That wasn't too cowardly, was it? Susanna summarised the official account of Jonathan's imprisonment and escape, and the alleged murder charge. She omitted her suspicions of Silvers. There was no point in landing Tabitha in trouble for inconvenient awareness: being confined in the Keep was bad enough.

"They're saying he killed..." Tabitha's face paled. "No! It can't be true! Someone's out to get him."

Her throat constricted. "It's difficult, but try not to dwell on it too much."

"Why not?" Tabitha scowled.

"They might decide you're a security risk if they over-hear you. Or mind-read you."

"I'm locked up anyway. What's the worst they can do?"

The girl was brave. And naïve. Like Jonathan. An image of Jonathan's face arose in Susanna's mind, his bemused expression the last time she saw him. The first time she kissed him. And maybe the last. Her hand trembled as she met Tabitha's glare. "They're supposed to treat you de-cently here, but I'm worried how far someone might go. You could be used as a hold over Jonathan. Or the other way round."

"That's—" Her voice dropped to a whisper. "That's something Jed would do. Isn't it? Jonathan warned me about him."

"Jed? Oh, Scientist Silvers. Maybe." She tapped a box. "We need to work on your power now, build on what we did last time. It's what Jonathan would want. Best to... stay be-low notice."

Tabitha nodded. In silence they connected the leads, at-tached their earclips and turned their pain boxes on. They clasped hands. As with regular mind reading, physical con-tact would give Susanna a clearer image. She needed all the help she could get.

While the girl stared at the weights, Susanna rode the

pain coming through her earclip. She centred her own sense of identity, allowing Tabitha's thoughts to waft through her like mist while spinning her own perception of them into distinct yarn-like strands, and then a textured weave.

With her mental model in place, Susanna bent her attention to examining Tabitha's mind while also monitoring the weights. Flickering images and fragmented voices danced across her perception, but she told herself not to heed them. Not today. She wasn't here to read Tabitha's mind, but to help her: to give her feedback on her power, so she could learn to control it.

She squeezed Tabitha's hand. "I'm watching now. Try pushing."

The weave of Tabitha's thoughts was far less complex than the orderly structured array of Jonathan's, or even the loose colourful tangle of Lester's. Perhaps organisation depended on maturity? Tabitha's texture was similar to Jonathan's in a few areas: areas he somehow flexed when he used his power. However, in places there was a wide gap between them. Working with Tabitha had enhanced Susanna's knowledge of powers, but she'd been unable to convey to Tabitha how to bend her power like Jonathan did.

"And again."

A thought strand quivered, then the movement fizzled out.

"Try, er, lower?"

Nothing.

Tabitha's grip on her hand increased. A set of strands tangled together and darkened, resembling the girl's hair rather than fabric. Susanna tried to regain her previous model, but her power wasn't cooperating. The weights and boxes blurred before her eyes. She blinked, raised a hand to her cheek and found tears. When had she started crying?

Tabitha's eyes were squeezed shut, and tears streamed down her flushed face. "No... no..."

Why did you have to leave? You said you'd look after me.

Jonathan's serious face hovered before her. He frowned and vanished into the tangled strands. He reappeared and took a bite of a scone before disappearing. Susanna shuddered. The vividness and clarity of the images made Tabitha's thoughts difficult to separate from her own—but the sense of betrayal, of abandonment, was certainly Tabitha's. She broke their handclasp and tugged off their earclips. "Time for a break."

"Why did he have to go?" Tabitha's voice was thick. She wrapped her arms around herself, shivering.

Susanna swallowed the lump in her throat. "I don't think he had any choice."

She picked up the pain boxes and replaced them on the shelf. This session was going nowhere, as evinced by Tabitha's distress and the stubbornly unmoving weights. Hearing sniffles, she took her time, allowing the girl some privacy.

Scraping and rattling overlaid the sounds of grief, followed by a clatter.

Sighing, she turned to face Tabitha, who remained hunched on her chair. The largest weight lay on the floor.

Susanna shook her head. If only she'd been paying attention, she might have salvaged some good out of this exercise. Pain wasn't the only stimulus. Grief and sorrow could provoke as strong a response, but they were harder to control and possibly more cruel.

After escorting Tabitha back to the residents' floor, Susanna returned to the barracks. In the captains' lounge, she requested a tray of tea to be delivered to her quarters. She'd need it for her next challenge: Lester.

As she walked towards the doorway, Richard arrived. Their eyes met, and he paused, blocking her route.

Remembering his unsympathetic attitude towards Jonathan, she pursed her lips but suppressed her initial urge to push past. Antagonising him wouldn't be helpful, and she'd rather they were on the same side.

She regarded his sallow face, the fine lines around his mouth and the shadows beneath his eyes. Maybe he had problems of his own. Finding things might be as draining for him as mind reading was for her. Even now, her ear tingled at the memory of the pain box. "Richard. Are you well?"

He licked his lips and looked away. "I've been busy. More demands every day. I'm already working flat out to locate stolen goods, but now they're on at me to find mislaid items too. Carelessness, not crime." He touched the light stubble on his chin. "At least I'm being paid extra."

... should I tell her?

She stiffened as she glimpsed his thought, placed a hand on his arm. "Can I help?"

It might not be–Richard glanced down at her hand and twitched his arm away. He stepped back, nearly colliding with a waiter, who swayed out of the way and kept walking.

"Ah, no. But thank you for the offer." With a jerky nod, he moved around her and continued towards the dining area.

Damn. She'd gone and put him on guard with such a blatant move. Following him wouldn't help. Patience, she counselled herself as she returned to her room. But she'd had enough of being patient.

When Lester knocked on Susanna's door, she raised an eyebrow at his tatty tunic and wet hair.

He sat down with an embarrassed grin. "Thought a workout would help settle me."

She poured tea for both of them. "How did you get on with the maid?"

"I'd no idea Staunton lived in the nobles' quarter." He sipped his tea. "His house is pretty small, isn't it? Not nearly as big as Isabel's. She must rattle around in that house, all by herself. Did you know she lives right up by the Royal Compound wall? I guess being the queen's cousin—"

"Yes, Lester. I've been there. About the maid?"

"Oh, so you have. I forgot. It wasn't really so difficult. I followed her, lifted her purse, then pretended I'd found it after she dropped it. Yesterday was her evening off, so I took her out. We ended up in a tavern."

That was no surprise. "And?"

His hand wobbled as he set the teacup down. "I... had a tankard of ale. So did she. It was a real treat for her, she doesn't have a night out very often."

"Good, good." Susanna's fingernails dug into her palms. "Did she say anything useful?"

Lester picked up a biscuit and started to crumble it between his fingers. "I mean, it wasn't that much. Even after I'd drunk it all, it was no problem keeping my power suppressed. I didn't need to use it, and it wouldn't have been fair—"

She sighed. "Lester, can you just tell me what she said? Please?"

He dropped the biscuit on the tray, dusted off his fingers and sat up straight. "Well. Staunton's in his study a lot of the time, reading and making notes. He has occasional visitors. She remembered Jonathan because Staunton received him in the back room. She's not allowed in there to clean, but she doesn't mind—less work for her. The butler turns his nose up and says, 'It's an offence to the master's position' to have such a messy room in the house. There's only one other visitor who goes into that room—"

"Silvers." Susanna's jaw clenched. It had to be.

Lester paused, mouth agape. "Yes. Silvers. All other visitors use the parlour."

Why? She rubbed her forehead. "Sorry, I didn't mean to interrupt. Carry on."

He slumped, leaning on the table. "Silvers visits a couple of times a month, often carrying a folder of notes. She overheard him as he was leaving once, said something about trying out Staunton's suggestion to increase the dose. Then he laughed and went off on his way."

How could she make sense of this? "Could they be working together? Voluntarily? Though it's more likely Silvers is blackmailing him. But why meet him and Jonathan in that room?"

Lester shrugged. "Dunno. That's all I got. About Staunton, I mean." He grimaced. "She was all full of plans for our next date... I'll need to lie low for a while."

"Thanks for all this, Lester. You did well." She patted his hand. "How much do I owe you?"

He shook his head. "It's alright. It was only two tankards, and I'm not that badly off. I asked if she wanted more, but she didn't dare. Staunton disapproves of alcohol—"

Susanna's head jerked up. "But he's a drunkard. Rather, Jonathan thinks he is. Isabel doesn't. Why?"

"Sorry," said Lester. "I've no idea."

She closed her eyes. There must be something she was missing, something that could explain things. Was Staunton cursed? Cursed or not, was Silvers blackmailing him for advice on how to curse people?

At the rap of knuckles on wood, she looked round. A paper slid under the door.

She picked it up and smiled at the words on the note. "We have a lucky break."

"Oh?"

"This is my next week's schedule for the monitoring interviews. I get to mind-read Silvers." Whatever the scientist was up to, she'd find out. And once she knew that, nothing would stop her from helping Jonathan.

Chapter 11

Eleanor clasped her hands and frowned at the grizzled guard standing in front of her study desk. "No signs?"

"I'm sorry, Your Majesty. We explored the lands to the east across a range of five miles, and there was nothing to suggest Captain Hanlon's presence."

Her grip tightened as her gaze drifted past the assorted family portraits on the wood-panelled walls. It had been a small hope, but the thought of Isabel lying injured or worse, far from help, had grown in her mind until she ordered a search party. "I see. Thank you for your efforts, Chief Guard Paton."

The tarnished golden buttons on his scarlet uniform glinted as he bowed. "She is, of course, free to do as she wishes... but, if you don't mind my saying, it might have been useful if she had left a clearer indication of her route."

Knuckles white, Eleanor drew herself up on her chair. "Yes, I quite agree. When I next see her, I shall make that point to her. Please consider her reprimanded. You may leave."

After Paton departed, she slumped, staring at the maps scattered over the desk. Her pencilled-in marks had given the guards some indication of where to search, but Eleanor couldn't in good conscience send the group too close to the burnt-out cursed mound without any warning: a warning she couldn't explain, and therefore one she couldn't give. Of course, Paton already knew about cursed powers though that just compounded the problem. If Eleanor confessed the blimp trip had gone so wrong, he'd never let her out of his sight again. At least Haslett knew to keep his mouth closed while arranging repairs.

She'd thought of Isabel as indestructible, a reassuring presence at her back. And now she was gone. Guilt settled on Eleanor's shoulders.

It's my fault, and I can't even admit my share of the blame.

True, they'd planned the excursion together, but Eleanor had sanctioned it: Isabel couldn't have obtained the blimp on her own authority. Still, any chance to combat beasts would have set her on the hunt. Whenever Eleanor suggested a new location, Isabel would go out on foot, wreak havoc on any beasts, then return with more information for Eleanor's models. Such trips might take a few days, but she'd always given warning of any absences in advance.

Privacy had been paramount to Isabel. She had even reported to Eleanor secretly after constructing a hidden doorway worthy of a cloak-and-dagger melodrama. Eleanor had used that same entrance to discreetly check if Isabel were home but incapacitated. However, the house had been empty.

In short, nobody else was to learn of Isabel's escapades. "Don't want to scare the grunts," she'd say. "Or get people suspicious. Witnesses are too risky."

So, Eleanor had to cover up those solo absences, and explain things away. She'd also had to maintain an official distance, so that if things went wrong—as they now had—she wouldn't be implicated. The queen might hold absolute power, but displaying fallibility might provoke civil unrest. Maybe that's why Isabel hadn't wanted the position, with all its constraints. Eleanor was stuck with the weighty responsibilities of the crown.

What could she do now? She couldn't waste Isabel's efforts, but she'd have to maintain plans both for a return and for a continued—or permanent—absence. Sighing, she flipped through her pile of official reports for the latest Council minutes. Even though she couldn't stomach their meetings, she should keep abreast of what they were saying.

The door creaked open, and Martha carried in a tea tray. "Here you are, my dear. Good and strong, the way you like it. And two more letters." She set the letters by Eleanor's elbow.

While Martha laid out the tea, Eleanor opened the first letter. It was scrawled on a page torn from a notebook.

My abject apologies, but I will be unable to visit you today. I have been taken unwell and am confined to my bed with a fever. I really am very sorry to inconvenience you like this, and I hope you will still look on me kindly.
Your loyal subject,
Artur Granville

An ache tightened around her forehead. Had she misjudged him? Was he reconsidering his agreement to help her? Or maybe he really was ill. She'd better send someone to enquire after his health. There was no point in moping, however. That wouldn't help.

The tinkle of a spoon on china reminded Eleanor she wasn't alone. "Martha, can you sit down, please? I'd like to ask you a few things. You knew my father for a long time, didn't you?"

Martha arranged herself on the padded chair beside the desk. "Oh yes, I worked for your father well before you were on the scene. And your mother too, Settlers watch over them both. Why?"

"I was wondering, did my father say anything about what he was working on, before he went to Settlers' Rest?"

"I'm a housekeeper, so he didn't discuss business with me, but he did have a few visitors outside of his regular meetings. Especially during his last months..."

"Do you happen to know who they were?"

"Of course! It was my job to provide refreshments. Let's see... Lady Nelson used to visit, though not so much later on. I got the impression they disagreed on a few things." Martha raised an eyebrow while Eleanor tried to maintain a neutral expression. "He sometimes chatted with Historian Gauntlett. The person he met with most often was... Kenneth Staunton. That's the name. The scientist who retired."

Martha's memory yielded no other names, and Eleanor released her to her duties.

After the housekeeper left, Eleanor sipped her tea. If her father's project wasn't a figment of her overheated mind, it probably included negotiations away from the Council. Why did politics have to complicate things? Even Artur might have got cold feet, and she couldn't blame him. Admittedly, she'd almost got him killed. And what had Eleanor spent the last year doing? Messing around with a blimp and in the library, seeking solutions to the curse. Bluntly, she'd been wasting time. A twinge of guilt struck her as she remembered Lady Nelson's words the other day. *You can't always do as you please, you know.* She'd been leaving things up to the Council rather than doing her job of reigning. Her father would have disapproved. She wished she'd picked up more of his knowledge, that she hadn't assured herself there would be plenty of time for that when she was older. But how were they to know—

Blinking away tears, she picked up the second letter. Unlike Artur's brief note, this one was two sheets of closely written text, probably some sad story with an appeal for a donation. She received one or two a month, from charitable organisations and occasionally individuals. She squinted at the handwriting. Odd. Why would someone bother writing in Noble Ascarite? That was for official communications only. This would take some time to decipher. She skipped to the signature, which was dated from last month.

Captain Jonathan Shelley

The chair clattered against the wall as she leapt to her feet. "Martha!"

The housekeeper bustled in and stared at the broken teacup on the floor. "No need to shout, I was just outside. Whatever is the matter?"

Eleanor pointed at the letter on her desk. "Where did this come from?"

Martha screwed up her face. "My friend Emily—she works at the barracks—found it while sorting some uniforms. She thought it must have been mislaid, so she dropped it off with me. Is there a problem?"

"Ah, no." Eleanor sat down again. "I was just surprised. Sorry for disturbing you. And sorry about the mess."

Martha raised a quizzical eyebrow, then her gaze fell on Artur's note. Her expression softened. "Never mind. I'll clear these away and leave you in peace."

Picking up a pen, Eleanor scowled at the letter and translated the salient points. Shelley—former convoy captain and suspected murderer—expressed his suspicions of Scientist Silvers. It had been Silvers who incarcerated Shelley, hadn't it? Shelley suggested that Silvers was attempting to deliberately curse people. As an example, he cited a mission where two of his guards were injured by beasts and cursed. Shelley didn't directly *claim* he'd been given inadequate resources, but his bare statement of his orders and the timings left little room for doubt. Eleanor's frown deepened. That must have been how Silvers obtained that live beast.

She massaged her neck. If the letter had really been written a few weeks earlier, it pre-dated Shelley's imprisonment and escape. If his suppositions were true, Silvers was more heinous than anyone else in history, with the possible exception of Denton, that captain whom Isabel had executed. Denton had been a prime example of how powers could be used unethically, manipulating people for personal gain. Would there have been less danger if everyone knew about the use of powers? On the one hand, public ignorance might prevent panicking mobs and riots, but on the other, public awareness might have reduced the harm he did.

If Silvers were performing such outrageous experiments, trying to create more cursed, how could he have been appointed? How could his colleagues tolerate him? It didn't sound at all likely.

It wouldn't be fair, however, to dismiss Shelley's words as falsehood. She'd have to allow for the possibility, no matter how small, that he was innocent. He might not have killed that guard, and he might not have killed her father. That said, he would still bear watching.

Investigating Shelley, or her father's death, wasn't Eleanor's job. The city captains and Paton would handle the work between them, deploying others as needed. She pursed her lips. It certainly wasn't her job—*not that I've been doing my job, let's face it*—but if her safety were at stake, she had a right to seek information, especially now Isabel was missing.

She nodded and wrote out two orders.

The first was a request for Kenneth Staunton's attendance at the palace. She'd find out from him what her father had intended.

The second was a directive to Paton, to investigate who Shelley's close colleagues and friends were, and to perform background checks. Once she had that information, she'd decide if they merited a closer look.

Should she summon Silvers? He'd seemed quite keen to share his findings about the beast, and she wouldn't have minded another chat with him. With that letter, however, things might not be so straightforward. She'd better speak with Staunton first.

She cast her eye over the first letter again, the note from Artur. She hadn't initially noticed, but the lower part of the page was creased. Unfolding it, she read his final line.

PS. May I see you at some later date?

Eleanor's lips curved into a smile. Maybe she wasn't completely alone.

Franka flexed her leg as she vacated the infirmary room, leaning on a cane, her white detainees' outfit swishing. It was good to be moving on after being stuck here for the past month, following her injury. A guard—a weedy, pasty-faced *Keep* guard—carried her meagre belongings while a larger one walked by her side, gripping a cudgel. She winked at him then waggled her eyebrows at his cudgel, but he responded with a blank stare. Oh, well, worth a try. She was out of practice. Though having someone else carrying her bag was a novel experience.

She wrinkled her nose at the odour of bleach in the corridor, at the guards posted outside each patient's room. Even though she was exchanging one confinement for another, the residential wing was surely an improvement. Scientist Fellows had assured her the rooms were well appointed, and she'd have access to reasonable privileges. Unfortunately, those privileges didn't include a key to the door.

Officially, she'd be observed to see if she threw off the curse. She knew fine well she wouldn't, although at least her power wasn't leaking out anymore. After those first few days, it hadn't taken much effort to keep it damped down, but it would take practice until she could demonstrate deliberate control. And if she did? She'd have the option of returning to the guard, probably as a captain. She pulled a face. That sounded like far too much responsibility, although it was a price worth paying to get out of this building.

The nature of the power she had been, well, cursed with—evoking fear in people—wasn't likely to help her in the field. She couldn't think of any situation where it would be useful rather than causing panic. Not like Jonathan's. It would be strange to call him "Jonathan" again, after a decade of "Captain Shelley". Last month he'd saved her life with his power. That was twice she owed him. Franka always repaid her debts.

What had happened to him? News of his imprisonment, his escape and the guard's death had buzzed around the infirmary like flies on a turd. She winced as she overextended her leg. He couldn't have killed the guard. If he had a failing, it was taking too much on himself. She could see him choosing to die to save someone, but murder was out of the question.

Still, there was little she could do from her position as a detainee. All she might manage was contacting Tabitha, as Jonathan had asked her. The poor kid's situation was indirectly the cause of Franka's injury and curse, but that was hardly the girl's fault. No, blame that stupid beast-catching mission. If Franka got the pair of them out of the Keep, she could call it quits with Jonathan and be on a more even footing with him. He'd said Tabitha's power was like his, but that she couldn't yet control it. Was that knowledge something they could use?

Franka limped up the stairs to the residential floor. There, the guard with her bag carried it into a room while her armed escort handed her over to the corridor guard.

"You'll be in Room Two." The corridor guard, a young lad with protruding ears, led her to the door. "I hope you find it comfortable. We'll bring you meals on a tray. If you wish to work on your, er... powers, we'll get someone to escort you to the practice rooms downstairs. Let us know if there's anything else you'd like. The scientists like to keep you happy."

Comfortable? Happy? Locked inside? She shrugged. He was just doing his job. "Thanks, I guess."

He swung the door open, and her eyes widened. This room was far bigger than she'd expected, even after Fellows' pep talk. Plush furniture, tasteful decor, as far as she could judge, and what looked like an attached bathing room. Maybe she could get used to this though the barred windows rather spoiled the view.

But first, she had a job to do.

She grinned at the guard. "Nice room, pal. I'm surprised you don't have people clamouring to stay here. That comfy bed looks like it could stand a lot of use."

He paled and took a step back. Franka's smile broadened. It seemed her reputation might be an advantage.

"I'm just curious as to the arrangements, should I wish to entertain anyone." She winked. "One of my colleagues who knows I'm here might want to visit. Do I have neighbours I might disturb, if we're a little, shall we say, noisy?"

The lad's Adam's apple bobbed. "I think the other residents would appreciate you being, ah, reasonably quiet." He pointed two doors down. "There's a young girl in there, and we'd appreciate it if you didn't disturb her."

"I'll do my best." *Two doors down, eh?* "And how about the rooms either side? I'm not sure I'll manage to stay *that* quiet."

"They're empty." He gulped. "If there's nothing else I'll, uh, leave you to it."

"Just a couple more things..." Franka placed a hand on his arm as she stepped inside. "I'll want to keep up with the news. Can you deliver the *Informer* daily? And, let's see, could I have some string? Something smooth, not that scratchy stuff. Never know when you might want to tie someone—I mean, something—up."

"I'll see to it right away, ma'am!" The boy saluted and fled, locking and barring the door behind him.

Franka's grin stayed while she unpacked her bag and inspected the room and amenities. Then it dropped off her face as she remembered the door being barred behind her. No matter how luxurious this place was, she was still a prisoner.

If Jonathan could get out, so can I.

Chapter 12

Susanna appraised the lunchtime buffet before spooning salad on to her plate, not wanting to risk any post-prandial torpor. She'd need her wits about her this afternoon, for her mind-reading session with Silvers. Her stomach fluttered. Finally she'd learn what game he was playing, even though she'd need to bend the rules and probe further than strictly allowed. If her suspicions were true, the implications for everyone would far outweigh her breaking protocol.

Other than David, who sat devouring a mound of beans and vegetables, the place was empty. Good. Her robust tablemate preferred eating to chatting, and she could use the time to think.

"Susanna, ravishing as always!" Lester's voice cut across the captains' lounge from the doorway. His hand brushed the top of David's cropped blond hair as he sauntered past the dining table.

She suppressed a smile at his cheery greeting. His buoyant nature hadn't been completely quashed by Silvers. David shot him a scowl. *Boys!* Though she could see why the other men found him irritating.

Lester's hair was neatly slicked back, his uniform crisp and freshly laundered. He picked up a plate, which he heaped high with roast potatoes and slices of pigeon pie.

"My favourite meal of the day." He winked. "No serving staff around to disapprove of my gluttony."

David cleared his throat behind them, and Lester raised

his voice. "*Some* people in the barracks eat even more than I do."

She nudged him with an elbow on her way towards the table. "Behave."

"For you, anything." He whistled a tune from a recent musical as he finished loading his plate.

After Lester joined them at the table, Susanna asked, "What's with the good mood?"

He held a hand in the air and bolted half his lunch before replying. "Sorry, I was really hungry. My appetite returned with a vengeance this morning."

"So I see." David frowned at his plate then cut a potato into neat quarters, speared a piece on his fork and popped it in his mouth. After swallowing, he patted his lips with a napkin. "What's caused you to lose your table manners?"

Lester smirked. "Good news, for all of us. Silvers is gone."

Susanna raised an eyebrow. "What do you mean, gone?" Surely that wasn't a euphemism?

"He's left the city. Headed out this morning, through the Ascar tunnel."

The fork clattered as she set it down, the salad forming a lump in her stomach. So much for their mind-reading session. "Not just for the morning?"

"I don't think so. Kind of far, isn't it?"

David coughed. "Actually, Silvers recruited some guards a couple of days back, for a trip he said would take two weeks." He snorted. "He had the nerve to tell *me* to lead it—does he think he's my boss? Of course I said no. It wasn't ordered by the Council, and I have better things to do with my time. The convoy guards weren't interested since so many of them had been out recently. I mean, on Jonathan's last trip."

"Nice that the scientists aren't breathing down *your* neck," muttered Lester to his potatoes. He looked up. "Uh, who's gone with them?"

"City guards, mainly new ones who don't know the difficulties of travel. I heard he was paying double rate, and out of his own pocket too."

Susanna gazed at the limp green leaves on her plate. What was the man doing? He couldn't have arranged this just to avoid his monitoring session. Where was he going in such a hurry? Why was he paying so much?

It *had* to be Jonathan. Her vision blurred with the realisation. "Lester, I'm not feeling well. Can you please escort me back to my room?" She stood and left the lounge.

Lester caught up with her in the hallway, a napkin-wrapped potato in his hand. "I hadn't finished eating."

"Never mind that, this is important!" She paced along the corridor, ignoring his protestations all the way to her quarters.

In the privacy of her room, she sat opposite him and spoke. "This is very bad."

"How come? Silvers won't be nagging us, and we can relax for a while."

Idiot. "Lester, if he's left the city going north, he's going after Jonathan. He's found some clue and a reason to follow it himself. And if he's paying them so generously 'out of his own pocket', I bet he's spending Jonathan's assets that he confiscated." She clenched her fists. If Silvers had been in front of her, she'd have hit him. If Jonathan stopped the man's heart, she wouldn't blame him. She might even cheer.

Lester sagged and gazed at the tabletop. "Oh."

Susanna placed her hands flat on the table. "Richard knows something. I caught a thought the other day. He was thinking of speaking to me but changed his mind. I hope he decides to—but I can hardly force him."

"Who? Oh, skinny Richard. He finds things? Fussy eater? Wears monogrammed shirts?"

She nodded. "I didn't know about the shirts, but that's the one."

Lester stared at her. "Do you think Silvers has set him to find Jonathan? I thought he couldn't find people."

"I believe he can't." She swallowed. "I don't know exactly how his power works. Maybe he can track a distinctive piece of clothing though I don't think Jonathan uses monograms."

"Wouldn't Jonathan rid himself of anything like that as soon as he could?"

"Of course he would. He's not stupid." *Even if he doesn't understand* techne. She shook her head. "I don't know. I'm guessing, but this feels like I'm on the right track."

"Anyway," said Lester, "what do we do now?"

"I'll speak with Lady Nelson, see if she can put the brakes on Silvers even though it's too late to stop this trip. She'll probably tell me about 'independent research' and 'non-interference', the way she always does. And then I have another request for you." Lester opened his mouth, but she held up a hand. "No more evenings with maids this time."

His eyes narrowed. "So what's it to be? Chasing after Silvers? Setting up an ambush for his return? Mind controlling the entire Council to forget about him?"

"No, there's someone vulnerable who'd benefit from your assistance." She took his hand. "Let's train Tabitha together."

Susanna sat with Tabitha and Lester in Practice Room D, each with a pain box close at hand. They had borrowed an extra table and chair from the room next door so Tabitha would have space for her weights.

"Do you think this will work?" Tabitha chewed her lip as she tied her hair back, today with an orange ribbon.

"I hope so. If I'd thought about it, I'd have asked Lester to come along before." Sighing, Susanna attached her own earclip. Maybe something would go right today.

She'd sent a note to Lady Nelson earlier this morning, requesting an appointment. The messenger had returned in short order with a refusal. Lady Nelson was under the weather and not up to receiving visitors, or so the message said. What was with the scientists, that they wouldn't talk to her? There was always Fellows, but Susanna doubted he'd be any use. With no initiative or backbone, all he cared about was his maps.

There was no point in dwelling on the matter. "I'll just recap before we start. Tabitha, you concentrate on using your power. I'll, er, perceive the shape of your mind while you're doing it. Lester, you focus on Tabitha and try to nudge her mind, direct her towards using her power. It'll be rather trial and error. I'll give you hand signals, the same as when we worked on your own power, to let you know if you're getting hotter or colder. Are we clear?"

The other two nodded and reached for their pain boxes. Tabitha's breath hissed in. Lester's jaw clenched.

Susanna's brows drew together as the pain hit her ear. "We should all hold hands when we're not adjusting the controls on the boxes."

Tabitha grabbed Lester's hand. He flinched and

squeezed his eyes shut, his nostrils flaring. Susanna patted his other hand. After a few rapid breaths, he opened his eyes and bestowed on Tabitha the most seductive smile Susanna had ever seen. *Whoo, no wonder he was so popular with his clients.*

Tabitha blushed.

"You... you can do this, Tabitha." His voice was husky.

They'd have been fighting over him. Susanna shook her head to dispel the image and grasped their hands. "When you're ready."

Tabitha's gaze dropped from Lester's face to the weight on the tabletop. Susanna reached out with her power, forming her mental model for Tabitha and comparing it with her memory of Jonathan's. A part of the weave fluttered, but in the wrong direction. Susanna tapped Lester's hand, which jerked, before returning her focus to Tabitha. A familiar nudge came from Lester, and the orientation of the weave swung around. Once Susanna judged it aligned with Jonathan's, she placed her hand flat on Lester's as a signal to maintain his position.

A gasp came from Tabitha, and she blew out a breath. She scowled.

The weight quivered.

"Again." Susanna held her breath. Had it been her imagination?

The weight slid a handsbreadth.

She licked her lips. "Lester, stop whatever you're doing."

Susanna's grip tightened on Lester's hand as the weight continued to move. It tipped over the edge of the table and floated downwards, landing on the floor with a clink.

Tabitha broke into a huge grin. "I did it! I could *feel* myself doing it!" She ripped off her earclip, jumped up from her seat and threw herself into Lester's arms.

... shitshitshit Jonathan will kill me shitshitshit... Lester's panicked thoughts and horrified face sent Susanna into a fit of giggles. She released his hand to allow the man some mental privacy.

Stepping away from Lester, Tabitha beamed. "That was great. It really makes sense now. See?"

She pointed at the weight on the floor, and it floated upwards and over the table. A crease appeared on her forehead. "Come on—" The weight clattered on the wooden surface, and she stuck out her lower lip. "Drat! I thought I had it."

Susanna smiled. "It's still an excellent start, Tabitha."

Lester stood and straightened his uniform, keeping the table between himself and Tabitha. "I can see you're a natural."

Her eyelashes fluttered while she gazed at his face. "But I couldn't have done it without you."

He stepped back. "Ah... but it was Susanna who had the idea. And without all her preparatory work, we'd never have got this far."

Poor Lester. Susanna placed a hand on Tabitha's shoulder. "I think we can agree we've all done very well, but that's enough for the day. Tabitha, we'll run your next session without Lester, just to make sure you can do this yourself. You probably don't even need me anymore, but I'll keep an eye on you at first."

Lester sidled towards the door and swung it open. He paused, a hand on the doorknob. "If you don't need me anymore, I'll be on my way?"

Tabitha slumped. "Oh, but—"

Susanna squeezed Tabitha's shoulder. "Thank you,

Lester. You've been a huge help, but I know you have other commitments." She waited until the door closed behind him before allowing herself to grin.

After they tidied up the room, Tabitha followed her up to the residential floor. "Are you going to tell Lady Nelson?"

"No, not yet. She was ill, and there's no point in disturbing her." *She can hardly complain at not being informed, after refusing to see me this morning.*

"So what do we do now?"

"We practise. Then you practise by yourself. The more you practise, the easier it will be to demonstrate to the scientists that you're safe. Does that make sense?" The girl was far too young to send out as a captain, but she might be able to bargain for some freedom. Susanna could help her with that nearer the time.

The girl nodded. "I see. But while I'm doing all that... can you help Jonathan?"

"I don't know. I'm doing what I can." Hopefully it would be enough.

They parted outside Tabitha's suite, under the narrowed eye of the corridor guard. Susanna left the date of their next session open. She'd need to spend time investigating Silvers. Though she wouldn't tell Tabitha that.

On the way back to her barracks quarters, she paused outside Richard's door. He'd been on the verge of saying something the last time they met, but she'd been a fool, too eager. She raised her hand to knock. Speak or not? Push him or not? Or even... no. She wouldn't deliberately mind-read him. That would be an abuse of her power, laying her open to trouble when she was next monitored. She wasn't yet that desperate.

She knocked.

Was that a footstep?

After knocking twice more, she gave up.

That evening, Susanna was embroidering a handkerchief when someone rapped at the door.

Richard stood outside in his shirtsleeves, rubbing red-rimmed eyes. "May I come in?"

"Of course. What can I do for you?" She put her sewing to the side and indicated a seat, glad she hadn't pushed him earlier.

He clasped his hands on the table. "Well. You know my power."

She nodded, peeking at his cuff and spotting a mono-gram. "Though not in detail."

"Broadly speaking, if someone shows me a picture of an item or describes it precisely, I can sense its location and where it's been previously. The difficulty is distinguishing it from similar items."

"I see." *Patience, Susanna.*

"I usually investigate jewel thefts, missing documents, that sort of thing. But Silvers told me he'd lost something. Said it was a trinket." Richard's lips twisted. "I hadn't thought of him as the type to keep lucky coins, although I could imagine him wearing some tacky piece of jewelry."

Susanna picked up her embroidery hoop and needle. If she wasn't watching him, he might feel less burdened by her attention. "And it wasn't what you thought?"

"Ah, no. He described a small gold disc, about so big"—he held his thumb and finger apart—"with one surface plain, the other engraved with his initials."

"As in, 'JS'. Yes?" The needle pricked her finger, and she bit off a curse.

"I located a dozen of them in his office, but he said there was one missing. Gave me the impression he'd dropped it somewhere. I tracked it to the basement of the Keep, then it disappeared for a bit."

"And?" Her grip tightened on the hoop.

"It reappeared in the northern fields and moved north." He met her gaze. "At a slow walking pace, roughly."

"You think Jonathan had it? Maybe stuck to his shoe?" She gave up on pretending to sew.

"The timing fits, though I'd say it was something more deliberate, like an identity bracelet. Say what you will about Silvers, but he's found a clever application of my power."

She took a deep breath. This was what she'd suspected. "Very clever. So you tracked where he was heading and told Silvers. And now Silvers has gone after him."

Richard slumped. "Yes. I mean, it's my job, and Jonathan's an escaped prisoner."

"I see." She massaged her forehead. "But why take the risk of telling me? And why now?"

He swallowed. "Since I wasn't accompanying Silvers on his trip, he asked where I thought the disc was heading. I suggested that town to the north, Maldon. But after he left, it stopped moving. I've sent a message to Maldon, to pass on the information when Silvers arrives there."

"Jonathan discarded it?"

Richard licked his lips. "I wondered about that, but Silvers told me it can't be removed."

"He's asleep?" *Or unconscious? Or–*

"Ah, no. Even if he were asleep, he'd move around a little. It's not moved by even a hairsbreadth for over a day."

Susanna's voice shook. "Richard, just tell me what you think."

Cheek twitching, Richard regarded her. "I think Jonathan's dead."

Chapter 13

I'm still alive.

Curled up on the ground, not daring to move, Jonathan took inventory of himself. His arms and legs ached, and the throbbing in his thigh reminded him of yesterday's butchery. He should be grateful his limbs were still attached. They might not remain so for long.

Melodious trills and chirps from dawn's chorus reached his ears. It was all very well for the birds: they were in no danger. As for him, he didn't dare open his eyes and face the threat before him.

Going by the warmth at his front, his fire had survived the night. And beyond it... lurked the beasts.

They hadn't tried to attack. Not yet. Several—he wasn't sure how many—had approached last night, halting just on the other side of his campfire. They'd clustered together and lain down, still and quiet, other than breath puffing in the cold air. Waiting.

From under his flimsy shelter, fighting off exhaustion, he'd fed the fire with the fuel close to hand. What had prompted him to pile up the rest out of reach? As his stock of wood dwindled, sleep overcame him.

Once the fire went out, would the beasts tear him apart quickly, or would they take their time, maybe eating him alive? His hands trembled and his chest tightened as he imagined the crunch of bone.

It was cowardice just to lie here. He'd need to open his

eyes, to assess the danger and then act.

Sure, Shelley. One naked old man, cold, injured, and lying down, taking on a pack of beasts. No problem.

To have any chance in this confrontation, he'd need to call his power. Using it to stop a heart would take too long. He'd have to bat each beast away. However, if they coordinated their attack—as they might well do—he was a dead man.

He kept his eyes closed and his breathing soft, even as his pulse increased. Surprise might make all the difference. He eased his hand down his thigh, preparing to squeeze yesterday's wound.

Jonathan opened his eyes a slit.

Embers and charred sticks met his gaze. He blinked and twisted his neck to see further. No beasts stood within his field of view.

He crawled out of his shelter and stood, hand on his thigh, head swivelling around.

Other than disturbed ground close to the fire and paw prints, there was no trace of the beasts.

Were they lurking close by, waiting for him to let down his guard before pouncing? What was the point in that? They could easily take him down without stealth.

For some reason, they had left him alive. All they had done was share his fire for the night then depart while he was still asleep. His forehead wrinkled. Maybe they weren't hungry.

He added more sticks to the campfire and peeled the uniform from the roof of his shelter. It was nearly dry enough to wear. He laid it by the fire and set breakfast to heat in his billycan. Wonderful, apple gruel again. He wasn't at risk of starvation—yet—but some variety would have been welcome. Maybe he'd find some onions today.

While breakfast cooked, he inspected his right thigh.

His makeshift bandage was bloodstained, and the wound gaped, but it leaked blood rather than pus. The redness from yesterday had diminished. He rinsed the bandage and applied a fresh one, then started to dress.

As he pushed his foot into a trouser leg, rustling from behind set him to grabbing for his broken sabre. He stepped on the other trouser leg, tripped, and landed beside the fire with an impact that drove the breath from his lungs and snapped the sabre's blade off at the handle. *Shit!*

Wheezing, he kicked off his impeding garment and scrambled to his feet, looking wildly around. His right hand clamped over his thigh wound while he extended his left to meet this new threat.

A single beast stalked into sight from behind the lean-to. Its grey pelt was shaggy, and its pointed ears reached the height of Jonathan's hip. Something pale dangled from its muzzle.

Pain. His power awoke as he squeezed his thigh, and he pointed at the beast. It met his eye, dropped its burden and skittered backwards several paces.

His hand wavered. It wasn't acting aggressively, and if it were going to flee, he might as well conserve his power. Or perhaps—

Behind me! He whipped around. Arm extended, he scanned the area. No threat presented itself, and his breathing slowed. He turned towards the beast again, half-convinced it would be gone.

It remained, head tilted to one side, regarding him. It padded forwards. A white patch on its snout caught his eye as it nudged its dropped burden towards him.

Then it turned and trotted away.

Jonathan gaped. He picked up a stout tree branch and approached the strange gift.

Crumpled on the ground was a dead animal the size of his hand. He bent towards it, noting the four legs and fur. Convoy protocol would have him move it to a clear spot with minimal handling, douse it with accelerant, and incinerate it. For the safety of all.

He lifted it. Still warm. Going by size alone, he'd have guessed this wasn't a beast. He frowned as he remembered the Ascar scientists arguing about teeth. He nodded as he inspected its mouth, ran his finger along its teeth. Flat, rather than pointed. Large rounded ears, short fluffy tail, cream pelt. He stroked the pelt. *So soft.*

Had he been given this in exchange for last night's fire? What was he supposed to do with it? Did beasts trade with each other, somewhere that people couldn't see them?

Beasts ate animals, didn't they? Was Jonathan a beast? Maybe he was, cursed and subsisting in the wilderness on what he could scavenge.

More immediately, was this food? *I'm cursed already. And this isn't a beast.* He salivated. *Besides, nobody's watching.*

With his rusty scalpel, he skinned and gutted the animal, jointing it and adding it to his pot. He'd pretend to himself it was chicken.

Later, a hot meal satisfying his stomach, Jonathan extinguished the fire and packed up his belongings, including the broken pieces of his sabre. He frowned at the paw prints. Were cursed beasts intelligent? His jaw clenched. Maybe Silvers had been right. Or... were *all* beasts intelligent?

He shook his head and set off, following the watercourse

further north. That was something for other people to debate over. As far as he was concerned, if he could exchange a nightly fire for freedom from attack, it was a reasonable trade. Something to eat would be a bonus, although he should be able to hunt birds and fish using his power. Since he'd already decided to explore alternative triggering methods, he might as well make it useful.

As he walked on, he kept a cautious eye on his surroundings. Naïve trust in beasts would be a serious mistake. He'd travel until he came across a more defensible site where he could set up a base. There, he would work on his power until he was ready. And then he'd go after Silvers.

Eleanor pencilled a cross on the map, then slid it across the library table to her visitor. "What do you think?"

Artur's hands trembled as he smoothed the paper out flat. "You think we should multiply... Oh." He leaned back in his chair, eyes closed, face flushed. "Sorry, I'm still not quite back to normal."

She chewed her lip. "Are you sure you're well enough to be here? I shouldn't be dragging you from your sickbed."

He smiled faintly. "It's fine. I really wanted to come." His eyes opened, and he blinked a few times. "I'm recovering, thanks to those pills your physician sent. Just occasional dizzy spells."

"If this is you better, I'd hate to see what the worst was." At least the pills had helped him relax.

"It wasn't all that bad. No pain, though I had quite a temperature." He laughed. "And I saw and heard the strangest things. For example, my uncle Reynard sat on the bed and said he had a headache."

"I'm sure he must have been worried about you."

"No, it was a hallucination. He passed on last year."

Eleanor's hand flew to her lips. "I'm so sorry!" Couldn't she say *anything* right today?

"It's fine. We weren't even that close when he was alive. He'd been declining, with his breathing difficulties and aching joints, and we knew it was only a matter of time. He's at peace now, Settlers watch over him. Oddly enough, it wasn't his chest that killed him but a bleed on the brain. At least it was quick." He rubbed his temples and leaned forwards. "Anyway, let's see this map."

She tapped the cross. "I've made a new model, including the new information from... that last trip. I'd predict another cursed mound in this area. It's remote enough that travellers wouldn't have stumbled upon it already."

"Hmm." He frowned at the map. "Seems plausible. You're thinking of groups of beasts settling at or near cursed mounds, aren't you? And every so often a family breaks away and migrates?"

"Maybe. In the absence of hard data, I'm really guessing. Nobody's observed beasts in their natural habitat." She looked down. "And I guess it's not a good idea to go out looking again. Not until we can do it safely."

His fist clenched. "I agree. But we can make detailed notes, something for use in future."

She waved a hand at the dusty bookshelves that surrounded them. "A great idea in theory, but there's a *huge* amount of information in this room, never mind the one next door. While some of it's well organised—like the *techne* notes I showed you—there are entire bookcases I've not even touched. There aren't enough researchers in the whole of Ascar to explore these, even if security clearance weren't an issue."

"Well, it'll be there if someone needs it." He met her gaze. "Are there any more maps you'd like me to look at today, or are we done with them?"

Eleanor's shoulders tensed. Of course he wouldn't forget her promise of answers. Maybe that was why he'd pushed himself to come today. She'd have to play fair with him. *Don't deceive people lightly*, her father had told her though he'd said nothing about partial truths. "No, that's everything. I really do appreciate your thoughts." She clasped her hands on the table. "I did tell you I'd explain, the night we made that blimp ride."

"Um, yes." He took a long breath. "Any word on Isabel?"

"I despatched a search party, eventually, but no signs." Her voice wobbled. "I'm afraid she's... not coming back."

Artur's face hardened, and he looked away. "You said you had a reason for leaving her out there. Alone. If you'd sent guards out as soon as we returned..."

Tears pricked her eyes. "I did have a reason. She told me to. Well, sort of." *She was always the decisive one. She'd have been a better queen than me.*

Artur shook his head while she told him of Isabel's solo excursions into the wilderness to hunt beasts and of her insistence on secrecy.

"... Sometimes she scared me, just a bit. She was so passionate about wiping them out, to ensure nobody else"— Eleanor coughed—"I mean, nobody in the realm could be cursed."

"Scary? I can't imagine why," he muttered. "But why the secrecy? And why alone?"

She shrank back in her chair, her guts roiling. This was the moment she had dreaded. The point of no return. "This is a state secret. So if you don't want to be involved, I shouldn't tell you. You can't speak of this to anyone, or the penalty—"

He silenced her with an upraised hand. "I promised Isabel my silence, and I said I'd help you. I'm a man of my word. Go on. Er, please."

"Right. Isabel is..." She swallowed. "Cursed."

"What?" Artur jerked upright then swayed in his seat.

Eleanor darted round the table and grasped his arm until he steadied himself.

She pulled up a chair and sat beside him, peering into his sallow face. "I said—"

"Yes, yes, I heard you. But how come? I mean, why's she—" He squeezed his eyes shut for a moment. "The cursed develop dangerous powers, don't they? She had one? You were hiding it from the Council?"

"Er, no. The Council already know."

He scowled. "And because she's nobility, they let her—"

"No! It wasn't like that." Eleanor winced. Admittedly, her father had decreed Isabel be exempted from the routine monitoring other captains underwent. He'd wielded his King's Discretion over that. No wonder. *She must know more state secrets than I do.* "I mean, Isabel isn't the only one..."

She briefly explained the arrangement between the scientists in the Keep and the Council, and how certain individuals were sent out to work in secret. Artur nodded as she concluded, "... Isabel's power over fire meant she could take care of herself. Because her power was so frightening, she insisted—insists—there be no witnesses."

He gazed around the library, at the corner where back copies of the *Informer* were stacked. "That makes sense now." At Eleanor's enquiring look, he continued. "When I was on bed rest I caught up on the news. The article on Captain Shelley concealing a cursed power caught my eye. I couldn't understand why he'd not been detected and detained already... but now you've told me all this, I guess they knew about it already. Sorry, I'm rambling."

Shelley again? Her fists clenched, and she forced them to relax. "You knew Shelley?"

Artur opened his mouth, then paused, gaze unfocussed. "Not well, but we talked about blimps a couple of times." He reddened. "You were there the first time—when you visited the blimp workshop. We continued our discussion a few days later, over dinner."

"What was he like?"

"Quiet, reserved. Polite conversation." His lips twitched. "Didn't like blimp rides. Oh, he had a black eye and some kind of hand injury. He didn't mention why though. Didn't drink the wine. I can't remember anything else. Sorry."

"No, that's fine." Eleanor wasn't sure what she'd expected, but Shelley sounded quite innocuous, other than the slight oddity of his injury. "When did he visit?"

"I don't remember the exact date, but my mother was really excited about it. That's it, he'd been out and killed some beasts a few days before. Hmm, they went in a blimp, but the operators didn't say anything about it afterwards. That's a bit odd, come to think of it."

"Maybe not." That must have been when Shelley captured the beast for Silvers. "The operation would have been Council-sanctioned. That is, your operators would have been barred from discussing it."

Artur frowned. "Do you really think all this secrecy is beneficial?"

Eleanor sighed. "Well, no. But I don't know what to do about it." He'd put his finger on the crux of her problems.

Chapter 14

Unexpected visitors arrived. Need medical attention.
Nothing serious, but ten of them. Bring all your dressings
and painkillers. G.

Annetta trotted towards the guesthouse beside the young
man pushing Giselle's small wheelbarrow. "When did they
arrive?"

"Around half an hour ago." Thomas' dark head bobbed
as he walked. "I was just outside town, gathering samples of
fallen leaves for tomorrow's lesson, and a bunch of strangers
walk straight up to me out of nowhere. I nearly jumped out
of my skin. Of course, I led them straight to the guesthouse
then went and found Giselle. She'd just sat down to write
our next census report."

Annetta smirked. Everyone knew how Giselle hated being interrupted. "I bet she had something to say about
that."

"I'm sure she wanted to, but there's some bigwig with
them." Thomas grinned back. "The look on her face was
priceless. There's enough in the guest-tithe to feed them
lunch, but after I've taken your stuff across, I need to go
scrounge more food for later."

Entering the guesthouse through the infirmary door,
Annetta peeked past the curtain into the main living area.

Was Giselle *sure* there were only ten? Bedrolls and bags
of all shapes and sizes lay strewn across the floor, some with

their contents spilling out. The travellers—all men in brown uniforms—slumped on benches along the wall or stretched out on the floor. One of them snored, and another prodded him with a toe until he rolled over.

She picked her way through the mess towards Giselle, who sat at her usual table, hands tightly clasped. Wisps of auburn hair escaped the woman's headscarf to straggle down her face. A man sat opposite her, his back to Annetta. His blue flannel shirt strained across his broad back as he leaned forward, elbows on the table. That was the bigwig? He was certainly big.

"... Sorry about not warning you." His accent was Ascarite, but less precise than Captain Shelley's. "However, I'd reasons for a surprise visit. Now you've passed me that message from my Ascar support staff, I see matters have changed." He lowered his voice. "I'll explain later."

Giselle sniffed. "I shall look forward to it." She nodded at Annetta. "I see our herbalist has arrived. Annetta, this is Scientist Silvers."

Scientist? Didn't they research the curse? This must be about Samuel. Her mouth dried up. "Hello? I'm Annetta. Maldon's herbalist. Sir." *Gah, nothing like repeating the obvious.*

The man leaned back in his chair and turned his head towards her. Under the expanse of a high forehead, his close-set eyes examined her as if through a magnifying glass. She shrank back.

He's only looking at you because he's curious. Be professional. She licked her lips. "You and the others need medical attention?"

He swung himself to his feet and gazed down at her. "Yes. City guards aren't used to walking long distances, so we're all a bit footsore."

That would explain the brown uniforms rather than the grey ones that convoy guards wore. She took a step back from his looming presence. "Is there anything specific I should know before I start? Sir."

Rubbing a thumb across his unshaven chin, Silvers stared at her. "Tell you what, call me Jed. I'm sure a lady with your sensitive nature would find that easier. I'm happy to leave our care in your capable hands. I trust your judgement."

See? He's considerate. No need to be anxious. She offered him a smile.

Giselle raised an eyebrow. "There's an infirmary area at the back of this building, and Annetta's brought the supplies she needs."

Silvers nodded. "Shall we queue everyone up who needs to see you, in order of severity? I'm a tad footsore too, although at least I had decent boots. After you've dealt with everyone else, is there somewhere less public you could have a look at me?"

Of course he'd want more privacy, being the boss. "My consulting room is only a short distance away. We can walk over there later."

In the infirmary area, Annetta shook her head over the ignorance of these travellers who had no idea about proper footwear. No wonder their feet hurt. Maybe she wasn't being fair, since their shoes were identical other than in size: brown in colour, no ankle support and leaf-thin soles. They were nothing like convoy guards' tough boots, or even her own walking sandals. She applied salves and dressings to an endless series of blisters and advised one blushing young fellow regarding the wisdom of roughage in one's diet. A few of her patients had non-medical questions, and she asked some questions of her own.

"Shops?" She shook her head. "We have weekly market stalls in the town square, but you just missed that. No, I don't think our shoemaker keeps a ready-made stock. If you want new shoes, it would take him a couple of weeks to construct them. Er... do you know why Scientist Silvers wanted to come here?"

The guard shrugged. "No idea. That scary-looking woman—Giselle, is it?—handed him a message after he arrived. Sounds like he might have changed his plans. I hope we didn't trek all this way for nothing, money or no."

After finishing with the guards, Annetta packed up her remaining supplies and approached Silvers. He had rolled up his sleeves and was leaning across the table to peer at Giselle's notebook.

Giselle continued scribbling. "That's fine, Scientist Silvers. I'll speak with Mayor Sutcliff and the others you mentioned. We'll gather at his residence tomorrow morning."

"Good. I know I can rely on you." He stood and smiled at Annetta. "I see our esteemed physician has completed her work. Lead on, please."

Giselle's sharp voice followed them to the doorway. "Annetta, don't forget you have an evening clinic here tonight."

Annetta blushed. "Of course I won't forget."

Silvers gazed around as they strolled across the cobblestones of the town square towards her workshop. "This is quite a change from the city. I'd no idea towns were so small."

For a representative from Ascar, he wasn't as pompous as she'd feared. She laughed. "I myself only moved here a few months ago, from somewhere far smaller. This is actually one of the larger towns, with a couple of thousand people."

"And you're the only healer?"

"Yes. I mean, other people help, but this is my full-time job." Annetta had shared some of her knowledge with Opal, who knew some field medicine from her convoy guard training. It was always useful to have a spare pair of hands. "Now I have a pill-maker, I can make batches of pills for other people to dispense. Quicker, and doesn't need my personal attention so much."

"What sort of pills?"

"Painkillers, anti-infective agents, calming remedies for stomach upsets..."

He glanced at the notice board. "Sounds fairly routine."

"Well, yes, common things are common." Annetta's shoulders drooped. No doubt Ascar physicians were more educated and saw a wider range of diseases. Her list hardly sounded impressive. "Oh, I once gave a visiting captain some remedies. Those helped with someone who..." She glanced at Silvers' lifted eyebrow. *He's a scientist. He knows these things.* "After being, um, bitten. You know."

"Annetta!" called a treble voice.

Samuel waved from the other side of the square. He pelted towards them and slipped on a wet cobblestone. Annetta gasped. Arms flailing, he somehow stayed upright as he skidded the rest of the distance, straight into Silvers' solid belly.

"Oof!" Samuel bounced off.

Silvers grasped his arm and held him steady.

"Sorry, mister." Samuel gaped up at Silvers.

Annetta winced. "I'm so sorry. Samuel's a bit, well..."

Silvers laughed and ruffled the boy's hair. "No harm

done, kiddo. I remember when I was your age, all knees and elbows. Had to run fast to escape the other boys. Didn't always have time to look where I was going. So, who were *you* running away from?"

"Uh, nobody, mister. Adrian sent me with a message for Annetta."

"Go on," she said.

"He says, do you want to join us for supper tonight?"

Drat. "Um... ordinarily I'd love to, but I'm afraid I'm working. After this consultation with Scientist Silvers I have my evening clinic. So, sorry. Not tonight."

"I'll let him know. Uh, and thanks for catching me, mister." Samuel beamed up at Silvers before walking away.

Inside Annetta's workshop, Silvers sat in her consultation chair with its adjustable footrest while she inspected his feet and ankles.

"You're right, it doesn't look bad at all," she said. "There's a bit of redness from rubbing, but the skin's not broken. I can give you a salve to toughen up the skin for your return trip. I suppose you *are* returning to Ascar at some point?" Surely he would be, but why had he travelled here in person? Her pulse increased.

He waggled his foot. "That would be great. Yes, we'll be returning, once I've sorted my business here."

"Er, is your business medical? Something I can help with?" *Oh, please say it's nothing to do with me.*

He puffed out his cheeks, gazing around her workshop with its shelves of salves, pills and infusion sachets. The chair creaked under his weight when he peered at the pill-maker on her bench. "Maybe. I'm impressed by your workshop."

She forced a laugh. "You come all the way from Ascar

and think a rural herbalist can help you?"

"I hadn't realised before this visit how well provided you ruralites are." He leaned towards her, eyes intent. "Meeting you is a real stroke of luck. You have no idea how difficult it is to find someone open-minded in the capital. The other scientists refuse to consider novel ideas. The physicians reject new medicinal formulations. Whenever I suggest something, they tell me nobody's ever done it before, so it isn't advisable. I mean, how do we learn unless we experiment?"

Annetta's spine stiffened. With such ignorant people in Ascar, no wonder he was frustrated. "That's ridiculous! If we had the same attitude out here, I dread to think how many lives we'd have lost, how many more people would have suffered."

"Exactly." His gaze bored into hers. "People with the curse are still people. It's a damn shame they end up mouldering in the Keep because their powers aren't something they can control. I'm sure most of them don't *want* to be a danger to those around them. I'm convinced it's possible to make a drug to help them suppress that power, so they can lead normal lives."

Her breathing grew rapid. *Herbalist's secrets.* Her predecessors had passed on their imperfect and incomplete knowledge. They'd been handicapped by the rarity of afflicted patients. Of course, one didn't *want* afflicted patients, but the lack of them made evaluating treatments difficult. The only reason for secrecy was so others wouldn't endanger themselves by experimenting with highly dangerous formulations.

Silvers was a scientist. His *job* was to learn about the curse. There was no reason to keep secrets from him, not about this. Here was a chance for her to make a difference, no matter what it cost her, to make up for how she'd harmed Captain Shelley.

Voice quivering, she spoke. "I might be able to help you..."

Chapter 15

Eleanor sat rigidly upright, her heart racing, while the servant admitted Kenneth Staunton into her study and closed the door behind him. It was time for some answers.

Staunton bowed. The formal robe over his shoulders slipped aside to reveal a suit with a fine grey herringbone pattern. "Your Majesty."

"Thank you for coming." She indicated the chair at the side of her desk.

"A pleasure." He sat. "How may I be of service?"

How should she best approach him? While Staunton wasn't a complete stranger, she'd only spoken with him at social gatherings. The faint wrinkles on his bearded face hinted at decades of knowledge. What confidences might he have shared with her father, sitting in this very room? He might find her a poor substitute. "Er, I have a few questions."

"Yes?" His face reflected bland attentiveness.

He's no mind reader, it's up to you to ask. "I believe you were working with my father last year, were you not?"

"Indeed I was. He'd taken a particular interest in the curse and its implications for society. I had the pleasure of several theoretical discussions with him though we never reached any conclusions."

"Oh. Do you remember any specific points?"

"Well, we discussed the afflicted and the abilities they develop." Staunton regarded her soberly. "I take it you're familiar with the training system, including how powers are triggered?"

Eleanor's gaze dropped to the pile of maps on her desk, the ones on which she'd tried to pinpoint Isabel's location. *Pain.* Small wonder Isabel had been so adamant about eliminating the curse. "Yes." She licked her lips. "It sounds horrible for those undergoing training as well as those in the field. I mean, Isabel was happy enough—even bloodthirsty—with brainstorming beast eradication, but when it came to powers, she'd always turn the conversation to something else. In fact—" Her throat closed up. Until this moment, she'd not appreciated how distressing the topic must have been. *I'm so sorry, Isabel.*

Staunton looked away and cleared his throat. "Your cousin has excellent control, and we're glad of it. I told your father about other, less traumatic, training possibilities, but had to admit our records show they've previously been tried and failed. The effects were too erratic. Mainly drugs, alcohol, even mesmerism." He frowned. "That last one resulted in some rather confused participants, but that was all. By the way, how is Captain Hanlon?"

She squeezed her eyes shut. Of course he would ask. What should she say? Her father had trusted him. "I don't know. She's missing. We had a blimp accident."

"What?" His hand gripped the edge of her desk. "Tell me."

Hoping she wasn't making a huge mistake, Eleanor told him of that disastrous blimp trip, of Isabel's attempt to destroy the mound and the consequences. Halfway through her account Staunton stood, pacing around the desk to stare out of the window behind her.

She finished speaking and sagged in her seat, waiting

for him to tell her what a fool she'd been.

He strode round the desk to face her, leaning on the desktop. "Were you injured?"

"Why, no." She blinked at him. He could see she was intact, couldn't he? "Just some bruising when we landed. Art—I mean, the blimp operator was fine too."

He eased out a sigh. "Thank the Settlers. Who knows what might have happened? I do hope Captain Hanlon returns safely."

Eleanor shivered. She'd certainly had a lucky escape. Even if Isabel hadn't.

He stroked his beard. "Your father mentioned your aspirations for public acceptance of powers and your interest in cursed mounds. He told me of your map surveys and your models of beast incursion patterns. He was proud of you."

Proud? She'd thought he'd just been indulging her. Her eyes pricked, and she bowed her head. "Thank you. Go on, please."

"But he'd have been horrified at the idea of your destroying them, in view of their potential value. Of course, we know beast bites can transmit the curse. I myself wondered if any flesh-to-flesh contact might be a risk. He hypothesised that something in the mounds could cause the curse without transmission via a beast."

Although she'd had a similar idea, of beasts becoming cursed from mounds, she'd not made that leap regarding direct transmission from mound to human.

Artur. Her blood ran cold. He'd been ill afterwards, with hallucinations. Had he been injured? What if she'd caused him to be cursed?

"Your Majesty, are you well?"

She stared up at Staunton. "Sorry. It's just a lot to take

in."

"I understand. This is a heavy burden for you, especially as your father's demise was so unexpected."

Tell him. "I think—" She cleared her throat. "I think my father was murdered."

Staunton eased himself back on to the chair, his hesitant movements a reminder that he wasn't young and spry. He sighed. "I fear he might have been. And... I was worried I might also become a target. That's one reason I retired."

Eleanor hadn't been alone in her concerns? Caught between relief and irritation, she said, "And you didn't say anything."

His forehead creased. "What could I say? His death was investigated, and nobody came up with any answers. I certainly couldn't add anything, other than my vague suspicions."

"But why? Who would want to? Why would someone hate him so?"

"I doubt it was hate, but he might have been standing in the way of many factions, especially with his new ideas."

It was Eleanor's turn to sigh. Historians, scientists and *techne* people, all pulling in different directions. Never mind those responsible for more everyday matters, like overseeing finance and the guards. How naïve she had been, paying them no attention. Shirking her responsibilities. "You're right. And Lady Nelson was right too. I should take up my proper role in the Council. Investigating the curse is important, but so is looking after the realm."

Staunton's nose twitched. "Lady Nelson and I don't agree on everything, but I'm with her there."

Something tickled at her mind. "You mentioned earlier... my father spoke of the potential value of mounds. Do you know what he was thinking?"

The retired scientist regarded the portrait of Eleanor's father that hung on the far wall. "This was theoretical discussion only, I emphasise."

"Go on." She held her breath.

"He did wonder whether it might be possible to bestow cursed powers on people, in a predictable fashion. Something that could benefit society rather than causing people to flee in fear."

Eleanor gasped. "Deliberately curse people? *My father* said that?"

Staunton held up a hand. "This was all theoretical discussion only. And we debated how one might do it without all the, ah, current unpleasantness associated with it. He was well aware of what reaction such an initiative might provoke, of the potential public outcry." He frowned. "Come to think of it, that was the last discussion we ever had."

"Could this have been related to his passing?"

"If someone overheard those conversations, if word got out, someone could have decided to... put a stop to the idea. We know that certain people can perform assassinations without leaving any signs."

Had one of the household staff or guards spoken out of turn? Or even deliberately set things up with Shelley? Eleanor's chest grew tight. "What do you know about Shelley?"

"Hmm? Oh, the former captain. Odd you should mention him. He visited me a few weeks ago."

"About what? What's your impression of him?"

"Conscientious. He was helping to train a young girl in the Keep, asked me if I had any ideas. I suggested he check the historical archives, which is where I'd found a lot of my information."

She exhaled. That must have been his companion, that day in the rooftop garden. Poor girl. Was that why he'd requested access to her library? Eleanor's cheeks heated. She might well have been maligning him, about her father's death if not that of the guard. "And he came to see you just to ask that?"

Staunton licked his lips. "Ah, he did speak about something else..."

Don't make me drag this out of you. She leaned forwards. "Yes?"

"He expressed some concern that my successor, Jed Silvers, might be trying to curse people."

"You mean, like my father had been thinking of doing?" *Or so you say.* She thumped a fist on the desk. "Could you not have mentioned this earlier?"

Beads of sweat appeared on Staunton's brow. "I wasn't sure whether Shelley was imagining it. He's not overburdened with brains. But you're right, putting all this together, it does seem possible—not certain—that Silvers has similar ideas." His lips twisted. "Although I suspect his methods are rather cruder than anyone would accept. I mean, if he were doing such a thing. I'm not saying he is."

Eleanor's fists clenched. "I wouldn't have believed Shelley's words alone, but you've helped me make up my mind. I'll certainly do something about—"

"Wait!" He grasped her arm then snatched his hand away. "This is not the time to intervene. If you investigate an appointed official on so little evidence, you'll cause panic and risk rebellion within the Council. Some will worry irrationally about their own positions, and others will seek advantage for themselves. Really, trust me on this."

Could she trust him? Using her Queen's Discretion, she could order him to be mind-read. But the procedure was mainly for suspected criminals, plus routine monitoring of working officials and captains. Eleanor shouldn't subject Staunton to such humiliation based on her own whims. Overriding his rights like that would lose her his willing co-operation. Her father had trusted him, and so should she. "So what should I do?"

He tugged his beard. "Ensure your hold over the Council is as solid as it can be. Then you can act with minimal dissension. It may take you a few months, but the time investment will be well worth it. Even if Silvers is up to something, he can't be working that quickly. The disruption of accusing him now would outweigh any benefit."

She sighed. He had far more experience of the Council than did she, especially as she'd been avoiding her duties. "You're right. The Council takes priority."

Further conversation yielded no new insights, and Staunton took his leave.

Cursing people deliberately? Eleanor's guts churned. Why had her father hatched such an idea? He'd shown no signs of being deluded, so he must have had some reason, whether right or wrong. His Council associates might have further information. *And I should really do my job.* She stretched, loosening the tension in her shoulders, then reached for her diary. She marked the date of next week's Council meeting and piled up the papers to review beforehand.

A knock at the door heralded the arrival of Paton. He entered and saluted, resplendent in his scarlet uniform with matching eyepatch. "Your Majesty, reporting on your last request."

She leaned back in her chair. "Speak."

"Enquiries reveal that Shelley only spent significant time with one other captain, name of Longleaf."

Even if Shelley was innocuous, his associates might still bear watching. "What's Longleaf like? Do you think he's trustworthy?"

Paton coughed. "Susanna Longleaf. She was a long-term convoy captain, but reassigned to city duties last year."

A woman? Ah. "What are your impressions of her?"

"No criminal records. Lives in the barracks. Prefers the... more expensive taverns." His tone was flat.

Eleanor raised an eyebrow. "Unlike yourself?"

He glowered. "I might indulge on a special occasion, but she's quite a regular. Even though she doesn't spend money on drink, of course, the owner greets her personally."

"I see." *And you have to watch from a table by the kitchen door.* Paton had many good qualities, but charm wasn't among them. She suppressed a smile. "Did she return to Ascar before or after my father went to Settlers' Rest?"

"Ah, before. By a month or so."

Coincidence or not? "Arrange to have her followed. Discreetly, of course. She might well be innocent, and there's no point alarming her. Report back to me in three days."

"As you wish. I'll see to it myself. Do you have any other requests?"

Her amusement vanished, and she swallowed. "Just one. Artur Granville is to have access to the palace, including the library and royal apartments, any time he wishes."

Her face heated at the senior guard's suddenly deadpan expression, but he merely bowed and murmured, "I'll notify everyone."

After Paton left, Eleanor leaned on her desk, head in hands, wishing she knew what to do. If Artur had been cursed, he'd be vulnerable to the scientists and locked up in the Keep. *And it would be my fault.* At least if Eleanor bestowed on him some royal connection, no matter how fabricated, she could protect him from that fate. That was, unless he became dangerous.

Jonathan tightened his grip on the stick and halted, glaring at the evergreen bushes. A low branch quivered then stilled.

"I know you're there," he growled. He placed his hand over his leg, ready to call his power. Good if he didn't need it, but better to be prepared.

With a rustle, a furry head popped out of the undergrowth, a white splotch on the side of its snout. Tongue lolling, the beast eyed him, its head bobbing as it panted.

"Why do you keep following me?" It wasn't as if he'd been feeding it. Maybe it was waiting for him to die.

A yip was its only reply, which was some relief: speech would have made Jonathan question his sanity, on top of everything else. Instead, it squeezed through a gap in the bushes and trotted ahead of him, tail flicking from side to side.

Shaking his head, he followed, taking care not to slip on the wet leaves. Where was it taking him this afternoon?

Two evenings ago, this same beast had appeared and led him to an overhang big enough to provide respite from the elements. He'd been too cold, wet and simply miserable to question its motives. Last night it found him a cave. It lay by his fire while he prepared for the night, then departed. It might not seem to be a threat, but it certainly shouldn't accompany him to Maldon. Even if he and the beast had formed an understanding, he couldn't allow it to endanger anyone else. Especially not after that young boy had been cursed: a curse that was partly Jonathan's fault.

While he walked, Jonathan kept an ear out for the watercourse he'd been following. It ensured he wasn't walking in circles, as well as keeping him supplied. Yesterday he'd even spied a sizeable fish. Mindful of the plans he'd made earlier, he'd triggered his power—barely—without resorting to squeezing his wound. However, he'd been too slow, and the fish had swum away. In frustration, he'd launched a few small stones into the water, which at least gave him some practice. Next time he'd try knocking birds from their trees.

Somehow, dispatching a bird with a missile felt less disturbing than using his power to stop its heart. Killing that old man had given him a memory suffused with self-disgust, even after so many months. At the time he'd resolved never to misuse his power like that again... but he'd gladly make an exception for Silvers.

Silvers. He stopped, panting, while his power thrummed. The beast tossed its head and whined. Jonathan trudged onwards. *Patience. Let them think you dead.*

When the beast swung away from the watercourse, he frowned but decided it wouldn't do any harm to follow for a short distance.

The trees thinned. Jonathan's knees protested at the uneven footing while gravel crunched under his tatty shoes. Catching up with the beast at the edge of a clearing, he scowled.

Before him lay a heap of irregular grimy shapes, part-buried in a mound of dirt. A few blades of yellow grass represented the only adjacent plant life.

Damn stupid beast, bringing me to a cursed mound. What use was that? Was this its home, as was claimed in children's stories? He eyed the mound with suspicion, but nothing moved. A sniff of the air yielded no hint of dead meat. So much for the old tales. Still, it might have served as a den in the past. The advice for travellers to avoid mounds was still wise.

Hmm. The beast had shown some rudimentary intelligence, and they'd benefited a little from each other. It might have its own reasons for bringing him here. He dropped his belongings and took a few steps forwards, peering at the ground for hazards.

Something glinted. Jonathan crouched, brushing away the soil. His fingers touched something cold and hard, and he pulled it out.

His eyes widened. He held a metal knife handle, its blade broken and pocked with rust. It seemed unlikely there had been a previous visitor. Perhaps beasts were like jackdaws, gathering items to hoard. If that were the case, what else might Jonathan find here? This side trip might be useful after all.

Breath catching, he approached the bulk of the mound. It was as if some giant had thrown lumps of debris down, not caring about their position. Glancing around, he noted with relief a lack of giant footprints. He snorted. *Descending into superstition, are we?* With a hesitant hand, he stretched out towards the closest piece. It was covered in grime, but disc-shaped and with a smooth contour.

Grasping it with both hands, he tugged, sliding it off the pile. It was heavier than he expected, and he dropped it with a thud.

He squinted into the gap it had left, and his neck prickled. Squashed into the cavity was fabric, like mud-coloured heavyweave. It disintegrated at his touch.

With this evidence, he had no further doubt. Someone must have been here. Someone with clothes and a knife. Had they been lured here and killed by the beasts?

Fear rising in his chest, Jonathan backed away. He scanned his surroundings, but they showed no signs of life. Even the beast that had led him here was gone.

Get out, Shelley!

Jonathan stumbled away from the cursed mound and back to the sanity of his watercourse. *Damn beast.* Had he been so desperately lonely to fantasise it might be a friend?

Chapter 16

Annetta arrived at the mayor's residence rubbing grit from her eyes. After yesterday's talk with Silvers, her sleep had been plagued by dreams of Captain Shelley, of the distress on his face when he lost control. She'd contributed, if only in part, to the trouble.

Sutcliff opened the door and scowled at her. "You're late. Everyone's waiting for you."

She scowled back. "I had patients to care for." Even if one of them was in a dream.

Her eyebrows rose when he led her past the usual meeting room and pushed open a different door. It bore a brass plaque reading "Queen's Representative."

Silvers was stationed behind a polished wooden desk while Adrian, Giselle and Opal sat in front of him. Judging by the scrape marks on the wooden floor, the mismatched chairs had been brought in from some other room.

Sutcliff headed for the remaining empty chair, but the scientist wagged a finger. "I think we need another chair for our herbalist."

Just imagine, a high-up from Ascar being so considerate. Annetta bit her cheek to keep from laughing as Sutcliff stopped mid-pace, hunched his shoulders and scurried out. A brief chuckle escaped Adrian before he dropped his gaze and adjusted his tool belt. Giselle frowned at her notebook, a hand over her mouth. Opal gazed up at the ceiling, humming softly.

After Sutcliff returned, Silvers began. "I've spoken with some of you individually, but I'll just recap why I'm here. You'll have received a message about Shelley, who's visited here in the past. About how he's cursed and dangerous."

Annetta's stomach churned. The danger was partly her fault, even if it had been an accident. When she confessed about the dareth leaf and told Silvers that some of her formulations might affect cursed powers, he'd nodded understandingly. It had been such a relief to confide in someone knowledgeable, someone who took pains to set her at her ease. *Though I can't think of him as "Jed". Doesn't seem right.* Silvers had reassured her he'd been watching Captain Shelley even before then, concerned about signs of his increasing instability. Unfortunately, they'd not finished their talk because of her evening clinic.

The wrinkles on Sutcliff's face deepened. "Yes, shocking news."

Silvers leaned on the desk. "I detained him when he arrived back in Ascar after his visit here. If I'd known he'd be so ruthless as to kill that poor guard with his dangerous powers, I'd have kept him in a more secure cell. Fortunately, anticipating potential trouble, I used some *techne* to ensure I could track his location. An experimental method"—his gaze lit on Annetta—"but one I plan to implement more widely."

"Tracking *techne*?" murmured Adrian. "What if you took..." He reddened. "Sorry, carry on."

"The tracking system is based in Ascar. The prediction was that Shelley would travel here."

"What?" Sutcliff grew pink. "To terrorise us decent townsfolk?"

Opal glared at him.

Silvers shrugged. "I don't know why, just his direction. But that's beside the point. The person in Ascar monitoring his position sent me a message with updated information. It seems he's not heading here after all. I didn't learn this until I arrived and read the message. I'd thought I could apprehend him."

Annetta's shoulders eased. If Captain Shelley was somewhere else, that was one less complication, though she still owed it to him to help, to make up for the damage she'd done.

"However," continued Silvers, "I'm glad I did come to Maldon. Very glad indeed. We hadn't debriefed Shelley fully when he escaped. I now gather he in fact confirmed that one of your townsfolk was cursed. I appreciate Giselle's frankness on the matter, in informing me about your victim, about Shelley's own terrifying manifestation of a cursed power and about his mendacious attempt to ensure your silence about it. And, most of all, his assault on Annetta. Attempted murder, no less."

Not *exactly* attempted murder. Annetta squirmed under Sutcliff's disbelieving glare. It had been more like a scuffle...

Giselle's lips turned down. "To be fair, Captain Shelley stressed we must be completely honest with any representative of Ascar. He warned us of the consequences if we didn't, that could affect the whole town."

Sutcliff's head swung around as he regarded everyone, his mouth open. He jumped up from his chair and spluttered, waving his hands. "You're joking, surely! I knew nothing of the sort. This is outrageous!" He turned on Adrian. "It's that boy, isn't it? He's always getting into trouble. And you didn't warn me."

Adrian bowed his head. "Yes, it's Samuel."

"And you! What use are you as a herbalist? You assured me he was fine!"

Flecks of saliva spattered Annetta's face, and she hunched.

"That's enough, Sutcliff." Silvers stared at Sutcliff until he resumed his seat. "Don't blame Annetta. The signs were very subtle, even for an experienced practitioner. Those in the know were sworn to secrecy by Shelley as I've already mentioned."

Ha, not much fun being told off, is it? She smirked at Sutcliff while wiping her face with a sleeve.

"Have I got the gist of your information?" asked Silvers.

Annetta joined the others in nodding while she got her head around what he wasn't saying. He hadn't mentioned the wide use of cursed powers, so it seemed he planned to keep Mayor Sutcliff in ignorance. That was hardly a surprise. Obviously Silvers had good judgement as to whom he could trust to keep secrets.

"Yes," said Giselle. "Captain Shelley said... since Samuel was so young, and not doing any harm, he'd ask the Council if we could give him something close to a normal childhood here."

"Ah, so Shelley's capable of original thought." Silvers regarded the desktop for a moment, a hand over his lips. "But he misled you. The Council would never have approved such a decision, made by a maverick captain. It's lucky I apprehended him before they learned of it and issued sanctions against the whole town. Or maybe that was Shelley's plan, to gain a hold over you and blackmail you in future. At least he wasn't so lost to humanity as to insist you conceal his actions from officials such as myself. I can see it wasn't your fault. Anyway, I'm taking Samuel off your hands. He'll travel with me back to Ascar. He can't do any damage with his power there."

Sutcliff's eyes narrowed. "What power?"

Adrian sagged on his chair. "He can see things from a distance. Like, what people are doing, or other places."

"Can he see what *anybody* is doing? At any time?" Sutcliff paled.

"I don't know," said Adrian. "We don't know what sets him off, and he doesn't seem to understand what he's drawing. We didn't want to encourage him or make a big deal of it. Looking after him properly has been... difficult."

Silvers rapped the desktop. "The thing is, a power like that in the wrong hands could be very dangerous. I suppose it might be worth considering Shelley's serendipitous suggestion, for those with trivial harmless powers, but the Council would have to discuss and approve it first. And it wouldn't work for Samuel. Imagine if someone used the poor boy to gather blackmail information, or to spy on people. The possibilities are endless. No, it's too dangerous to leave him here. Rest assured I'll look after him personally and ensure he's well treated."

Giselle sighed. "We'd hoped to keep Samuel, but even Captain Shelley hadn't been certain the Council would agree. We trusted him, and I'd like to think he meant well at the time, but you bear the authority of the scientists. We're not going to challenge your decision."

Eyes wide, Sutcliff nodded. "Yes, Samuel definitely needs to go."

"So that's settled." Silvers gazed at each of them, stopping at Annetta. "I'd also like to borrow your herbalist, see if she can help with our medical formulations."

As the others stared at her, Annetta's heart raced. This

was what she'd been thinking, wasn't it? Where her conversation with Silvers had led her? Her chance to help, not just the people of Maldon, but maybe the whole realm. If her special recipes proved useful, she could make a huge difference. It would be tough, but she wouldn't let them down. Not Silvers, and not Captain Shelley, whether or not he deserved her assistance.

Adrian's gaze darted between Annetta and Silvers. "Don't you have enough pharmacists of your own? What possible use could Annetta be to you?"

Her mouth dropped open, and she stiffened. "Excuse *me*, Adrian. I have ample experience of treating illnesses. I bet the herbs around Ascar are different from those here, and nobody from the city has ever researched them. I could be of *plenty* use to Jed. Um, Scientist Silvers."

Silvers leaned forwards, addressing Adrian. "Your young lady here has an immense store of knowledge that I believe the Ascar researchers are unaware of. Her endeavours, properly channelled, could help the whole of society, not just this one town."

See, Adrian, he *thinks I'm useful, even if you don't.* It was obvious the scientist was after her skills, nothing else. Silvers meant the herbalists' secrets, of course, which weren't exactly Annetta's own invention. But this was a unique opportunity, with an Ascar scientist learning of her work. Although Keep detentions were common knowledge, laboratory work was kept quiet. And no wonder. Why raise false hopes of a cure? If she didn't do this, who would? She swallowed. "Someone should go with Samuel, and it makes perfect sense for it to be me. You know the... accident I had with Captain Shelley. This is my chance to make things right." As Adrian's face fell, she relented. "It won't be forever."

Silvers turned his attention to Opal. "You should travel back with us too. Be useful to have a convoy guard on the journey. I'm paying double rate."

Opal straightened in her chair. "Sorry, sir, but no." Silvers frowned, and she added, "You're not my commanding officer. It's not my duty to follow instructions from a civilian. No offence, sir. I was instructed to remain here until another captain commands me otherwise."

Clenching a meaty fist, Silvers pushed his chair back from the desk. "If you know what's good for—"

Pulse rapid, Annetta raised a hand. "I think Opal really should remain to provide medical cover. She's been supplementing her field medicine training with my teaching. Fortunately I've already produced several batches of pills for various indications. They'll remain potent for several months. Adrian's machine was very helpful." She stopped and drew a breath. Why couldn't Opal have been less blunt?

Silvers stared at both of them for several heartbeats before resuming his seat. "I suppose that makes sense. We'll depart with Samuel and Annetta."

She glanced at Adrian, but he kept his gaze towards the floor.

Annetta spent the next day organising her workshop and regular supplies for Opal's use before packing for her imminent journey. Her herbalist's bag bulged with her rare ingredients and secret remedies, although her general bag held embarrassingly few possessions. Maybe she could obtain more clothes in Ascar. She double-checked that the secret compartment under her bed was empty. Not only would she need the special supplies for her work in Ascar, it would be dangerous if anyone else came across them by accident.

In the evening, she had supper with Adrian, Lisa and Samuel.

Lisa ladled barley stew on to their plates. "It'll be odd with you and Samuel gone. Quieter, for a start. Less mess to clean up."

"Yeah." Annetta gazed at the stew topping the mound of mashed potatoes. Good plain cooking. Would city food be to her taste, or would she be too unrefined to appreciate it? She picked up her fork.

"It'll be fun," mumbled Samuel around a mouthful of food, "though I bet they don't cook like you. Jed said if I behave myself, he'll send me on a blimp trip. I'd love to fly in the air like the messenger birds do. I bet I'd see fun things from the sky."

"Are you all set? How long will it take to reach Ascar?" asked Lisa.

Annetta shrugged. "A week or so. Opal's moving into my house, makes it easier in case of emergencies. I wouldn't have minded a bit longer to put things in place for her, but Scientist Silvers insisted on leaving tomorrow."

She sneaked a glance at Adrian. He kept his gaze on his plate, chewing and swallowing as if he couldn't taste the food. Well, he couldn't, could he? That's how he'd ended up poisoned... *And he nearly died.*

Wincing at how she'd snapped at him earlier, she cleared her throat. "Adrian, would you like me to keep an eye out for anything particular in Ascar? Any information or devices?"

He set his fork down and raised his head, not meeting her eye. "No. Well, actually..." He stared into the distance, reached for a folder on a shelf and pulled it over to the dining table.

Lisa snatched his plate with its half-eaten meal before he could drop the folder on top of it. "Pa!"

Adrian blinked. "Sorry. I was just thinking."

Annetta's lips twitched. "I guess that means you would like me to find you some things while I'm there?"

Pages rustled as he flipped through them. "I wonder if you could..." He pulled out a pen and started to scribble.

Lisa shook her head. "Is everyone else finished eating too? Samuel, help me clear up, then we can sort your packing."

After the two children headed upstairs, Annetta watched Adrian writing for a few minutes then coughed. "I hope that's not a shopping list."

"What?" He reddened. "Oh, no. I started drawing something else. The only thing I'm thinking about would be something to help make pictures. They have daguerreotype *techne* there, and I'd love to try it out."

"I'll keep an eye out, when I have time. Adrian..."

"Yes?"

She clasped her hands. "This isn't going to be a holiday. I hope you understand. I have to go. This is bigger than the two of us." *Not that there's any "us".*

His shoulders slumped. "I know. I hope you won't forget me when you're famous."

She gazed at the tabletop. "Of course not."

The following morning, after handing her workshop over to Opal, Annetta arrived in the town square with her bags. Samuel was already there with Adrian and Lisa. Fortunately his walking sandals still fitted: he'd not been in Maldon long enough to outgrow them.

They made small talk for a few minutes—what was left to say?—until the guards arrived with their handcarts.

The last traveller to enter the square was Silvers. Giselle accompanied him, with a basket of provisions she placed in a handcart.

The scientist ruffled Samuel's hair. "Ready, lad?"

The boy beamed. "Sure thing! It'll be exciting, won't it?"

Silvers grinned back. "I'm sure it will."

Chapter 17

Picking her way along the deserted narrow street, stepping around piles of refuse, Susanna wrinkled her nose at the stench of effluent from the nearby underground waterway. She pulled her oldest cloak around herself and tugged the knitted hat down over her ears as the evening chill descended.

Sweat prickling her back, she meandered up the street. *Act natural, as if you belong here.* A likely chance. She probably stood out like a blimp in the Armstrong Tunnel. Well, what *did* one wear to go spying? It wasn't as if she'd been trained for this, but there hadn't been anyone else she could ask to help. Lester might not have minded, but his face was too unforgettable. Unlike hers, as a middle-aged nonentity.

She steadied herself against a broken lamppost and allowed a bout of wooziness to settle. Eating something earlier would have been wise. But she'd had no appetite. How could she?

I think Jonathan's dead.

That's what Richard had told her, what he'd suspected from using his power to track Jonathan. Was he right, or could she allow herself to hope? Not just for herself, but for Tabitha, whom she'd not visited since Richard's revelation. She couldn't inflict her uncertainties on the poor girl. All she could do was focus on exonerating Jonathan—or avenging him. She would make Silvers pay.

Silvers lived in an area of the city Susanna had never visited. She wished she didn't have to. When her enquiries had yielded his address, she'd blinked and asked the records clerk to recheck the information. Even if he'd grown up here, why hadn't he moved away at the earliest opportunity? She'd shaken her head in amazement that he'd risen so far from such humble beginnings to become one of Ascar's most prominent scientists.

Even though she'd lost her chance to mind-read him, his trip out of the city gave her another opportunity, an opportunity she wouldn't waste. If only she could gain proof he'd set up Jonathan, or had blackmailed Staunton, or planned to curse people... surely she could find *something* to incriminate him. Letters, notes, even people's thoughts— she'd take what the situation offered. *Using your power for personal gain? And against a scientist too!* She pushed the concern away.

She walked along the row of cramped terraced houses, each one propping up its neighbours. Their shared side walls raised a problem she'd not anticipated. So much for finding a hiding place where she could watch and be unobserved. With a huff, she squinted at the faded house numbers.

There! Slowing her pace, she allowed her eyes to linger on the entrance to Silvers' house. A metal number was screwed into the freshly painted front door. He might not have moved away from his roots, but he clearly wasn't still living in squalor. A frown creased her forehead at the ostentation, given the surrounding area.

From Susanna's perusal of the public records at the city hall, Silvers had a live-in married couple working as handyman and maid. Servants would be unusual for this district. She wondered if he remained here to show solidarity with his neighbours or to rub his new affluence in their faces.

Now that she'd arrived, what should she do? She'd thought there might be an alley where she could lurk, maybe an open window. But with these terraced houses, their doors all opening on to the street, she could hardly avoid notice if she waited around.

The door swung open with the barest creak. Susanna bent as if to tie her bootlace while two pairs of feet stepped into the street. Grimy boots and tatty slippers: both the household servants.

"He's away, what's it matter what we buy? He'll never notice. He's loaded," said a harsh male voice over the click of a key in the lock.

"He'd notice, alright, even with his new money. Let's see what's on offer for cheap. And don't forget he wants glue," replied the woman in a nasal tone.

The voices faded as the footsteps moved off.

Susanna's breathing quickened. The house should be empty though she couldn't think how to use that to her advantage. She clenched her fists. Breaking in would be foolhardy, and she'd probably get caught. It hadn't been part of her training to detect or evade pursuit, and she wasn't young enough to be agile.

Still, there were acceptable things she could do. She strolled a little further down the street, turned, and approached Silvers' door again, slowing as she passed his front window. Glancing inside, she sought a clue, anything that would help her.

The room appeared, well, functional. Plain wooden table, a place setting at one end, a few papers piled in the middle. Doubling as a study and dining room, maybe. Some odd shape stood at the other end. That would bear a closer look.

Her gaze skipped along the neighbouring houses. How could she remain unmemorable? There might not be people *on* the street, but she could imagine curtains twitching and gossip being passed on.

Steeling herself, she stepped up to the door and knocked, her knuckles barely grazing the wood. She tilted her head as if listening for noises from within, allowing her a further glance at the window. Then she shook her head, stepped in front of the window and openly peered inside.

A small metal box lay on the table with two clamps attached, a second box close by. Beside them was an unrolled cloth case, within which metal instruments gleamed. A glass jar containing a brush—*the glue, I suppose*—completed the ensemble. What was all that about? She'd never seen anything like—

A heavy hand grasped her shoulder, and she flinched. It belonged to a squash-faced bruiser in a stained singlet and shabby trousers.

"Lookin' for someone, lady?" Beery breath and halitosis wafted into her face as she tried to shrug his hand off.

Blast. She couldn't risk a scene and doubted whether she could defend herself if he got aggressive without screaming for help. And just what kind of help might arrive? "Just seeing if my friend is in." She swallowed. "Ah... Jed, I mean. Looks like he's not, so I'll be on my way..."

He looked her up and down with bloodshot eyes, his gaze lingering on her face. "You're not his type. Too scrawny. And he wasn't expectin' you." The man stepped closer. "Now, if you want me to keep my trap shut about the lady with the hoity-toity voice..."

"No!" She tried to slide away.

He grabbed her wrists and pinned her against the window. The weight of his body pressed against hers, and her chest tightened. Why had she come out unarmed?

His mouth sought hers and she twisted her head, pulling one hand out of his grasp. She scrabbled behind her for anything she could use: a brick, a piece of stone, even a sharp nail. Only smooth glass met her hand. She tried to kick his ankle, but he was faster and stamped down on her booted foot. *Pain.* What use was her power? She didn't need it to know what he intended. This visit had only achieved more trouble, fool that she was. Blood rushed in her ears, and her vision grew hazy.

... stupid woman...

Running footsteps pounded up to her.

The pressure from the man's body eased as he was yanked away. Another, larger man gripped her assailant's collar. As Susanna gasped for breath, a hand to her chest, her rescuer felled her assailant with a single, clinical punch to the jaw.

Her stammered thanks dried up as she noticed the eye glaring at her from beneath his heavy hooded cloak. His other socket held a mass of scar tissue.

"You're an idiot," he snarled. "Leave, and don't come back."

Trembling, barely able to hold back tears, she left.

Chapter 18

Franka glowered in frustration while she stared out of Practice Room B's observation window at today's volunteer. The skinny man scratched an armpit and returned his attention to the cards on his table. She squinted. Bah, it was obvious. Knave of stars should go with seven of rings.

The stimulus clip on her earlobe tugged as she shook her head. She was supposed to be scaring the man, not getting distracted by his solitaire game or wondering when—if ever—she'd next play with the guys in the barracks. Of course, he wouldn't know that—he was being paid to sit in that room for the morning and note down anything odd. They'd have told him they were testing some new *techne*, not that someone afflicted was working her wiles on him.

Wrinkling her nose, she turned the calibrated stimulus generator's setting up another notch. *Pain.* This was hardly fun, but if it got her out, she'd put up with it and push on through. It would be better than mouldering in that stupid suite, wearing this stupid white costume and making stupid useless wishes.

Ah, there it is. Something moved inside her, the power she'd been keeping suppressed. Calling it wasn't so difficult, but directing it was more challenging. That Scientist Fellows—soft-looking chap—had told her what happened when her power first manifested in the Armstrong Tunnel. She'd sent a wave of fear out, enough to scare off the other guards. Only one person had stayed to look after her.

Jonathan.

Following interviews with the infirmary staff, Fellows had concluded Franka's power was directional rather than... *concentric waves, was that what he said?* That kinda made sense. It might even prove useful, despite her initial doubts. Crowd control, maybe, if she could keep it low level and not cause panic. Ha, they'd probably make her use it in interrogations.

She scowled at the volunteer, who'd given up on that game and was reshuffling the pack. *Fear me.* His lips moved as he laid out another spread, then he peeked at the second card in the pile. Pressure grew in Franka's head as she focussed her will on the oblivious man. Her power surged. *Be terrified, you cheat!*

The door behind her crashed open, breaking her concentration.

Franka pulled off her earclip. "Dammit, I nearly had—"

The two guards who'd accompanied her here crowded each other in the doorway, their faces pale. One levelled a tranquilliser gun at her while the other clutched a baton in his shaking hand.

She swallowed, slowly spread her hands on the table. "Did I do something wrong?"

The guard with the gun frowned before lowering his weapon. "We thought you'd lost control. Your power was pushing out so strongly we, uh, decided to end this session."

Right. Directional. Though not the way she'd been thinking. "Sorry about that, guys. I think I know how to sort that. Just one more try? Then I'll go along with you quietly."

She reached for the discarded earclip, and they didn't stop her.

Franka's shoulders tensed as she again focussed on the test subject. He would earn his keep today. She groped for her power, held it ready and took in a deep breath. *Pretend it's a fishing pole. Cast it towards him, not behind you.* Exhaling, she *let go.*

The man's head jerked up, and his cards scattered on the floor.

Gotcha. She smiled.

Back in her suite on the residential floor, Franka ordered and ate a leisurely lunch while considering her next problem: Tabitha. How was she going to make contact? If she proved herself and became a captain, she'd be allowed to visit whoever and whenever she wanted. But working up to that would take too long. What might Tabitha go through in the meantime?

Discreet enquiries—as discreet as she could manage—had shown the corridor guards to be of two types. The majority were city guards who wanted an easy life: only here for the regular hours and pay packets. A few others were ex-convoy, with experience of beasts and the wilds, and more sense of responsibility towards their charges. She'd spoken a few times with Michael, a former convoy colleague.

Michael had sighed. "I'm sure Cap—er, Shelley would have approved of your wish to help her. You always kept us straight while on convoy. But rules are rules. The afflicted people detained here must be kept separate. We corridor guards are monitored, to ensure we're not... colluding." He gazed down the hallway. "We try not to intrude on your privacy, but if anything untoward came to my attention, I'd have to report it."

Was that a hint he might not watch her too closely? Or maybe a warning to be prudent. *Prudent? Not my style.*

Could her power of fear be of any use? Maybe she could send signals by pulsing it or something. She'd better be sure she could control its direction, however, or else she'd give the game away. Parking the thought of using her power, she turned to more practical plans. First, she'd better deal with the problem of being watched at any time.

The observation hatch in her suite door was just big enough for someone to peer through, though covered by a sliding wooden panel to allow the illusion of privacy. Franka tied the hatch shut using some of the string she'd requested from the corridor guard the day she arrived. Guards usually looked in on the residents after each meal, so she wouldn't have long to wait.

Franka stripped, tossed her clothes on to the bed and began a stretching routine. The deep-pile rug was comfy on her toes. *Bet it's even nicer on my back.* Even if this failed, she'd be getting herself in shape again.

After a few minutes, just as she was warming up, a rattle came from the hatch, followed by voices.

She increased her efforts. With her back to the door, she planted her feet a shoulder-width apart and bent over to place her palms on the ground. *Ahh, nice stretch, not too painful on my scar. Now, hold it.*

There was the sound of a heavy bar sliding aside, and a key rattled in the lock.

The door swung open, and Franka grinned at the guard framed in the upside-down doorway. His bristling moustache, purpling complexion and open mouth were everything she could have hoped for.

She maintained her position for a few seconds longer then straightened, turned to him and winked. "Well, I wasn't expecting a visitor. Come to keep me company? Or just for the view?"

The man spluttered, his gaze darting around the room before it settled on the unlit fireplace. "Preposterous!"

Catching sight of a grinning Michael behind the man, Franka raised an eyebrow. "Hey, *you're* the one who walked in on *me*. I need to keep in shape, y'know? Can't be lazing around, getting a fat arse."

"Your hatch was fastened shut." The guard glared. "Of course we had to open the door, check you're not doing anything inappropriate. Though your lack of clothing is absolutely inappropriate."

"Hey, fair's fair. I'm in my private quarters here. I'm not running a peepshow. You want to see me, open the door so I can see you too." Her gaze drifted from his red face to his brown boots.

Drawing himself up, the guard opened his mouth, but Michael murmured, "Since detainees are kept isolated, it doesn't matter what they wear, does it? Or don't wear, rather. We can always knock on the door first."

Franka shrugged. "Doesn't matter to me whether you do or not, if ogling me's part of your job. But don't complain if you get an eyeful."

Michael's voice quavered. "I, uh, don't think this comes within our remit, Paul. The monitoring people might ask questions. And if a resident becomes a captain..."

"Bah, fine!" said the guard. "We'll knock and let you make yourself decent before checking on you. But if you don't reply when we knock, we're coming straight in."

"Don't know about *decent*." She grinned. "But I wouldn't mind a chance to... prepare, you know?"

The guard glowered. "I'll be watching you."

"Please do." Franka ran her tongue over her upper lip

and resumed her stretching.

The slam of the door and the thud of the bar were sweet satisfaction.

She finished her routine uninterrupted, took a bath and occupied herself reading the recent news sheets until after they'd collected the plates from her evening meal. Now for the next part.

In the fireplace, she found a charred stick and a palm-sized piece of coal of the right weight. With the stick, she made a quick scribble on an old news sheet:

F in 2

She stuffed the coal and paper into a sock. The whiteness of the sock wasn't ideal, but at least the Keep abutted Ascar's city wall, and these rooms faced the mountains. If some brave fool were wandering in the wilds outside, they'd hardly pay attention to a sock. *Hmm.* She rolled her package around in the soot. *Better.*

For the third time since she'd arrived, Franka paced out the length of her suite and the distance from the walls to the barred window. She measured out her remaining string—an arm span more than she needed—and cut it to the right length. Ideally she'd have doubled it, but there wasn't enough. The boy who'd provided it had apparently been assigned to other duties, and she didn't want to raise suspicion by asking for more. She knotted one end of the string as a marker and tied the sock closed with the other end.

Time to see if her idea would work. She approached the window and opened it, casting her gaze over the evergreen trees that covered the mountains' southern slopes. The faint scent of pine made her smile.

Sock in one hand, free end of the string in the other,

Franka extended her arm through the bars, allowing her wrist to overhang the edge of the windowsill. She let a length of the string slip through her fingers and started swinging the weighted sock.

Easy does it. She continued to swing, allowing the string to play out gradually through her fingers. Starting was easy—a trivial effort—but she'd have to keep the rhythm perfectly regular through the entire attempt.

As the string lengthened, her wrist started to ache, but she persisted, allowing the arc to increase. If she'd judged right, by the time she reached her marker knot, the weight would reach Tabitha's window at the end of the swing. Of course, whether Tabitha could catch it, whether Tabitha would even notice it, and whether anyone else on the floor below would notice it, was another matter...

Sweat trickled down Franka's back, despite the evening cool, and her wrist felt like it were on fire. *Nearly there. Breathe in, breathe out.* The knot slipped through the fingers of her non-swinging hand. *Just a few more swings, and we're there.*

Her vision blurred, sweat dripping into her eyes. Her swinging hand cramped, and she bit the inside of her cheek, bracing herself to keep the rhythm steady.

From deep inside, her power awoke, pushing against her control. *Shit.* Could she control the swinging and her power, or should she just give up for the evening? She didn't know if she could do this again. *Fishing rod, fishing rod.* It was worth a try.

Nearly cross-eyed with concentration, Franka *let go* in the direction of Tabitha's room, expending her power. *Sorry, kid.*

Her eyes told her that the benumbed fingers of her

swinging hand were tightening on the knot. *We're there. About fucking time.*

Franka flicked her hand at the top of her final swing. *Go on, land on the window ledge.* Her hand had lost all sensation.

A cacophony of squawks and fluttering wings reached her ears. She started, and the knotted end of the string slipped through her fingers, falling from her grasp, no doubt to land in some useless tangle of bushes outside the city wall.

Bugger.

Chapter 19

Jonathan frowned as he peered at Maldon's outskirts, checking for any signs of nighttime movement. He'd need to leave the concealment of the trees outside the town if he were to accomplish his objectives.

Was this visit wise? There was little choice. Going after Silvers would demand all his skills and ingenuity. Arriving back in Ascar a ragged, half-starved wretch would give him no chance of success. He'd considered his options and decided that the best plan would be to enter Maldon quietly, seek information, steal what he needed, and depart just as quietly, leaving the townsfolk blameless. Thus re-provisioned, Jonathan could then stroll back to Ascar and confront Silvers at a time of his own choosing.

After some two weeks in the wilderness on his own, his shoulder blades itched at the idea of encountering people, especially people who might be hostile. From the guard's words at the tunnel, they were after him for murder, but Silvers might have blown up the accusations still further. He could have spread a lot of lies from the centre of his spider-web in Ascar. Had Tabitha and Susanna been dragged into this, viewed as guilty by association?

The beasts didn't care about Jonathan's reputation. After he'd visited that cursed mound, he'd seen no further signs, with even the one that had followed him noticeable by its absence. Thank the Settlers for that.

All was quiet. He shoved his tattered sack with its dwindling supply of grain beneath a bush. No point in encumbering himself when he wanted stealth and silence.

When he shifted his weight, his wound ached, but the discomfort was trivial compared to before. Even better, he didn't need the pain. Two weeks of practice, of going against his prior conditioning, had taught him other ways of activating his power at will. Pain remained the most reliable and controllable stimulus, but no longer essential. Wouldn't that surprise Silvers?

He approached the closest building. Pausing at a corner, he checked for lit windows along the next part of his route. All remained silent and dark, and his breathing eased a touch.

He drifted through the town square to the notice board. The moonlight glinted off its glass covering as he scanned the announcements. He nodded at Ascar's message about him, which was much as he'd expected.

Reward for capture or neutralisation.

Well, the townsfolk might not try to kill him on sight. He'd take care not to escalate any encounters.

From previous visits, he knew the locations of the food storehouses and laundry, which should yield decent pickings. But first, he'd try his luck with a more challenging source of loot: Annetta's house. She kept medicines which might affect powers. She'd told him as much after their inadvertent skirmish. Such medicines were worth taking a risk to obtain, and he could try them out somewhere isolated.

The problem was that she stored them under her bed.

It was unlikely she'd be out visiting a patient, and laughable to hope she'd sleep too deeply to notice him. As

Jonathan approached her house, he winced. If she woke, he'd have to ensure she didn't raise the alarm. He didn't *want* to attack the poor woman, but at least she wouldn't attract any blame for his actions. This time, he was in control of himself and could easily overcome her without harming her or using his power. *And I won't let her get the better of me again.*

He circled the house, pausing to listen at her bedroom window. Soft snores reached his ears. Damn. At least she was asleep.

After turning the front door handle, he pushed gently, meeting no resistance. How fortunate that ruralites trusted their neighbours, so he needn't expend his power on a lock. He eased the door open and took a slow step inside. A potpourri of herbal scents assaulted his twitching nose. In the dimness of the workroom, he shuffled forwards, one hand patting the wall. The room seemed larger than on his last visit.

After an age, his hand pushed open the living room door. It creaked, and he held his breath. No sounds of alarm met his ears, and he slid inside. In contrast to the workshop, a glow from the stove illuminated this room. He nodded in satisfaction.

Jonathan's gaze turned to the shelf holding a dozen jars of Annetta's infusions. One of those had stimulated his power by accident. She'd called it dareth leaf. *Hmm.* Far safer to steal one of these jars than attempt the medicines under her bed. That would do. If she woke up—and he hoped she didn't—he'd restrain her and steal her medicines. Otherwise he'd leave her alone.

As he considered the next step, he grimaced, remembering the sack he'd left outside the town. It would be impossible to carry all these jars in his hands. Which was the right one?

He recalled the dareth leaf's aroma, a deep rich earthy one. Picking up the first jar, he opened it and sniffed. His nose wrinkled at the bitter scent. Not that one. The second jar was too floral and tickled his nose.

He sneezed, clapping a hand to his face to muffle the mini-explosion. *Shit!*

Sweat trickled down his temple as he listened for a reaction from the bedroom, but all that met his ears was the crackle from the stove. He let out a breath and turned to the next jar.

The bedroom door crashed open.

Jonathan spun round, poised to grapple. He gaped at the figure charging him, at the glimpse of tattooed bare skin. *A man?*

As the muscular figure reached him, arms outstretched, Jonathan twisted out of the way and gave him a shove. The man thudded into the wall beside the stove.

The stove's light illuminated the man's snarling face. Marcus, not Adrian. Damn, the pudgy craftsman would have made an easier opponent than the farmer. And he'd seemed more Annetta's type.

Concentrate, Shelley! The farmer growled and charged again. Jonathan ducked. *Just get out!* Annetta hadn't yet appeared, but she might have climbed out the bedroom window and even now be raising the alarm. A confrontation with more people would force him to use his power, especially if he were injured. Such an escalation could lead to panic and deaths, including his own.

He backed towards the door, trying to avoid the farmer's fists. A punch caught him on the shoulder, and he staggered.

Pain. He grunted, and his power rose. His breathing grew heavier as he put effort into suppressing his power.

"Gotcha!" Marcus kicked at him.

Jonathan dodged and stumbled over a chair. As he fell on his back, he grabbed Marcus' sleeping shorts and used the man's momentum to topple him.

Marcus landed on the table, the teapot falling off. The crash as it hit the floor was echoed by splintering furniture.

It was pointless trying to escape now. Jonathan rolled over, seized an arm and leg, and bent them to immobilise the farmer.

"Annetta, let's talk," he called over Marcus' curses. The quiet herbalist wouldn't fight, especially if he were restraining her lover. "All I'm after is—"

Cold metal touched his neck.

"Let him go, Captain Shelley." The voice wasn't Annetta's.

"Opal?" Jonathan's grip slackened, and he raised himself on his knees, lifting his hands, the blade following his movement.

Marcus wriggled out from beneath him and stood with a glare. "You bastard! If you hadn't had the advantage of surprise..."

He drew his leg back to kick, and Jonathan tensed himself to receive the impact. *Down, power.*

"That's enough." Opal's voice was cold. "Put on more clothes and call the mayor."

Lighting a lamp, Marcus frowned. "Wouldn't it be safer if you went?"

"I'm the guard. This is my job. I know how to handle a weapon, and I don't go attacking suspected murderers with my bare hands. Now, go!"

Marcus disappeared into the bedroom for a few moments and returned wearing a shirt. He gave Jonathan one last glower before departing.

Jonathan swallowed, not liking the weight of the blade on his neck, nor the fact Opal stood behind him. However, this was an opportunity to escape, if only she weren't a guard. Or... might he appeal to her for help? No, even if she agreed to assist him, that would land her in trouble again. "May I turn around?"

"Slowly."

"I'm an old man, Opal. I only do slowly."

Opal lifted the sabre, and, still kneeling, he eased himself around until he faced her. The padded guard jacket and linen nightshirt were an incongruous mix.

Her scowling visage was little comfort. "Why did you have to come back? You must have known they'd be after you!"

He spread his hands and raised his chin, glancing over her shoulder. There were shelves on the wall behind her. Shelves with more jars. Jars he could use as missiles. His power whispered to him. "Look at me, Opal. All I have are these clothes I arrived in, and they're not even mine. I had to try *something*."

The sabre remained pointing towards him. "They said you were a murderer."

"I'm not." He pulled the pain from his shoulder and directed it at his core. "Can you tell me what's been happening? Please?"

Opal snorted. "Plenty. The message came from Ascar couple of weeks back, saying you were a murderer, dangerous, a price on your head and all that..."

"I see." He took a breath, focussing on the jar behind her. He'd only get one chance. *Keep her talking.* "And what else?"

"Then it got worse. Samuel's gone. Annetta's gone. That Scientist Silvers gives me the creeps."

"Silvers?" Jonathan jerked forwards, halting himself as the sabre's tip touched his chest. "Why?"

"He showed up with a gang of city guards." Opal's breathing was rapid. "Spoke to Giselle, Annetta, Adrian."

And I told them to cooperate if someone from Ascar showed up. Jonathan ground his teeth. At worst, he'd expected another captain to visit Maldon. Not Silvers.

The sabre wobbled. "Silvers was delighted to find a boy who can 'see things at a distance', never mind Annetta and her herbal remedies. So he took both of them away, offered Annetta a job with the scientists."

Cold sweat ran down Jonathan's back at the thought of Samuel in the Keep, and how Silvers might subvert Annetta. She had knowledge of more than dareth leaf. This was even worse than he'd imagined. Why hadn't he warned them about Silvers when he was here last time? His power surged, and he pushed it back down. Now wasn't the time. His thoughts raced over how he could reach Ascar quickly without making Opal complicit. "I suppose Mayor Sutcliff will inform Ascar."

"Yep, and we'll hang on to you until a squad shows up to take you back."

"Yes..." He met her gaze. "For my trial. I didn't kill the guard. Mayor Sutcliff needs to emphasise that I'm demanding a trial, to prove my innocence. If the messenger bird's sent to the Keep rather than the public posthouse, the message will reach the Council quicker." The bird would certainly arrive before Silvers did, and the scientist wouldn't have a chance to intercept the message.

"You're keen." She raised an eyebrow at him. "If I were you, I'd have kept running."

"This is the best chance I'll get to clear my name. I won't try to escape. You have my word on it." His fists clenched at the thought of Silvers visiting Maldon, but this was also a lucky opportunity. If Jonathan's capture were publicised, he couldn't be disposed of quietly. Being collected by a squad of guards would be faster and safer than travelling alone, especially in his condition. They might even send a blimp. He shivered. *I'll cope.* It would get him close to Silvers. And after that... it wouldn't matter.

"Hmm." She shrugged. "It's your funeral."

As long as I can take that bastard with me.

Chapter 20

Indigo skirt swishing as she approached, Eleanor inclined her head to the guard outside the Council chamber. She hoped her palpitations weren't visible through her jacket. Were it not for her red-clad escort, she might have changed her mind and retreated. But Catherine Nelson and Kenneth Staunton had been right: it was time for the queen to prove herself in office.

The guard saluted, thumping a fist to his brown-jacketed chest. "Your Majesty."

After swallowing, she raised her chin. "I am here for the Council meeting."

He bowed, stepped aside and swung the door open. Murmurs from within died away.

Before she entered, Eleanor turned to her two guards. Considering her intentions here, she should demonstrate her trust in regular security. "There's no point in your waiting here for the whole morning since the meeting room is already capably guarded. Just make sure you're back before the meeting finishes. You may leave."

The younger royal guard awkwardly saluted. "Your Majesty, Chief Guard Paton ordered us to remain within hailing distance at all times. We shall stay. Ah... if you don't mind, that is."

"Oh." Eyeing the man's earnest expression, she gnawed her lip. Of course he'd say that. Sometimes Paton's zeal could be oppressive, although on this occasion it was a slight relief. "Very well, then. You may stay."

She straightened, took a deep breath and entered.

A faint scent of wood polish and old cigar smoke met her nose while she hovered at the threshold of the gloomy chamber, allowing her eyes to adjust. Four silent figures stared at her from the U-shaped table.

The centre-most chair scraped back as Chief Councillor Hastings rose. He bowed, one hand on the tabletop, the other placed over his chest. "Your Majesty! This is, ah, an unexpected honour. How may we be of service?"

The two other men at the table also rose, murmuring greetings. Historian Gauntlett bobbed his head and blinked at her through thick glasses. Security Councillor Martek's lanky frame folded into a bow, exposing his balding pate.

Lady Nelson remained in her seat beside Hastings, dabbing her lips with a handkerchief. She raised her head and smiled at Eleanor before mouthing something. *Good girl.*

Eleanor stepped further into the room and faced them over the table. "I must apologise for being remiss in my duty. I am immensely grateful to you, Chief Councillor, for heading the Council while I... dealt with other commitments. Today, I am pleased to relieve you of that burden."

Hastings frowned. "We've already commenced the meeting. It might confuse the issue to change the presiding officer in the middle. Plus, according to statute, any changes to the Council structure and membership should have advance notifi—"

"Thank you for your comments, Councillor Hastings." Her back heated under the jacket. "I believe I am already a member of the Council. Its head, in fact. Please inform me if I am incorrect."

"Of course, of course, but this is most irregular. In order

not to disrupt due process, perhaps you could observe this time, and then maybe next meeting..."

Eleanor's shoulders tensed. Of course he wouldn't want to give up the salary bonus or the status associated with the position. What could she say, without attracting his enmity by outright contradicting him? Her mind flicked over what she'd read of him. Should she suggest—

Lady Nelson gripped Hastings' sleeve with a claw-like hand. "There is, however, scope to be more flexible in conditions of instability. With that rogue captain on the loose, potentially threatening the whole realm, it's perfectly appropriate for the queen to take over."

I never thought I'd be grateful to Shelley, though she's laying it on a bit thick. Eleanor forced her shoulders down. "Indeed, Lady Nelson is correct. I should take direct responsibility from now on. It would be a shame if the Chief Councillor were to attract censure for decisions that should rightfully be mine."

Grim-faced, Hastings muttered his acquiescence. He picked up his papers and moved further down the table. Gauntlett and Martek resumed their seats.

With measured steps, Eleanor walked around the table to take up her rightful position in the central chair. *The chair's chair, ha.* Sticky with sweat, her hands clutched its wooden armrests, worn smooth by previous occupants. She flinched as someone touched her arm, but it was only Lady Nelson, who pointed at the agenda.

Grip tightening, Eleanor spoke. "I see we are now on Item Two. That is, matters of urgency. Councillor Martek, what word on the Shelley pursuit?"

Martek shook his head. "Nothing concrete so far. No assaults, sightings or mysterious thefts."

Lady Nelson muffled a cough in her handkerchief. "At our last meeting, Jed demanded we fund guards to escort him to Maldon, insisting that's where Shelley was headed. But he couldn't provide any proof, so we declined. I've no idea why he's so fixated on that place."

"I see," said Eleanor. "Please continue with your general report, Councillor Martek."

He perched a pair of reading lenses on his nose and peered at his papers. "Kyleth Village, nothing to report... Keighley Village, nothing to report... Despite Scientist Silvers' concerns, Maldon Town has nothing to report..."

The mundane information flow continued, and the tension in Eleanor's chest eased. Her role wasn't to run the departments directly—that wasn't what her absolute power meant—but to ensure they spoke to each other and to maintain an overview. All she needed was to listen, keep things balanced and give a few judicious prods when discussions stalled. If she needed to bang heads together, she'd find the strength from somewhere.

Let everyone have their say. Hastings spoke on regulations, Gauntlett on historical precedent, and Martek chipped in when he perceived threats to safety. As for Lady Nelson... Why was she so quiet?

Eleanor's gaze turned to the chair beside her. Eyes closed, Lady Nelson held a handkerchief to her lips: a handkerchief smeared with blood.

"Catherine, you're unwell!" Eleanor pushed her chair back and knelt, patting Lady Nelson's hand. She waved at the others. "Martek, send for my physician. Gauntlett, arrange a stretcher. Hastings, is there a nearby room where she can lie down? Don't just sit there gaping, go!"

The men hurried out, and raised voices issued from the

hallway.

Lady Nelson's eyes opened, and she rasped, "Don't end the meeting." She gripped Eleanor's arm. "You need to carry on. Assert yourself. If the first meeting you chair is half-baked, they'll never believe you capable."

Still kneeling, Eleanor held the old woman's bloody hand until her physician and the stretcher arrived. *Damn, she's been coughing for weeks. I should have paid more attention.* She stood back as they lifted their patient up, the physician shaking his head.

After Lady Nelson had been taken away, the three other councillors re-entered the room, Hastings in the lead.

"We should reconvene at a later date. I'm sure this incident has been distressing for you." Hastings' voice took on an oily tone. "If you're too busy to attend next time, I could assume the chair again..."

No, the man wouldn't relinquish his position easily. *Assert yourself.* "I appreciate your concern, but it would be wrong to interrupt governmental process merely because of an individual's indisposition. After all, we are concerned with the welfare of *all* citizens. As you so astutely stated earlier, due process should be followed."

"But Lady Nelson's absence—"

Eleanor held up a hand, displaying the bloodstains on her wrist and cuff. "Her absence is unfortunate, but you ran meetings readily enough in *my* absence." She sat. "If any of you gentlemen feel too disturbed to remain, you may leave. The rest of us will continue after I co-opt replacements."

All three men resumed their seats.

Gauntlett blinked at her. "Your Majesty, I believe I'd been giving an overview of road construction in the past, before the interruption?"

"Indeed." She tried to ignore the empty seat. "Continue." *They'll be calling me Queen Eleanor the Heartless.*

After drawing the Council meeting to a close, Eleanor looked in on Lady Nelson, who was asleep on a sofa in a side room. Arrangements were being made for transport back to the Nelson mansion. She ordered the physician to keep her informed, then returned to the palace, her escorts trotting to keep up.

The suit was tossed on to the floor as she headed into the bathing room, leaving Martha exclaiming over the bloodstains.

In the relative privacy of her bath, Eleanor's whole body shook while tears leaked from her eyes. What had she done? What would they think of her, carrying on after a Council member's collapse? And a long-term friend of her family, at that. She sniffed, knowing what Isabel would have said. *Who cares what they think, as long as they know you're in charge.*

She leaned forwards, sloshing water onto the floor. Although Lady Nelson had pushed her to do this, Eleanor hadn't expected the woman to speak up on her behalf. That mention of Shelley had been a masterful touch. And the other Council members hadn't even questioned just how dangerous one man, even a cursed one, could be to the whole realm. Well, yes, Eleanor herself had been concerned about assassination, though even that was looking dubious. But threatening national security? All the publicity about his escape was really to maintain the secrecy of powers. Secrecy that shouldn't be necessary.

After donning a comfortable house robe and picking at a light lunch, Eleanor summoned Paton to her study. The man might be overprotective, but he was loyal. He'd paid with an eye for his loyalty to her father, and she was lucky to have him.

He saluted. "Your Majesty. Do you wish my report on Captain Longleaf?"

She nodded. "Carry on."

"As instructed, I arranged to have Longleaf followed. I followed her myself on the first day."

"Did she notice she was being followed?"

"No." His lip curled. "She made little effort to hide her movements."

"Maybe she has nothing to hide."

"True," he conceded. "But she went to Scientist Silvers' house."

Eleanor's attention sharpened. Maybe not so innocent, then. "Could you find out what they did?"

"Silvers was away. So she left."

"Odd that she didn't ensure he'd be at home to receive her first. Did she speak to anyone else while she was there? Presumably she left a calling card with his butler."

"Er, no. She did look through his front window, but there was nobody in."

"She just went there, discovered he was out, and departed?" Eleanor frowned. "And after that?"

"She returned to the barracks. I'm told she's remained there since then, presumably performing administration."

Leaving me no further on. Was Longleaf colluding with both Shelley and Silvers? After receiving Shelley's letter, Eleanor doubted they were all working together. "Paton, are you sure nothing happened when she visited Silvers' house? Maybe she left something for him?"

Sweat beaded his lip. "Definitely not."

She sighed. "Look, if you happened to lose sight of her

and aren't sure what she did, that's fine. Or even if she noticed you. But just tell me. Be honest."

He scowled. "Of course I didn't lose sight of her. And she'd no idea who—" He cleared his throat. "I mean, I observed her whole visit. I'm confident she's not a threat to you, although she may be investigating Silvers for her own reasons."

If Longleaf and Shelley were allied against Silvers, that made more sense. Or even Longleaf and Silvers against Shelley? *My head hurts. As long as they're not allied against* me. But what had got Paton so rattled? Hmm, he was a widower, wasn't he? "Do you think she's attractive?"

"What?" His fists clenched. "No, not at all."

Eleanor hid a smile. Perhaps he wasn't so impartial, but his spying might make future encounters with the woman awkward, especially if he met her socially. "I trust you when you say she's not a threat. But just to set my mind at ease..."

"Yes, Your Majesty?"

"Please continue to follow her. But assign someone else to do it, not yourself. You may leave."

He bowed and left, back stiff.

Martha knocked on the door and entered, a frown crinkling her face. "I didn't want to bother you..."

Now what? Surely the stresses of the day couldn't get worse. "Yes?"

"Artur arrived, such a polite young man, and with good taste in flowers too. I was going to let him wait in your sitting room. But he looked so pale I put him to bed. May I send for your physician?"

"Of course!" Had he pushed himself too hard?

"And if you don't mind, maybe the doctor could check my ears when he's done? I was sure Artur mentioned seeing ghosts, but that can't be right."

"Wait, no." Anxiety gripped Eleanor's chest. If Artur were cursed, she couldn't afford witnesses. "The doctor's busy taking care of Lady Nelson. I'll, ah, decide what needs done after speaking with Artur myself. Oh, and cancel all my appointments for the next week. If something urgent comes up, I'll be working in the palace."

Chapter 21

"Go away," muttered Susanna, but the knocking at her door continued. She rolled on to her side and pulled the other pillow over her head. *Just leave me alone.*

She squeezed her eyes shut, trying to ignore the knocking. Trying to ignore everything. Trying to ignore her foolishness at visiting Silvers' house. Bile rose in her throat at the memory of that disastrous trip. Silvers' cronies would warn him on his return, and he'd make her his next target. She'd wanted to help Jonathan, and instead she'd made everything worse.

Jonathan, I'm so sorry. Are you even still alive?

"Susanna!" The knocking intensified.

Lester. She burrowed further under the blankets. He could look after himself. He didn't need her dubious assistance either.

"Susanna, are you alright? I've not seen you for a couple of days."

Of course I'm not alright.

"If you don't open the door, I'm fetching Emily."

Susanna groaned. The housekeeper would clean the room, tidy the dirty clothing scattered on the floor and clear away the detritus of untouched snacks. Knowing Emily, she'd wrinkle her nose and push Susanna herself into a hot bath. It wasn't worth it.

She pushed herself up, pausing as the room spun around her.

"Susanna?"

"I'm coming," she croaked.

After easing her aching body off the bed, she wrapped the blanket around herself, shuffled to the door and opened it.

Lester gawped at her, then slipped inside. "What happened?"

"I was stupid." She waved at the chair and plonked herself on her chaise longue.

He moved her dirty plates into the corridor and opened the window. Ignoring her half-hearted objections, he nipped into her bathing room and returned with a glass of water which he pushed into her hand.

While she sipped, he pulled a paper bag out of his pocket and opened it, offering her a misshapen piece of toffee. He waggled his eyebrows. "Hey, my emergency rations. You're worth it."

She had to laugh as she accepted it. "Oh, Lester. What would I do without you?"

"I'm sure you'd have sorted yourself out, eventually." He sat at the table. "Care to talk about it?"

Susanna nodded, wincing as she chewed the vile confection. Trust Lester to have a sweet tooth. At least it was helping her alertness. She swallowed. "Since Silvers was away, I went to check out his house..."

Lester's eyes widened as she filled him in on her trip to the slums. "You've got some nerve! Even I'd be wary of returning to that neighbourhood. You're right. You were stupid."

"Thanks. I was lucky that man rescued me though I don't understand why."

"What, a huge fellow, muffled in a cloak, and he only

had one eye? Probably a lookout for some dodgy deal, didn't want trouble on his doorstep."

"I guess." She straightened up. "What's been happening while I was wallowing in misery?"

"Plenty. I thought you ought to know." He handed over that day's *Informer*.

A LOSS TO THE SCIENTIFIC COMMUNITY
Lady Catherine Nelson, Chief Scientist, passed away peacefully at home last night after a brief illness. Famed for her discovery of the curse's three day incubation period, a discovery which has benefited every citizen in the realm, she led scientific research in Ascar's Keep for nearly four decades.
Queen Eleanor stated, "Lady Nelson was a close friend to the royal family. She will be sorely missed."
A private cremation will be held this afternoon.

On reading the article, Susanna pursed her lips. Could Silvers have somehow been responsible? She shook her head. He was out of the city, and his unsavoury associates wouldn't pass unnoticed in the nobles' quarter. "Who's taking over?"

"Word is it's likely to be Fellows." Lester's jaw clenched. "Though I wouldn't put it past Silvers to shove his way in. How do they decide?"

"Given the seniority of the position the Council would choose. I suppose that means Hastings' favoured candidate. We'll just have to wait—" Susanna's heart leapt into her throat. "Damn! I need to visit Tabitha." She stood and grabbed a uniform, the blanket puddling at her feet.

Lester averted his gaze and cleared his throat. "Why the rush?"

"She was under Lady Nelson's protection, and that's gone now. Granted, it was so Silvers couldn't use her as a hold over..." *Oh, Jonathan.* "If Jonathan's gone, it might not matter, but I should see how she is. I've not visited for a while. Didn't want to tell her about Jonathan."

"Poor kid." He winced. "Do you want me to come along with you?"

And distract Tabitha? Tempting. "No, that's fine. Thanks for visiting."

"Good luck."

She shooed him out and readied herself for a visit to the Keep.

Why the delay? Susanna tapped her foot as she sat in the reception area. However, she should be grateful: the wait for permission to be granted was an opportunity to compose herself. Breaking the news about Jonathan would be draining for both her and Tabitha. The seconds crawled past, and she clasped her hands in her lap. Her foot nudged her sewing basket. She'd brought it in case Tabitha was upset enough to need an extended visit.

When three guards marched past her, she eyed them speculatively. Might she sneak in after them? No, that would be conduct unbecoming for a captain. She'd just have to be patient.

She was inspecting a part-embroidered handkerchief when a whistle sounded. The lad manning the reception desk put the speaking tube to his ear then said, "Captain Longleaf, you can go up now. Sorry about the delay."

"Thank you." She approached the stairs leading to the residential floor. It wasn't the boy's fault. Maybe Lady Nelson's death had caused unrest with the detainees, although she doubted many of them would care. They might not even know about it. *I'm sure Tabitha doesn't. She's probably never even seen the* Informer.

Upstairs, Susanna followed the guard to Tabitha's door. He slid open the observation hatch and pulled out his keyring.

"Knock when you want to leave," he said.

"I may be some time. Lady Nelson had a special interest in Tabitha, and I need to break the news." Her grip tightened on the sewing basket's handle. *And some other news too.* "I'm not sure how Tabitha will take it."

"You have until dinner time." The guard tugged his moustache. "Tabitha's quiet, undemanding, not like some of the other detainees." He swung the door open just wide enough for Susanna to enter.

Tabitha turned from the window and smiled. "Susanna! Where have you been?"

Susanna's heart lurched. *No excuses.* Only the crackle from the fireplace broke the silence. "I've had quite a bit on my plate." She set her basket on the table, knocking a crumpled news sheet on to the floor. She tossed it into the fire and sat. "I'm sorry I didn't come earlier. Have you been practising?"

"Sure." Tabitha scooped breadcrumbs out of a bowl and scattered them on the window ledge.

"That's good." Susanna retrieved her embroidery hoop. "I need to tell you some things."

"When you're done, I've a bit of news too. I'm just keeping an eye out for the red-beaked wren that came along a couple of days ago."

She shook out a skein of magenta floss. "Lady Nelson has passed on."

Tabitha faced Susanna and scrunched up her nose. "That's sad. I remember Jonathan made the arrangement with her. She visited me a couple of times, told me to behave. She was kind of short with me, but I guess she meant well. How does that change things?"

"I'm not sure." After threading a needle, she snipped the floss to the right length. "While you were under her guardianship, the other scientists weren't allowed to visit you. Remember, the concern was that Scientist Silvers might pressure Jonathan by threatening you." *I refuse to call him "Jed".*

"Oh, I see." The girl gnawed her lip then turned to the window. "But if nobody knows where Jonathan is, I'm not valuable in that way? Jonathan isn't at risk?"

The floss snapped in Susanna's hands. Chest tight, she rose and joined Tabitha at the window. "I've had some news about Jonathan."

"Did he manage to contact you?" Tabitha extended a hand through the window bars towards one of the birds.

I have to tell her. Now. She closed her eyes. When she opened them, a brown bird was perched on Tabitha's wrist.

Susanna blinked. "That's a messenger bird."

"Is that what they are?" Tabitha extended her other hand, some breadcrumbs on her palm. "I've had a few showing up. They prefer pastry crumbs to bread, which is odd."

Grasping at the excuse to put things off a little longer, Susanna pointed at the bird's leg. "They're domesticated. See, there's an attached message tube. There's a post station on the rooftop here for incoming messages. I guess the birds are stopping off here for a snack on their way."

Tabitha's hand curled around the breadcrumbs. "Is that

a problem?"

"Hopefully not. We'd better remove the tube."

Susanna fetched her snippers while Tabitha crooned to the bird, stroking its feathers. Tabitha held the bird gently as Susanna removed the message tube.

"There we go." Tabitha tossed the bird into the air.

"I'd better check if this is an important message." She slid the paper out of the tube. "We don't want your permission to feed the birds withdrawn, especially as you didn't intend for this bird to land here."

She unrolled the paper and stared.

PRIORITY: Maldon request urgent assistance. After Scientist Silvers departed, fugitive Shelley arrived. Successfully captured by my citizens. Need guards escort Shelley to Ascar for trial. Also requesting reward money. Mayor Henry Sutcliff. PRIORITY.

He's alive! Tears filled her eyes, washing away her previous despair. Then her sensible brain asserted itself. Alive, but in custody. If Ascar sent guards to bring Jonathan back, he'd have no chance to escape. She, Susanna, had best ensure they didn't receive the message. It was all she could do to buy him time.

"Something important?" Tabitha brushed crumbs off her sleeve.

She looked down and swallowed. "Something better burnt than seen by the Council." There was no point making Tabitha an accomplice by telling her, although it was a relief she'd not mentioned her suspicions he was dead. She folded the tiny paper into a pellet and tossed it towards the fire.

The door flew open, and two guards burst in, each holding a flechette gun. "Don't move!"

Susanna froze, hands by her sides, facing Tabitha. Had they been watching all this time?

Tabitha's gaze flicked from Susanna to the guards, then to the floor.

Susanna dared to peek at the floor. Her heart sank as she saw the pellet lying just inches away from the fire. She glanced back at Tabitha.

Tabitha raised an eyebrow.

Was that an offer to move it? So tempting, but Tabitha might be facing troubles of her own. Susanna gave a tiny headshake.

One guard picked up the message and smoothed it out. He studied it and scowled at Susanna. "Destroying official messages? Colluding with a murderer?"

The other strode over to Susanna and gripped her arm. "We've been watching you, Longleaf. Looks like you're in trouble."

Susanna's shoulders slumped. If she didn't resist, they'd have no reason to detain Tabitha too. The girl was better off in the Keep than in some prison. "May I say farewell to Tabitha? She's nothing to do with this."

The guard with the message shrugged. "I guess so."

She looked Tabitha in the eye. "Look after yourself. He... would want that." *And now I'm abandoning you too.*

Susanna cursed herself for her latest idiocy while they waited for someone senior to arrive and deal with the prisoner. She should have stayed in bed. Until her impulsive attempt to destroy the message, her actions hadn't been illegal. They might have raised some eyebrows, questions and disapproval, but that was all. Now she'd crossed the boundary. *Respectable Captain Longleaf, committing a crime? For shame!* At least she'd not used her power, so her offence didn't come under the scientists' jurisdiction. The corridor guards might report to the scientists, but it would be a fellow city captain assigned to the investigation. Embarrassing for her, but Ascar's fragmented justice system might work to her advantage. Not that she deserved any advantage, with her stupid behaviour.

The door by the stairwell swung open, and a guard strode through. He had a distinctive bulky build, salt-and-pepper stubble and a red eyepatch to match his uniform. Royal red, not brown. *Paton.*

Susanna gaped. Now she recognised his shape, not to mention his missing eye. He was the man who'd rescued her outside Silvers' house. It had been no coincidence. He'd ordered the extra guards here? To watch her?

The two guards flanking her saluted. "Chief Guard Paton, sir. She was attempting a felony, so we apprehended her."

Paton stomped up to her. "You can't keep out of trouble, can you?"

Eyes wide, she studied his face. "You rescued me! Two days ago..."

He scowled. "You were making such a hash of things. Looks bad when officers are so stupid."

"You followed me? Ah... I'm tremendously grateful you did. Thank you." Her face heated. *How humiliating. I'd no idea.*

"Of course I followed you. I wouldn't have been hanging around there for fun. You're sticking your nose into too many things, Longleaf, and I'm fed up running after you. I'm putting you in custody."

Custody. Prison. She forced out the words. "With what am

I charged?"

"Other than the stupidity? We'll call it colluding with a murderer for the moment."

"*Alleged* murderer. He's not had a trial."

"That's as may be. Easier all round if you're out the way."

"For how long?"

"Queen's Discretion. We'll hang on to you until Her Majesty decides. But of course you'll know how royalty's absolute power works, being an *educated captain.*"

"Very well." She raised her head. "Bring on the shackles."

He snorted. "Spare me the drama. You lack the nous to flee a burning house."

She winced. He could be right. "Where will I be held?"

"The palace. Detention room there hasn't been used for a while, but it'll be a change from the normal routine."

Chapter 22

Annetta paused to remove a stone from her sandal while Samuel brandished a stick as if it were a sabre. Curses floated towards her from up ahead where the guards dragged the handcart up yet another slope. There was a chorus of groans as a few bags fell out. Was it going to be like this all the way to Ascar? Travelling to Maldon with Captain Shelley's convoy hadn't been nearly so much effort, despite the heavily forested route that time. At least today's weather remained dry, although it was hard going with the uneven terrain.

A shadow fell over her. "Tired?" Silvers mopped his brow.

"Oh! Not so bad, thanks." She smiled at him. "We can move a bit faster if you want."

His eyes narrowed at a guard to their left who trudged along with eyes on the rocky ground. "It's not you holding us up. They've no idea what they're doing. He's supposed to be on beast patrol, not watching his shoes."

"I suppose that's a downside of picking guards who've not been on convoy."

His jaw clenched, and his nostrils flared.

Annetta winced, wishing she hadn't provoked him. "Um, you weren't to know they'd find it so difficult. And you had to be sure Shelley hadn't influenced them."

"Jed?" Samuel piped up.

"Hey, kiddo." Silvers crouched and looked Samuel in

the eye. "What's up?"

"You said you'd tell me all about Ascar."

"Sure. Let's walk on, and I'll tell you about the city..."

Annetta trailed behind them, keeping an eye out for plants that might survive in this poor soil. She listened with half an ear.

"... It'll be a while before you can go into the city, but it's full of clever people and things. You'll see lots of places and people you want to draw, huh?"

"I bet I will!"

"I'll give you plenty of paper, and pencils of all colours..."

She inspected a stunted shrub, stroking a glossy leaf. *Evergreen like waxy thornbrush, but smaller. I wonder if it'll have the same effect on the flux.*

"Will there be other children to play with?"

Silvers tilted a hand from side to side. "Not to start with, but yes, later on."

"Oh." Samuel stopped walking and scuffed at a rock. "So who's going to keep me company?"

Tucking a leafy sprig into her bag, Annetta caught up with them. "I will, of course. Jed, where will we be staying?"

Silvers waved a hand. "We have a whole floor of luxury suites in the Keep, where our special guests stay. Although they're kept in secure accommodation—for everyone's safety—it's very important that they feel comfortable." He regarded her. "You're an exception, Annetta, in that your movements won't be restricted. You can rent lodgings in the main city. Or I guess you could share a suite with Samuel. Your choice."

The main city? *Rent?* Her breathing quickened while she imagined a florid landlord sneering at the few coins in her purse. Should she ask for... No, she didn't want to bring up the topic of money. "Um, what are the suites like?"

"Spacious, even partitioned for two of you. Believe it or not, they're more comfortable and better furnished than my own house." He patted his belly and grinned. "And the food's decent—scientists and residents get the same fare. Also, because the rooms are in the Keep, you'd be close to the infirmary and laboratories."

"I guess I'll go for that then, especially if I might get called on during the night. Could I request some things?"

Silvers' brows drew together. "Such as?"

Don't get greedy, Annetta. "Equipment? Is that alright? I've heard of special glassware for distillation..."

His face cleared. "That's fine."

Annetta smiled. He was making every effort to see to their comfort. She hoped she wasn't demanding too much.

Later, while the guards entertained Samuel with stories, Annetta had a chance to speak with Silvers more privately. They were crossing dusty scrubland with good visibility, and the two of them lagged behind to talk.

"Jed? This might be a good time to plan what I'm doing in Ascar. I mean, I don't want to stay there forever."

"Right. What would be really helpful is a formulation to neutralise dangerous powers completely. We'd used painkillers on Shelley, but I suspect he overcame them somehow. So we need something that works differently." He lowered his voice. "The other thing is something that could activate powers without the need for the current stimulus. Obviously Shelley managed that, and we'll need to... learn how he did it."

She nodded. Captain Shelley had told her about the pain used in training, and Silvers hadn't contradicted his words. It was clear the scientist wanted to make a difference, to make life better for everyone. They might not be able to prevent the curse, but if they could suppress its more dangerous manifestations and activate the more beneficial ones without pain, that was a worthy aspiration. "I found something in my notes that might work for your first request. As for the second, my dareth leaf did have an effect on Shelley. So that's a start."

"Ah, sounds promising." He eyed her. "Did you try it on Samuel?"

"What?" She stumbled on a rock. "No! I mean, we didn't *want* him to be drawing stuff. He's too young to understand what he's doing, and it's just that..."

"Fair enough. And yeah, you're right. It's probably better to wait until he's older before asking him to think too hard about his pictures. Though your dareth leaf is certainly worth considering. I'm sure you'd view it as more acceptable than... pain, yes?"

She swallowed. If she found an alternative stimulus, she could support Samuel with his training. In the long term that might help him out of custody. No point being squeamish about the matter. "Do you have, um, people I could try out my recipes on? I mean, ones who're distressed and suffering because of their powers?"

"Sure. One poor lad was cursed while acting under Shelley's orders, on a mission that should have been straightforward. Dreadful manifestation. His power causes pain to anyone he touches."

"The poor boy! Of course I'll help. I don't think any of my recipes will have permanent effects, but at least I could give him, and those around him, some relief."

Shouts from ahead interrupted their conversation.

"Stay back." Silvers jogged after the guards in the lead.

Following more slowly, Annetta drew level with Samuel and his escort.

"I'd better see what's going on," said the guard, breaking into a trot.

She blinked when they caught up with the rest of the group, which seemed to have grown. The city guards milled about, and a new group of grey-clad figures stood or squatted, checking their weapons and backpack contents.

Seeing a figure in a dark grey uniform, she tensed. A captain. But of course it wasn't Captain Shelley. This man was far burlier and younger, and his close-cropped hair was fair rather than grey. He and Silvers were talking.

Silvers grinned. "The irony of it, he must have arrived the day after we left. Don't let him slip through your fingers, Buchanan. Shelley's a sly one."

"No fear of that, Silvers. We're old acquaintances." He lowered his voice. "Your colleague Fellows supplied me with plenty of painkillers to use on the way back."

"To prevent him calling his power? You'd better be careful though, it might not—"

The big captain frowned at Silvers. "I'm not a novice. The Council trust me not to need micromanagement."

Annetta relaxed. It didn't sound like the newcomer was a friend to Shelley.

Silvers' jaw clenched before he glanced at Annetta and shrugged. "Well, don't complain if you run into problems. How come you went to Karsten rather than Lady Nelson?"

"I guess you won't have heard. Lady Nelson went to Settlers' Rest a few days ago. Chest problem, she pushed herself too hard in some meeting."

Poor woman. I wonder if it was the lungbleed cough.

"Did she now? Interesting."

The captain's lips turned down. "Somehow I thought you'd say that."

After a little more conversation, the other group formed into ranks and marched off, while Silvers waved his guards to move on.

Annetta resumed her conversation with Silvers. "Did I hear right? Shelley's been captured?"

"Yep, in Maldon. We just missed him. Or rather, he missed us. Maybe he was coming after you."

Her mouth dried up. Because of her herbalism, she was a threat. And she'd once thought the rogue captain was a kind man. "I hear he was a good captain, for many years. It's such a shame he went mad. Do you really think he killed that guard?"

"I can't suggest anything else. There was nobody else around. The guard's relief went in and found him dead. Who else could it have been?"

"Shelley didn't strike me as a killer. Though—" Her chest lurched as she remembered his attack on her, her terror when she'd kicked and head-butted him. She'd experienced his violent nature herself. *Attempted murder*, Silvers had said. She hadn't thought of that at the time, but he was right.

"Oh, but he was. He killed an old man on his last convoy trip. While the man was asleep."

She wiped sweaty palms on her trousers. "What trip?" Maybe it had been a different trip, to some different area.

Silvers' brow creased. "It was about four months ago."

Her heart raced. "Not Gerald?"

"I don't know the name." He smiled and snapped his fingers. "Ah! Now I remember. It was on the way to Maldon. Isn't that funny?"

She choked off a whimper as she noticed Samuel watching them. "I was on that trip! And so was Samuel. Gerald was bitten... was he cursed? But he wasn't dangerous. No more dangerous than Samuel."

"Who knows what was going through Shelley's mind, killing innocent civilians. That death was completely unnecessary. What a waste."

Who knew indeed? Though she'd hate to think of any death as "necessary". Annetta walked on, her hands trembling while she thought over her narrow escape. And what about Samuel? If Shelley had killed Gerald, such a harmless old man, would he have considered killing Samuel too? She clenched her fists when she remembered how Shelley had spoken with Gerald's family, claiming he'd died of natural causes. She'd thought Shelley was smoothing things over for her, but he was really covering up after himself. And all that time she'd spent worrying it was her fault the poor man died.

Her spine straightened. Whether she pitied or reviled Shelley for his deeds wasn't the point. The point was... she'd have to work extra hard and find a suppressant for cursed powers, whether to benefit unfortunate sufferers, or to protect innocents from deliberate exploiters. She regretted she'd not had any to supply to Captain Buchanan, but she'd have something ready for when he arrived back in Ascar with Shelley. *I won't be caught out this time.*

Opal poked her head through the doorway. "They're ready."

Jonathan clambered to his feet and glanced round the ramshackle shed where he'd been held for the past week.

Although his muscles ached from inactivity and sitting on the floor, he'd had little time for boredom, using the time to practise calling his power at need. Satisfying though it might be, killing Silvers would take more than bare hands.

The townsfolk had provided clean clothes after Giselle pronounced the brown uniform only fit for rags. He tucked his donated shirt into the cast-off trousers, still a touch on the loose side despite the regular meals he'd been given. A civilian outfit felt strange. But Jonathan wasn't a guard anymore, just a prisoner.

He straightened and stepped outside, blinking in the mid-morning sunshine. "I'm ready too."

Sabre in hand, Opal gestured for him to precede her towards the town square. The soles of his scavenged shoes flapped as he walked. After an attempt to repair them, Maldon's cobbler had admitted defeat, and there were no replacements immediately available.

Despite it being nearly lunchtime by rural standards, the streets they traversed were deserted. No doubt Sutcliff had ordered the townsfolk to remain indoors, for fear of the dangerous criminal. Typical of the man. "What did they say?"

Opal's words floated over his shoulder. "It's Captain Buchanan. He interviewed me and Marcus about how we caught you." Her tone shifted from professional to amused. "He also met with Mayor Sutcliff. Since he and the guards arrived at the guesthouse late last night, I suppose he also spoke with Giselle."

David Buchanan. Not the worst choice for this assignment. Tough, practical and with no power of his own, making him less inclined to sympathise with a cursed prisoner. The Council weren't taking chances. "Are you travelling back with us?"

"No. I told him I'm providing medical cover for the town until Annetta returns. He saw her on the way, so he'd no reason to doubt me."

Jonathan glanced back at Opal. "How far out from Ascar did they meet?" Perhaps he could escape *en route* and catch up with Silvers before he reached Ascar.

She smirked. "Captain Buchanan had been travelling for one day, so maybe two days out for Silvers' group. Those soft city guards were having problems."

For a moment, Jonathan smirked with her, forgetting his situation, then he sighed. There was no chance of overtaking them. "Which guards are here now?"

"He's picked a dozen hefty, experienced ones. Like Morris, Graham, Victor, Tony..."

That made sense. They'd no way of knowing Jonathan didn't intend to cause trouble. Not until after they delivered him, hopefully straight into Silvers' clutches.

On arrival in the town square, Opal directed him towards the group of guards waiting in front of the town hall. She exchanged a salute with them. Sutcliff lingered behind them on the steps. There was no sign of any other townsfolk.

Out of reflex, Jonathan also saluted, attracting stares from his former subordinates. His ears heated, and his hand fell to his side, but then the rugged David stepped forward and returned the salute.

"Shelley." David's gaze travelled from Jonathan's face to his feet.

Resisting the urge to look down or tug at his clothing, Jonathan looked up into David's face, his neck tensing. "Captain Buchanan." He'd lost his right to address the man any other way.

"I'd hoped we could meet under better circumstances."

"I also. But we will again, after my trial. I'm innocent."
Of that, at least.

"He's lying!" called Sutcliff from the back. "Fomenting unrest and making me look bad."

That idiot can look bad without any help. Jonathan's fists clenched.

David turned to address the group standing behind him. "Shelley's guilt or innocence is not for us to decide. Our job is to return him to Ascar and to deliver him for his murder trial in good condition. Even if he's innocent, he'll need to be detained in the Keep, like any other afflicted."

Jonathan wondered if he'd ever get there. And with all the publicity about his curse, he would never be freed, even if he were acquitted of murder. Too many people might suspect there were other afflicted folk at large, working for the Council. Still, no matter. They might detain him near Tabitha's room, and he would perhaps have a chance to say goodbye. Would she remember him with affection? As for Susanna, she might regret his troubles, but it was just as well they hadn't—

David's boots scuffed the cobblestones. "A few things to sort before we go. Scientist Fellows provided some pills for you to take. Painkillers." He pulled a bottle out of his pocket, tipped a pellet into Jonathan's outstretched hand and waited for him to swallow.

Trying not to grin, he obliged and opened his mouth to show he had done so. Despite his practice while free and in custody here, he'd not had the chance to try calling his power after ingesting a painkiller. They'd just delivered him the perfect opportunity. An excellent surprise for Silvers.

David raised his voice to include the guards. "The scientists tell me that pain can worsen cursed unnatural powers. These painkillers reduce the risk that Shelley will manifest anything along the way. No guarantees though, so don't provoke him. I don't want accidents, and I'd rather not execute him on the journey."

"I'd rather not be executed either." Jonathan assessed each guard's face, relieved at the lack of outright hostility.

"We're travelling light and fast," said David. "Backpacks only, no handcarts. You need to carry one too." He gestured, and a guard handed Jonathan a backpack. "I brought this one for you. It contains clothes for the journey, but once you've put them on, we'll fill the bag with supplies."

Jonathan opened the bag and tugged out a padded yellow jacket. "Yellow?"

David grinned. "It's warmer than what you're wearing." His smile disappeared. "And more visible."

Beggars can't be choosers, Shelley. Reaching further into the bag, Jonathan pulled out a pair of sturdy grey boots. Surely not? "You brought *my* boots! My own ones..." He resisted clutching them to his chest, but his hands trembled, and he blinked.

"Sure, saves time if you're not limping. I want us back in Ascar within three days. No civilians, no handcarts. Perfectly doable. Put them on, and I'll assign the first watch." David turned away.

Sitting on the bench, Jonathan kicked off the tattered shoes and pulled on his boots. His feet slid into them like embracing old friends, and he wriggled his toes at the luxury. Opal handed him a canteen and another bundle, murmuring, "Rations." Jonathan placed the rations in the backpack, donned the yellow jacket and slung the canteen over his shoulder. He stood and put on the backpack, his back muscles tensing at the unaccustomed weight. *If they can carry these, so can I. Just because they're bigger, younger, fitter... that's no excuse.*

David was concluding his briefing. "... I want three guards watching at all times. Keep your flechette guns ready, and don't crowd him. Safer if you spread out. I'll be walking beside him much of the time, need to inform him about the trial process."

Jonathan tried not to sag. What kind of reputation did he have?

"Sir," asked a guard, "what if he attacks you with his, er, cursed power?"

After strapping on his backpack, David shrugged. "That's why you'll be watching us at all times. If I happen to mysteriously keel over, fire away."

Jonathan snorted. "I'm not suicidal enough to attack you. But I do hope you don't have a bad heart." He glanced at Opal. "Opal can confirm I've been behaving myself."

She nodded. "Yes, Cap—er, Shelley hasn't been any problem at all. Whatever he's done, he deserves a fair trial."

David clapped him on the shoulder. "And I'll ensure he gets one." He raised his voice. "Right, moving out."

As he walked out of Maldon, surrounded by guards, Jonathan didn't look back. There was no point.

Chapter 23

With slumped shoulders and aching legs, Annetta trailed the group of guards through the sparse trees bare of foliage. At least they'd left the depression of the scrubland behind, and there was the promise of green come springtime. Samuel skipped ahead with Silvers. How could the boy have so much energy? It wasn't even midday, and already she wanted to rest. Maybe she was getting old.

When she passed the last of the trees and beheld Ascar's northern farming area, a sense of familiarity caught her by surprise. Stubbled fields extended before her, interrupted by clusters of dormant fruit trees. Scattered workers pruned branches, cleared ditches and dug the hard-packed soil. Despite her nostalgia at the sight, she was grateful she didn't have to join in. Farming was hard work.

Other than the scale of the farms, the major difference from Maldon was the backdrop of the Cleon mountains, their snow-capped green slopes rising before them. *Nearly there, just the other side of those mountains.* That's what Silvers had said.

"It's a lot bigger than Maldon, isn't it?" asked Samuel when she caught up with him. "There must be at least a hundred people out working! Do you think there will be more when we get there?"

A population a hundred times that of Maldon's, Opal had told her. Annetta licked her lips. "There will be a lot more people in Ascar. And many more out in the fields after winter passes."

"How will I remember their names?"

She had to smile. "I don't think you'll need to remember them *all*."

"Don't worry," said Silvers. "We'll introduce you to just a few people at a time."

Samuel beamed. "Who do I meet first?"

"Why, the people who'll be looking after you—the guards who sit outside your room and keep you safe." As Samuel ran ahead, waving his arms at some crows, Silvers turned to Annetta. "Can't have someone like Shelley breaking in because he wants to eliminate you as a threat."

Silver was right. She shuddered. It had been a close call.

They walked along smooth, straight-paved paths that demarcated the fields, traversed by pedestrians and an occasional pedal-powered cart. The ground was hard beneath Annetta's feet, even with her reinforced walking sandals, but at least she wasn't tripping over roots and rocks every few steps. The guards pulling the handcarts increased their pace, no doubt eager to arrive home.

Annetta panted for breath as she walked up the final incline, past a few warehouses and a windmill. Adrian had been exploring wind-powered devices, but nothing of this size. She'd have to write and tell him about this. Maybe Samuel could do him a sketch.

When she arrived at the opening of the tunnel, the guards had parked their handcarts and were milling around. Silvers was already speaking with a squat, muscular chap wearing short trousers. Didn't that man know it was winter? A few men with similar builds stood behind him.

"I'll make it worth your while," said Silvers. "Something

extra if you can take us all in one trip."

The man barked in laughter. "You're on, sirrah! That's a prize I don't want to miss." He waved at the men behind him. "Mitch, Guido, Lance. Priority run with all these passengers. One long train, pedallers front and back. And quickly! We'll need to be back before the workers finish for the day."

Annetta massaged her legs while the guards and pedallers entered the dark tunnel and loaded up wagons with their belongings. Samuel wandered around, peering into the wagons, but not—*thank the Settlers!*—touching anything.

Silvers waved her over to the wall, indicating a black mark. "See this?" As she squinted at the dark smudges, he continued. "When Shelley escaped, he ambushed his pursuers by blowing up the tunnel. The damage has been mostly fixed, but this is where it happened."

She gasped. "How dreadful! And with all those poor people inside? He needs to be stopped."

Samuel tugged at her sleeve. "They're ready now."

"Hop in, lad!" said the chief pedaller. "And you too, miss."

Silvers hefted Samuel into the front wagon where he started quizzing the pedallers about how it all worked. Patting her bag, Annetta clambered into the rear wagon and squished herself between a couple of the guards.

With a metallic whine, the train of wagons lurched into motion, accompanied by raucous laughter from the pedallers. They headed into the tunnel, and the sunlight dimmed behind them. Annetta ducked. *Of course it's high enough, silly.* At least nobody would see her blush while their eyes adjusted to the darkness.

Annetta's eyes opened, and she raised her head from the shoulder of the sleeping guard beside her. She glanced around to see if anyone had noticed. Thankfully, she hadn't drooled on him. In the front wagon, Samuel and Silvers still murmured to each other, but the guards all seemed to be sleeping. The metallic humming from the rails had been strangely soothing.

"Good nap?" asked the pedaller behind her.

"Yes, thanks." The flickering dim light brought on queasiness, and she squeezed her eyes shut. Chewing an easemint leaf would be a waste, especially if she couldn't replenish her supplies. How could she distract herself? She took a deep breath. "Um, Lance, is it? All that pedalling must be good exercise. I bet you're all very healthy."

He laughed. "Yeah, good lungs and good legs. Most of us started off working the battery then got permanent jobs in the tunnel."

"Battery? What's that?"

"You've not heard of it? I guess it's your first trip to Ascar."

"That's right." Her palms grew clammy at the thought of her imminent responsibilities. People would be depending on her, and she'd promised to look after Samuel. Anxiety or not, she had a moral obligation to help. She could hardly turn around and leave now.

Lance spat over the side. "When we work the battery, we pedal machines in the inner city—where the factories are—and that fills power cells. The power's used in other machines, to provide light without naked flames, and I think the convoys have battery-powered equipment too. There's never enough power to go round. Us really good pedallers get poached for the tunnel. Ain't that right, Guido?"

His neighbour elbowed him. "Apart from you, you mean. Save your breath for pedalling."

Lance snorted. "Anyway, we're nearly there. See it's a bit lighter ahead?"

Soon afterwards, the train stopped. Annetta's breathing eased. She wouldn't want to make that trip regularly. The pedallers helped them unload their belongings. She gaped as they then climbed back into the train, pedalled it round in the turning circle and disappeared back into the darkness.

"That was a fun trip." Samuel clapped his hands. "What's next?"

"Hold on a minute," said Silvers. "I need to finish up with these guards."

Annetta gazed around while the scientist spoke to the guards. They stood in a cavern with handcarts, crates and other items surrounding them. Scattered openings interrupted the walls, which appeared a mixture of natural rock and bricks.

Samuel picked up a chisel and tapped on the side of a crate. "Is anyone in there? No? Maybe they're out."

She eyed the openings in the walls. *Stop imagining monsters!* "Don't wander off, Samuel. We'd never find you again."

"Aww, I bet there are great hiding places here." He grinned. "Maybe I can come back and play hide and seek with some other children."

Silvers raised an eyebrow at them but continued speaking to the guards. "I'll want to call on you again in a few days for something else, so be ready."

"Sure thing, sir. As long as we don't need to do all that walking again."

He laughed. "No, no walking. Just regular guarding. I'll be in touch."

Annetta wondered at his words. Silvers must have a lot of responsibilities if he needed to employ extra guards. At least she could help him with something.

The guards picked up their belongings and filed out while Silvers addressed Annetta and Samuel. "Right, one formality before we take you upstairs. You need to pass through an interview room, but it shouldn't take long. Those guards are doing theirs just now, so we'll give them a few minutes. Essentially, you declare you've not been spreading secrets. Samuel doesn't need to do it this time since he's taking up residence here."

Plus, he's only ten. She forced a laugh. "I may have learned some secrets, but I certainly don't go around talking about them. That would be unprofessional. Do you have to go through this too?"

"Yep. Of course, people with different roles have access to different information."

She nodded. That tied in with what Shelley had told them, so he hadn't been lying about that part. "I guess you know a lot more than most people, but as long as you don't tell anyone, you're fine?"

"You got it."

He led them to a door beside a staircase, told them to wait, and disappeared inside for a few minutes. When he reappeared, his face was lightly sheened with sweat. "No problem. Your turn now. Just go in, take a seat, and answer the questions they ask. You don't need to hide anything."

There was no need to worry about this new requirement. It sounded like something lots of people went through. She entered the tiny room and perched on a high wooden stool. What had got Silvers so stressed? The place looked boring rather than frightening. Other than the stool, the room contained a metal column with a hole in it, maybe an artistic sculpture.

At a crackle from the wall, Annetta jumped and clutched her bag. "Oh, you startled me! Scientist Silvers told me to sit here. Was that alright?"

A sigh issued from somewhere in front of her. "Place your hand through the hole in that column in front of you."

Oops, it hadn't been a sculpture. At least she'd not *said* anything ignorant for anyone to hear. She stuck her hand in. "Like this?"

"That's right. Now, push the top of it down until it clicks."

After doing so, she found her wrist snugly held in the gap. "Wow. What's it do?"

"It's a lie detector."

"Oh, like it takes my pulse? How clever." She'd have to let Adrian know his speculations had been right.

The voice wobbled. "Something like that. What's your name?"

"Annetta."

"And why are you here?"

"I'm a herbalist. Scientist Silvers said I might be able to help curse victims, so I'm going to do some work in the Keep."

The voice asked her what she knew of the curse and powers, and the oath Shelley had extracted from her, when he was still Captain Shelley. She gave as much detail as she could remember before grinding to a halt. "I think that's everything."

"You may leave."

The gadget around her wrist loosened, and she slid off the stool. "Thanks. Er... have a good day?"

Another sigh followed her out of the room. *Well, that wasn't so bad.*

Seeing Samuel sitting on the stairs by himself, paper and pencil in hand, she blinked. "Where's Jed?"

"Said he was nipping upstairs to make arrangements for us, so everything's ready when we arrive. Told me to wait here."

And you did? That was progress, for Samuel. Maybe he'd found a good role model.

Silvers returned shortly afterwards. "Sorry about the wait, but I wanted everything to be just right for you. Let's head upstairs now. It's a few flights."

Annetta and Samuel followed him, Annetta clinging to the bannister. *Four floors up!* And to think she'd been impressed that Adrian's house had an upper floor. For all his bulk, Silvers moved pretty lightly and didn't even sound out of breath as he held the door open for them. "Here we are. This is the residential floor."

They stepped inside, Silvers behind them.

The grubby off-white walls and hallway floor were a touch disappointing, although the generous spacing between doors suggested the rooms might be quite large. Two guards in brown uniforms faced them: an older one with a moustache decorating his florid face, and a younger one with wide blue eyes. The third door along was ajar, from which came thumping and scraping noises.

"Our two guests," said Silvers. "As agreed, they'll be in Room Three. Samuel is one of our special guests, so he'll need to stay in the room. Annetta, however, is carrying out important work here. She can move freely between the room, the infirmary and the laboratory floor, although she'll need an escort—at least, at first. Can't have her getting lost."

She swallowed. "Er, hello. I'm Annetta, and this is Samuel." *Drat, I've done it again!* "I mean, nice to meet you." She turned to Silvers. "I can start work right away if you want."

Pulling out a pocket-watch, he shook his head. "It's a bit late in the afternoon. Spend the rest of today settling in, and come to the second floor first thing tomorrow. That's where the infirmary and laboratories are."

First thing? She'd better get an early night. "Is an hour before sunrise early enough?"

Silvers' lips twitched. "That's a tad on the early side for the city."

"Oh." Her face heated. "Sorry."

"That's fine, good to see you're keen. Tell you what, I'll send someone to collect you, but it won't be as early as that." He nodded to the older guard. "Looks like we're sorted for Doctor Annetta and Samuel. Any other news while I was away? I've already heard about Lady Nelson, and Shelley's capture. Bumped into Buchanan on the journey."

Doctor Annetta? She tucked that away for future enjoyment.

The guard chewed his moustache. "Captain Longleaf was arrested here around a week ago."

Silvers whistled. "Was she, now? What was all that about?"

"Samuel!" Annetta grabbed for the boy's collar as he wandered towards the open door. "Let them do their work." She kept an ear open for the continuing conversation.

The guard's voice lowered. "Seems she tried to conceal the message informing of Shelley's capture. The messenger bird landed outside Room Four, and she happened to be inside."

"I'd better go have a chat with her. Didn't realise she was one of Shelley's accomplices. Is she being held downstairs?"

"No. Queen's guard took her away."

Annetta trembled and stared at the men. Shelley's influence had extended even this far? It was lucky the guards had caught the woman.

Silvers' brows drew together. "Damn. They really shouldn't interfere with what goes on here."

"Sorry, sir, but it seems the queen issued standing orders about her."

"Well, I dare say Longleaf will get what she deserves. And she's been disturbing the residents too? Lady Nelson's death seems to have brought out the worst in people. Maybe I can pick up the pieces." He addressed Annetta. "I'll leave you now. Enjoy the rest of your day."

"Thanks." After Silvers left, she turned to the older guard. She might as well be friendly. "Since I'm here, do any of the residents need medical attention? I'm happy to help."

He frowned. "It's against regulations for the residents to communicate with each other. Might be a bit different for you, not being confined and so on, but you'd need to get permission."

"Oh, of course." How silly of her. It hadn't occurred to her the Keep would have such restrictions, but his words made sense. Some of the residents might be dangerous. Still, it was a shame they couldn't offer each other mutual support. "I guess I'll be working more downstairs."

The younger guard coughed. "Miss, the room's ready now. I hope it's suitable." He ushered them into the suite and closed the door behind them. It swung to with a reassuring thunk.

Even with partitioned-off sleeping areas, there was plenty of space for them both. Annetta's spirits lifted at the plump pillows on the beds, deep-pile rugs and blazing, crackling fire. She opened a wardrobe to reveal several sets of beige overalls. Smile broadening, she stroked the fabric, so different from her homespun garments. On the floor of the wardrobe were three pairs of beige slip-on shoes with cloth uppers and rubberised soles. She wriggled her toes in anticipation of their comfort.

A second wardrobe contained a pile of white overalls in something approaching Samuel's size. They probably wouldn't stay white for long. Who did all the washing?

"Wow." Samuel pointed at piles of drawing paper and a case of coloured pencils on the desk.

Annetta's first thought was much the same.

He wandered over to the open window. "Hey, Annetta, have a look at this."

She joined him, and her eyes widened. Before them lay the mountains' slopes covered in evergreen trees. She craned her neck, but couldn't make out the snow at the top. Then she looked down, and her hands clutched the bars. So far down! No wonder they had bars across the windows. If they didn't, she'd be terrified of falling out. Why did they make buildings so tall?

A knock came from the door.

"Hello?" called Annetta.

A hatch in the door slid aside and a pair of blue eyes

appeared. "What would you like for dinner?"

"What's available?"

"Just tell us what you fancy, and we'll see what Cook can rustle up."

Annetta smiled. This really didn't seem so bad.

Chapter 24

Eyes closed, hands crossed over her chest, striving for an empty mind, Susanna lay on the detention room's folding bunk. She'd pulled it down earlier and unintentionally jammed her fingers in the hinge. While stifling a yelp of pain, she caught a mental flicker from outside the room. She wondered who the mind reader was. Not that it mattered: they'd just be doing their job. As one of the weaker mind readers, Susanna could only put up a token resistance, but that was no reason to make things easy for them.

It proved impossible to think of nothing at all, and she didn't want to dwell on her culpability over that message. Instead, she concentrated on Jonathan's innocence. *Breathe in... he's been framed... breathe out... he's innocent...* Unfairly accused, unfairly detained and unfairly used by Silvers.

She opened her eyes and gazed around the room. Painted-over picture rails halfway up the walls made an odd combination with the heavy door lock. Maybe this was a converted anteroom. For how long would it be her home? No doubt the queen had other priorities, and Susanna couldn't imagine herself high on the list. *Queen's Discretion.* Days? Months? Would they notify anyone where she was? Her disappearance would be a mystery to Les—No. She wouldn't think of him. She wouldn't drag him into this too. *Breathe in...*

Heavy footsteps approached. She swung herself upright while a key turned in the lock. The door creaked open, and

Paton's bulk filled the doorway.

"You're in luck, Longleaf," he grunted. "Maybe. Her Majesty had palace commitments she wanted to concentrate on. She'd already cleared her schedule for the week. When I told her I'd detained you, she ordered your interrogation today."

"I see." Susanna stood and smoothed down her creased captain's jacket. "Lead on, Chief Guard Paton."

She followed him along a hallway with scuffed wooden floors. Duty rosters were pinned to the walls, and the smell of burnt toast made her nose wrinkle. They passed several red-clad guards, who saluted Paton while staring at Susanna. She kept her head high and her gaze straight ahead. She'd *trained* some of those guards before they'd been offered royal duties. What must they think of her now?

The interrogation room's walls and floor were tiled. In the centre was a rusty stool bolted to the floor, and an adjacent restraint column. Beyond that, a partition with a viewing grille divided the room. At Paton's nod, she sat and thrust her arm through the column's aperture.

She winced at the clunk when Paton pushed the column down. Monitoring was hardly a new experience though she was more often on the other side of the grille. But being interrogated as a prisoner? Tiny holes in the wall caught her eye. Sniffing, she detected only a faint floral scent. Apple blossom? Not one of the usual punishment gases. She'd never administered one, but some odours lingered... The room grew hazy. She stared at the grille while Paton strode beyond the partition.

Breathe in...

Murmurs and the scrape of furniture floated through the grille.

"Identify yourself." Paton's voice.

"I am Susanna Longleaf, a captain with the city guard." Though maybe not a captain much longer. Her shoulders tensed at the tickle of another mind reader in her head.

"Your veracity is being assessed by a mind reader. Lying will be punished."

"I am aware of that. I shall answer your questions truthfully and to the best of my ability." They'd witnessed the worst she'd done already, so what did the rest matter? And she knew nothing definite about Jonathan, just guesses and speculation. If she could make life difficult for Silvers through this interview, she'd count that as a minor gain.

"First of all, what prompted you to parade down Silvers' street like a festival display?" There was a rap of knuckles on wood. Paton coughed. "I'll rephrase that. For what purpose did you visit Silvers' house?"

She swallowed. "I had learned that Jon—Captain Shelley might be dead, and I was sure Silvers was implicated."

"Shelley was imprisoned by Council decree. He broke out. You thought Silvers helped him escape then killed him? Perhaps even that Silvers killed the guard?"

"Well, no, but Jonathan had become suspicious of Silvers. He'd thought Silvers was attempting to spread the curse—"

"What was his proof?"

"He'd hardly have written evidence! But Silvers sent him out to capture a beast. Such an order can't have been—"

Behind the screen, paper shuffled. "Scientific Committee's request, approved by the Council. Two guards injured and cursed. Attributed to poor leadership."

Susanna glared at the screen. "It wasn't Jonathan's

fault."

"Ha, I suppose you were there."

"Of course not." Why was Paton being so obtuse? Admittedly, he wasn't the one being interrogated. *Breathe in...*

A soft voice murmured.

"Moving back to the reason for this interview, you conspired with Shelley, who's known to be a murderer."

"*Alleged* murderer. He's not been convicted. Anyway, I wasn't conspiring. He knew nothing of what I was doing." And maybe he would never learn of it.

"It seems rather convenient you were in the Keep just at the right moment to retrieve that message." Scepticism dripped from Paton's voice.

"It *was* a coincidence!" Her chest tightened. "I was visiting Tabitha to bring her up to date. Jonathan had asked me to help her."

"Help her? Don't claim you went there to help feed the birds."

"Of course not. I'd been working with her in the training room, helping her learn to use her power." *Damn, I walked into that!* "We had permission, really we did. Lady Nelson had directed Jonathan to train Tabitha. She allowed me to stand in while he was away." *Breathe in...*

"Funny how the two parties to *that* little agreement aren't around to corroborate your claims."

"Your mind reader will confirm I'm telling the truth. It was Jonathan's last request of me." Her voice choked off, and she bowed her head.

Slumped in her misery, Susanna only vaguely noticed mutters and whispers in the background, with occasional rumbles of protest from Paton. After a few more mutters, someone exited the room, a door behind the partition slamming shut.

She flinched. Had they cleared the area in order to deliver a punishment? "Queen's Discretion" could mean so many things. Eyeing the holes in the wall, she cleared her throat. "So, what's next? Bring it on." Small comfort nobody could hear her wavering voice.

Her eyes widened as the young woman stepped into view, her hair in a no-nonsense bun.

Queen Eleanor pushed up the sleeves of her lilac pullover and folded her arms. "I've dismissed the others in order to speak with you in private. No mind readers. No guards."

No witnesses? Susanna half-rose from her stool and attempted a bow, constrained as she was by the column. "Your Majesty. How can I help?"

"A moment." The queen dragged a chair from behind the partition and sat opposite Susanna, frowning. "You're aware of how the afflicted develop control of their powers. Isabel wouldn't tell me much, but... pain. You learned in isolation. Completely self-directed."

"We all did. That was the protocol." Until Tabitha. Was Susanna in more trouble? Sweat slicked her wrist against the metal of the restraint column.

"But you went beyond that because of the girl, Tabitha."

Damn. "That's right. We—I mean, I had the idea of providing feedback through mind reading. It could speed up acquisition of control and make it easier on the subject."

"I see." Queen Eleanor nodded. "And it worked? Tabitha can now use her power at will?"

"No. Activation still needs pain..." Susanna blinked at the memory of Tabitha's tears. "Or strong emotion. And she still needs to practise control. But my feedback gave her a head start."

In the silence that followed, Susanna shifted uncomfortably on the stool. She cleared her throat. "Your Majesty? Your questions... I have difficulty seeing how they relate to the charges against me or Jonathan. He's innocent, I'm sure of it."

"Maybe. I see that's what you believe, anyway. Why are you so convinced?"

Because he's Jonathan. "Because I know him. He did kill someone once. With his power. To maintain secrecy. The Council agreed it was necessary, but that killing's preyed on his mind ever since. He'd be devastated if he were forced into it again..." She sniffed, and it turned into a sob.

The queen's footsteps moved away, and the restraint on Susanna's wrist loosened with a click.

Susanna withdrew her arm and massaged it while she sought a less painful topic. "And your questions about the training?"

"Those were in regard to a different issue." The queen reappeared from behind the partition. "Captain Longleaf, I don't think you're guilty of anything other than, well, possibly unwise decisions." Her lips tightened. "Settlers know we're all guilty of that, from time to time. But your detention here is fortunate for me. I could really do with your help."

"What about Jonathan?" Susanna's eyes narrowed. Was the queen offering her a deal? Might as well push it. "And Silvers?"

"Rest assured, your... friend will have a fair trial. I'll see to it myself when he arrives. As to Silvers, he'll have to wait. There are more pressing matters. Talking of which, I'd like you to meet someone..."

The cooking fire crackled, and a few off-duty guards murmured amongst themselves while setting out sleeping rolls. The three assigned to Jonathan remained silent and unmoving.

"A word with you, Shelley." David's voice cut across the clearing where they'd stopped for the night.

Bowl in hand, Jonathan stood and approached him. "What's up? Uh, sir." David had been... not exactly a friend, but a respected colleague.

"Walk with me." Carrying his own bowl, he led Jonathan towards a nearby stream. He rolled his eyes at the guards who followed hard on their heels and waved them back out of earshot, although they continued to watch from the tree line. "Since you've been making things easy for us, I'll tell you about arriving in Ascar. So you know what to expect."

"I'd appreciate it." He kept his voice low enough to just carry over the trickling water. Advance information from David would help Jonathan plan his own unexpected moves.

"Right." David gulped a spoonful of stew. "Because of public concern about the 'mad cursed captain' you'll go to trial pretty much immediately on arrival."

"I'll be ready." The sooner the better. Jonathan had spent the day's travel in clandestine practice, making the most of this precious opportunity to try calling his power while under the painkiller. Nobody had commented on an unusual frequency of snapped twigs and startled birds.

David raised an eyebrow. "Someone's keen."

"Of course I'm keen. I want to get this over with. Prove my innocence. Who'll be there?"

"It's a closed trial because of, well, powers. Council, scientists and captains."

Good. Silvers wouldn't miss this, even if he didn't arrive to gloat over Jonathan beforehand.

David continued. "Because it's private, you'll be mind-read. Means it should be quick, none of this verbal fencing to guess who's lying."

Jonathan nodded. Although mind readers could have simplified many court proceedings, the secrecy around their existence precluded relying on them openly. It was hard on the mind readers too. "Quick is good. I can live with that."

"You seem very confident."

"No reason not to be. I'm no murderer." At least, not of the guard.

David scraped his bowl with the spoon. "But you're an escaped prisoner, obviously. And as I hear, they detained you for losing control of your power, nothing worse. So what prompted you to break out rather than letting them put you through retraining?"

Jonathan paused. He didn't expect to survive his trial, not if he killed Silvers in the courtroom, or even before they arrived there. Better to make his suspicions known now, in the hope David would care enough to prevent another Silvers from rising. "You're right. I did break out after being imprisoned with that justification. But Silvers' real reason was to use me as a source of cursed flesh, attempting to curse people deliberately. He'd failed to transmit the curse via a beast I captured for him, so he took a sample from my leg. I guess he was going to..." The stew in his bowl glistened unappetisingly. "Uh, feed it to someone?"

Spoon in the air, mouth open, David didn't interrupt

Jonathan's account.

"He'd misjudged the painkiller dose, so once it wore off I escaped," concluded Jonathan. "Wouldn't you have done the same? But I really didn't kill the guard. I believe Silvers murdered him. I suspect he wanted me to be blamed so he could hang on to me permanently."

David made a face at the congealed mess on his spoon then dropped it back in the bowl. "You expect me to believe that? Do you have proof?"

Yes, that thing I dug out of my leg. Why had he discarded it? The last person to butcher his leg had been himself. Jonathan sighed. "Nothing concrete, only what he said. Believe what you will."

"I suppose nobody else was there when he spoke to you."

"Well, no. Apart from the guard who died. It's my word against Silvers'."

"That's a far-fetched story."

Jonathan shrugged. "I know. I guess you wouldn't understand."

"Still..." David lowered his voice further. "I can understand the appeal of having more people around with powers."

Pain. "You can't understand what it's like, what they put us through. Did you wonder about the painkillers, why they had to be so strong? I have to pay for every use in pain!" *Easy, Shelley.* He took a deep breath.

"Surely it can't be that bad. I mean, being able to do such things would be worth it, no?"

Of course David had no idea how gaining control could be so traumatic. He'd never been through it. How could Jonathan make it clear? "David, you have children, don't you? I remember you mentioning them previously."

"Yes, a boy and a girl. Twins, age eight. Why?"

"There's a girl in the Keep. She's called Tabitha, and she's only fifteen. I sent her there after she was cursed. You know how it is..."

"So young?" David's downcast gaze confirmed he was no stranger to such responsibilities.

Jonathan continued. "I tried to help her, but Silvers got wind of it. The scientists can treat detainees in the Keep however they want. I was worried what Silvers might do to her, so I asked Lady Nelson for protection. She agreed, but on condition I train Tabitha. I hooked the poor girl up to that damned box that causes pain, and... I didn't even have the guts to switch it on. Tabitha had to do it. That was the hardest thing I've ever done, making her inflict pain on herself." He wiped his eyes while waiting for his voice to steady. "Of course, it was even worse for her."

"Hmm." David pushed his spoon around the bowl. "I see what you mean. But at least after your trial—once you've proved yourself innocent—you could turn the tables on Silvers. A counter-claim should be straightforward." He smirked. "Or perhaps you're thinking of 'accidentally' broadcasting all that information about him when the mind readers take your evidence?"

Jonathan cleared his throat. "Maybe." *If I'm not dead.*

"Oh, I just remembered." David frowned. "You won't have heard. Lady Nelson has died."

"What?" He gaped, registering a sense of loss. Not that the old woman had been an ally, but she'd not been on Silvers' side either. Tabitha would be left vulnerable. "I did ask Susanna to keep an eye on Tabitha, but she doesn't have the authority to—"

"Susanna? She's disappeared."

Jonathan's knuckles tightened on his spoon. "What do you mean, 'disappeared'?"

David's lip curled. "Lester said she'd been holed up in her room for a couple of days, not talking to anyone, and he'd even wondered whether to break in. Anyway, he finally spoke to her, and she rushed off to the Keep to do something. But then she didn't come back."

Jonathan's mouth dried up. This seemed like too much to be coincidence, although at least Silvers couldn't have been responsible, not if David knew of it before leaving Ascar. Not unless Silvers had an ally. Would it be selfish to wonder if Susanna had run into trouble on his account? "When was this?"

"Mmm, the day the message arrived announcing your capture. Council assigned me to come out here, I was up to my eyeballs trying to prepare, and I told Lester I'd punch him if he asked me *one more time* whether I'd seen Susanna." He regarded Jonathan's face. "Hey, it was only one day. You know how Lester gets. She might well have returned while I was on my way out."

"Look, David. I mean, Captain Buchanan. May I request a favour? Not for myself. I'm worried about Tabitha." Susanna could look after herself, he hoped, but Tabitha was just a child.

"I'll consider it if it's within reason. What do you want?"

"To save time, since I'll be busy with my trial, could you check up on her, as soon as we arrive back in Ascar? She's been in the Keep for months, with nobody else looking out for her. Her parents already rejected her when she became cursed. I guess, I've been the closest she's had to a father..." *And now she'll lose me too.*

David eyed him askance. "You're talking like you don't expect to see her again."

"Of course I do. Expect to see her, I mean." *Don't mess this up.* He swallowed. "But... I worry."

"I can understand that. You'd better turn in now. We start moving early tomorrow."

Chapter 25

Annetta fidgeted with her bag strap while she waited for Silvers to arrive at the infirmary.

The elderly infirmier eyed her over the rim of his half-moon glasses. "Impatient?"

"Not exactly, more nervous." Although she'd left her regular preparations in Maldon for Opal, her entire collection of special herbs had accompanied her to Ascar. She'd spent the previous day flipping through all her notes, deciphering her mentor's tortuous handwriting and selecting the recipe with the greatest chance of success. Without the need to gather ingredients, she'd been able to focus on preparing them. The laboratory's advanced equipment—including distillation flasks—yielded double the volume she'd expected. However, this was still an untested remedy. "Louis, what if this doesn't work?"

He shrugged. "Then we try something else."

She chewed her lip. "I don't want to disappoint Scientist Silvers when he needs it in such a hurry. If we can suppress Shelley's power without knocking him out, it would make for a fairer trial. Whatever he's done, he should have the chance to speak."

Louis opened his mouth, but shut it again as the door from the reception area opened.

Silvers entered, rolling up his shirtsleeves. "Good, you're here. All set?"

"As much as I can be." She patted her bag for reassurance. "It's time, I suppose."

Poor Terry. This initial test would be an attempt to help the guard who had been attacked while under Shelley's command. The young man had truly been cursed with the power to inflict pain on others, although only through direct contact. How difficult that must make treating him. If her remedy worked on Terry and on others, the afflicted could be... not *cured*, but perhaps freed from long-term detention.

With Annetta and Louis following him, Silvers approached the guards outside Terry's door. "Let us in."

One guard moved aside while the other unlocked and opened the door.

Louis picked up a tranquilliser syringe from the adjacent emergency trolley. "Just in case."

I'm glad one of us knows how to use those. Since syringes and needles were only produced in Ascar, she'd never used one before yesterday. Rural folk relied on salves and pills instead. She was grateful for the good-natured volunteers who'd offered their arms so she could practise.

Silvers rubbed his nose. "Good idea, after what happened last time. You remember that, Louis? You had to tranquillise him."

Lips tightening, the infirmier nodded.

Annetta's heart sank. "Did Terry have an accident?"

"Ha, no. *Shelley* had the accident and made a mess of the room. Luckily Louis was standing by with his syringe." Silvers scowled. "And then the bastard assaulted me with his power when I offered to help him up. Gave me a nosebleed."

"That's a dreadful abuse of his ability!" Her spine straightened. So Shelley really had been dangerous even before that encounter with her. Malicious, even. A couple of times, she'd wondered if Silvers might have exaggerated, but here was Louis backing him up. A twinge of guilt struck her that she'd doubted the scientist. "I do hope this works, so he can't attack anyone again."

"Me too. It would be a shame if he had to be neutralised because he was too violent to detain. That would be a real waste. Anyway, in you go. Ladies first." He bowed and gestured to the doorway with a flourish.

The smile fell off Annetta's lips as she entered. Terry slumped at the table, chin on his hands. A calibrated stimulus generator lay before him.

He raised his head. "Oh, hello, Annetta. I hope this works."

Me too. "I'm sure it will. You'll be fine."

"How are we doing this?" He clipped on the earpiece.

"You'll need to use the box to call your power and keep it active." She reached into her bag and pulled out her syringe, the one with her special formulation. "Then I'll inject you with this, which should suppress your power, even when you're still connected to the box and, um, in pain. I'll be as quick as I can. Does that make sense?"

"Sure." Terry nodded. "Wish me luck."

"Hang on," said Silvers. "Shouldn't we check if Terry's power is working? Otherwise we'll have no way of knowing."

Her pulse raced. Why hadn't she thought of that? Of course someone needed to touch him. It was her remedy, so testing it ought to be her responsibility. "Sorry. I forgot about that bit. Um, Louis? If you can take my syringe?" She gulped. "I'll hold Terry's hand and let Scientist Silvers know if his power's affecting me. If you can inject him. Anyway, you're better at injections than I am." Her neck tensed in anticipation.

Silvers shook his head. "No, that won't do. You need to assess the dosage and so on. *I* will be the, ah, victim." He flashed her a smile. "Though please act quickly."

"Oh! Thank you!" Annetta beamed at his commitment. He really believed in her.

Terry switched on the box and winced, then he nodded, laying a hand on the table, palm up.

After placing his fingers on Terry's wrist, Silvers took a deep breath. "His power's certainly working. Louis, stay back. No interrupting the experiment. Annetta, would you mind?"

It took the needle in Annetta's trembling hand a few seconds to find an arm vein without her touching Terry. Seconds in which Silvers' breathing grew ragged. Why hadn't she put a tourniquet on first? The vein wobbled away from the needle tip as she chased it around. Silvers grunted, face flushing. *Drat, I'll never get it at this rate!* She gritted her teeth, clamped her hand around Terry's arm and shoved the needle in while lancinating pain surged up her arm into her shoulder.

"Gaah..." She thrust the plunger down.

The relief was nearly instantaneous.

Panting, she blinked at her pain-free hand. It was almost as if nothing had happened. "Wow. Terry, are you alright? And Jed? Um, Scientist Silvers."

Terry pulled off his earclip and puffed out his cheeks. "Yeah, that was weird. Pain was still coming through my earclip, but the power thing stopped."

Behind them, Louis coughed. "Since you all survived, I'll return to my other duties. The infirmary's been filling up recently." He slipped out.

Silvers grinned despite the sweat trickling down his face. "I can't believe how fast that worked. It wasn't fun, but there's nothing like personal experience for getting an understanding of things. This is great!"

Annetta grinned back. "We're really on to something." Her face fell. "Oh, drat. Remember, my ingredients only yielded two doses, so we now have just one left. And I didn't notice any bitter pinkweed on the way. It'll take me a while to find some more."

After they left the infirmary, Silvers walked Annetta back towards her room, asking, "How long will that dose last?"

"According to my notes, a full day. I'll check on Terry again later." She sighed. "If I'd known that recipe would be so effective, I'd have spent more time gathering pinkweed, rather than maintaining a full set of everything mentioned in my notes."

"One dose is better than none. Now, when Shelley killed that old man, it took a full minute, according to his debrief. Your remedy works much faster than that, so I can rely on you to prevent him from doing any harm, to keep everyone safe when he arrives. That will get him through his trial. After that, at worst, we can drug him unconscious until you can make some more or come up with another bright idea. Well done."

"Oh, thanks!" She blushed at his appreciation, though she hadn't quite followed all he said. Debrief? After he'd *murdered* someone? Maybe the word had a special meaning here.

Silvers left Annetta at the residential corridor, saying he'd call her when Shelley arrived. The guards paused their card game and let her into the suite.

Seated at the table, a piece of cake on his plate, Samuel swallowed and wiped his mouth with a sleeve, smearing it with jam. "Annetta, you didn't tell me there was a festival!"

"What festival?" Even though she'd been working, she'd have noticed someone mentioning one.

"Look." He tugged her sleeve, pulling her towards the open window, and climbed upon a stool. "They've got decorations outside, really colourful! Though nobody's been singing."

Her brow wrinkled. Since they faced the back of the city, who would bother placing decorations here? Maybe it was a city thing.

"See? Just outside." He wobbled on the stool and pointed.

Holding the bars, she leaned forwards, and her eyes widened.

Running horizontally past the window ledge was a rope, for lack of a better word. It appeared to be several pieces of ribbon and fabric strips, all tied together. She was pretty certain it hadn't been there before.

At a loss for words, she watched as it began to move sideways, as if someone were pulling it from one end. It slid past her gaze in a parade of colours: pink, orange, red and blue... She blinked. Was that a grubby sock?

She prodded the sock as it crept past the window. *Maybe I need glasses.* Paper rustled inside.

Then it clicked. Residents weren't allowed contact with each other, but someone had found a way around it. How clever, and it kept them occupied. Isolating afflicted people might ensure safety—like quarantine—but it seemed cruel to bar all communication. Even with dangerous powers, what harm could sending notes do? No, what the guards didn't see... didn't concern them.

She swallowed. "Samuel, I'd like to borrow your pencils and use some of your paper..."

Chapter 26

Jonathan's knees nearly touched David's as they sat facing each other in the wagon. The big captain's eyes glinted in the low illumination. His gaze had been fixed on Jonathan for the whole ride through the Armstrong Tunnel.

Don't worry, David, I'm not trying to escape. "Soon you'll be rid of me," muttered Jonathan, over the hissing wheels on the rails.

David's eyebrows lifted. "Assuming you told me the truth, we'll be dining together in the captains' lounge soon enough."

"Right." He placed his hand on his right thigh, felt the lumpy scar from his injuries, but no pain. Focussing, he called his power, and it responded. Good, it still worked. "You'll... remember to check up on Tabitha?"

"Sure. We're nearly there now. I've been ordered to handcuff you. They stay on until you get to the courtroom in the Council building. Left to myself, I wouldn't bother—"

"That's fine." Jonathan shrugged off the garish padded jacket and held out his hands. He didn't *need* them to direct his power, and the more harmless he looked, the better.

The train reached its destination in the Keep's basement, where six city guards stood. Jonathan peered at them as he climbed out of the wagon, spying a bulky figure at the back. Was it Silvers? Tendrils of anticipation quivered in his chest.

The convoy guards arranged themselves around

Jonathan, and David led them towards the waiting group. The frontmost city guard half-heartedly thumped his chest. Jonathan's lips tightened at the sloppiness.

David crisply returned the salute. "Handing over the prisoner, Shelley, as directed by the Council."

A figure nearly as large as David pushed through the brown-clad guards. Jonathan clenched his fists, his arms tensing against the restraints. Vengeance was nearly within reach.

"Good," said Silvers. "I'll take things from here. Run along now, Buchanan, I'm sure you've got plenty of other duties."

"Guards, dismissed." David signalled his guards, who filed toward the exit. Then he leaned towards Silvers so closely their noses nearly touched. "Treat him properly."

"Oh, I shall." Silvers stepped back. "He'll get what he deserves."

Jonathan's jaw tightened, and he took a deep breath. *Not yet.* He'd better wait until David left before making his move.

"I'll see to it once I've reported in." With a nod at Jonathan, David walked off.

"See to what?" asked Silvers, but David's brisk stride continued without a pause.

Jonathan grinned. "You wouldn't understand. It's a captain thing."

Silvers scowled. "You're an ex-captain now, Shelley, and don't forget it. And with your power neutralised, you're in no position to harm anyone. You're safely in my care."

"Until my trial." Jonathan stared at Silvers' jowly face, allowing his anger to ignite. "After that..." His power arose, expanding to fill his core. "We'll just have to see, won't we?"

He *let go*, his power coursing through him to seek out his opponent's heart and one of the tiny blood vessels that supplied it.

Silvers paled and clutched a hand to his chest. Jonathan managed one step forwards before two of Silvers' guards leapt to grab him. Ha, they didn't know what was happening. It would only take a minute, and then he'd be finished. He and Silvers both.

Breath hissing through his teeth, Silvers spoke. "Annetta."

A figure darted forwards from behind the guards. Jonathan caught a glimpse of metal before Annetta seized his arm. She bent over it for a few seconds, pressing his elbow.

Pulling the syringe out—of course he hadn't felt any pain from the needle—she stepped back, looked him full in the face and spat, "Murderer!"

He gaped at the venom in her voice, his concentration interrupted. Then he grasped for his power, but it slipped away like a minnow, disappearing into the turmoil of his thoughts. Shit!

"What have you done to me?" His voice was hoarse.

Waving a finger in Jonathan's face, Silvers smirked. "She's neutralised your power, Shelley. Can't have you trying to murder even more people. I suspected you'd try something, so I took steps to ensure you'd fail. Good to know my predictions were correct. We can call this experiment a success."

"You're the real criminal! You've convinced Annetta to go along with you. And these damn city guards are in your pock—"

One of the guards slapped him.

"I? A criminal?" Silvers raised an eyebrow. "You're the one who just tried to kill me. That can go on your record sheet too."

"I trusted you, you monster." Annetta's eyes narrowed. "I didn't want to believe that you'd killed Gerald and covered it up. I'm glad I realised my mistake and could stop you this time. May Gerald's ashes come back to choke you." Panting, she addressed Silvers. "Going by Terry, this will be effective until tomorrow. It's such a relief the injection worked. I hope the full extent of Shelley's crimes comes out at his trial."

Jonathan's head spun. *Monster.* He couldn't even deny it.

Silvers patted her shoulder. "I'll make sure it does, Annetta. And yeah, I'm relieved it worked too. Woulda been awkward if it hadn't." His belly shook as he laughed.

With a final glare at Jonathan, Annetta fled towards the stairs.

Silvers jerked his head at the guards. "Take him to the cells. He's safe to handle now."

With rough hands they gagged him and hauled him towards the corridor where he'd been held previously. Sweat soaked his back and his bowels cramped when they approached his old cell, four doors down.

Think, Shelley. No point panicking. This drug would last until tomorrow. Even if he couldn't use his power, the mind readers would find him innocent at his trial and free him. That was, unless Silvers had somehow bribed or blackmailed them all. But even if Jonathan remained imprisoned, he'd simply need to be patient and catch Silvers unawares at some future opportunity. He'd just have to survive until then. His shoulders eased.

"Wait." Silvers halted outside the second cell.

The guards stopped, still holding Jonathan's arms.

Silvers waved towards the hatch in the cell door. "Have a look, Shelley."

What was Silvers' game? Might as well play along. It could hardly get worse. He squinted through the hatch, and his breath caught.

Tabitha stared back from the bunk where she was shackled, her tear-stained face partly covered by a gag.

Jonathan lunged forwards, but the guards wrenched him back. His shoulder joint popped, although he felt no pain. If he could have torn off his arm, just to get through the door and reach her, he would have done it. But he couldn't, so he simply stood, panting.

"Just to ensure your good behaviour." Silvers pointed to Jonathan's old cell, telling the guards, "Chain him to the bunk in there, then wait outside."

Once his arms were chained behind his back, the gag still stifling his words, Jonathan glared at the guards before they left the cell. Their footsteps faded down the corridor.

Silvers entered, shaking his head as he looked down at Jonathan. "I really don't want to harm Tabitha, a young girl with her whole life ahead of her. Believe me, she's far more valuable to me alive and unharmed."

Rage burned in his chest, and his nostrils flared. *I'll kill you.*

"If only you'd behaved properly last time, it wouldn't have come to this. Still, you can salvage the situation before anyone else is damaged." He glanced in the direction of Tabitha's cell. "Understand?"

Jonathan nodded, his jaw muscles clenching as he bit down on the gag.

"See how easy it is to agree? I want you to plead guilty

straight away at your trial. Don't want the mind readers learning something they shouldn't. If they did... I'd be disappointed." Silvers reached into his pocket and drew out a small metal box with two buttons, displaying it to Jonathan. "See, this device can transmit a signal to Tabitha's cell. Its friend there contains a glass vial of... well, you wouldn't recognise the name, but it's a quick-acting poison gas. Would be a real shame if the vial were to break during your trial, wouldn't it? Do you get my drift?"

Shards of terror sliced into him. He nodded again, the gag digging into his neck.

"I'm so glad we're in agreement. In case you're wondering, Tabitha won't talk either. She knows better than that, now you're here."

Tears filled Jonathan's eyes, and he dropped his head. Silvers had won. For the moment. Well, what did it matter if Jonathan blackened his name by pleading guilty? Either he'd get an opportunity to kill Silvers after his trial or, more likely, he'd find an opportunity to kill himself. Whichever way things went, Tabitha would be safer, no longer a hostage for Jonathan's cooperation.

The cell door swung open and shut, and Silvers' footsteps moved away, leaving Jonathan with the darkness of his thoughts.

Chapter 27

Susanna flicked off her pain box. "I got a clearer sense of your focus that time."

"I'm glad one of us did." Artur rubbed the side of his head, leaving his sandy hair sticking up. "When you read me, it's kind of prickly."

"Sorry." She removed her earclip. "Some people can sense me working—I think it's because my power is quite weak. The stronger mind readers aren't so obvious."

Leaning back in her chair, she stretched her arms up as she gazed around the room, hoping for inspiration. Eleanor had directed them to work in the guest suite set aside for Artur and assured them of privacy. It was strange to set the pain boxes on a mahogany table—Paton had lugged in an entire dining set, cursing under his breath—and to have silk cushions on the chairs. Not that the surroundings gave her any clues. "What were you focussing on?"

He tugged off his earclip. "Following Eleanor's suggestion, I concentrated on my uncle and how he looked when I had that hallucination of him. Or whatever it was that told me how he'd died."

"Hmm." She frowned. "If you've been cursed without any beast contact... that's never happened before. Still, I can see Queen—Eleanor's reasoning, about that trip to the mound with Isabel and your illness. But I don't know whether we're on the right track or if we're wasting our efforts. That said, we've not even been at this for a week, and it's not the sort of power that would be obvious."

"But you did say my mind looks different from Eleanor's."

"Yes, but it's not like I've ever examined normal people." Susanna's lips twitched. The queen might be "normal" in terms of being unafflicted, but her behaviour was hardly conventional. Her willingness to act as a test subject had been remarkable, given royalty's absolute right to immunity from mind reading. Paton had glared and offered himself, but she'd overruled him. She'd insisted Artur was her responsibility.

Of course, a queen could easily make other, more ordinary things happen too. She'd assigned Susanna the suite next door and prevented her from collecting her things from the barracks. Paton had snorted and concurred. *Something's bound to go wrong on the way*, he'd said, *even if she goes out with a minder*. Susanna hadn't dared take umbrage. To be fair, the garments the housekeeper had provided were a cut above what Susanna was used to: the silk a more delicate weave, the dyes just a shade brighter. She wondered who they'd belonged to previously. They were a touch ostentatious for the current queen.

After a knock, the door swung open, and Eleanor slipped in. She wore a sober ink-black robe. "How are you getting on?"

Susanna wrinkled her nose. "Slow going, I'm afraid. We're doing our best."

"I know, and I hate to push you like this. But the sooner Artur can control his power, the less risk he'll be in. He's been a good friend. Especially with Isabel missing, I mean."

Susanna ignored Artur's blush. *Poor Isabel. All my warnings didn't help her. I hope she's alright.*

Eleanor continued. "I've invited someone else to help, to suggest some ideas. I hope you don't mind."

So much for secrecy. Susanna glanced at Artur, who shrugged. "Of course not. Just now?"

"Yes." Eleanor opened the door and beckoned.

Sporting a neatly trimmed beard and wearing a dark brown pullover and trousers, Staunton walked in. "Captain Longleaf. And Artur, I believe?"

Susanna rose, mouth agape. "You!" Then she remembered their hostess and sank back into her chair. *So much for my fabled aplomb.* "I'm sorry, I was just surprised, Scientist Staunton. I'd had some difficulty in contacting you previously."

Staunton sat at the table while Eleanor took the couch. "I had reasons for that, but they're not needed anymore."

"But why avoid me and not Jonathan?" Her cheeks heated. "We're... close. Fairly close." *Sort of.*

He leaned forwards. "But Captain Shelley isn't a mind reader."

Oh. "You were scheming and didn't want anyone to suspect?"

"No comment." He raised an eyebrow. "Though I believe I have your charming young colleague—or should I say, conspirator?—to thank for an unusually dust-free library. My junior maid has been most industrious, attempting to overcome her disappointment at his absence."

Drat. "Sorry. Er, you might be able to help Artur?"

"I'd appreciate it," murmured Artur.

"Certainly, that's the main reason I'm here. What have you done so far? Please summarise."

"It started with a girl named Tabitha..." Susanna told him of her work training Tabitha, both with and without

Lester. "However, it was easier with Tabitha than it's been with Artur. I was trying to mould her 'shape' to be more like Jonathan's because they have similar powers. With Artur, I don't have a model to work towards."

Staunton steepled his fingers and gazed at the wall, then he beamed. "That's wonderful! And you managed all this in how many sessions?"

Before she could reply, someone knocked at the door. Eleanor let Paton inside.

"Prisoner's just been delivered to the Keep. They're gathering for the trial, Your Majesty."

Prisoner. Trial. Susanna's palms grew clammy.

"Damn, and I shouldn't make them wait." Eleanor smoothed her skirts. "Susanna, he'll be fine. Just a quick mind read, and we'll be done. Have to follow due process, that's all."

Susanna winced. "Jonathan hates having his mind read." She couldn't even go and support him since she was technically in custody.

"Same as with his monitoring interviews, he won't be given a choice." Eleanor smiled. "And who would plead guilty just to avoid it?"

The door closed behind Eleanor. It was comforting to know the queen was on their side.

Staunton coughed. "I know you're a bit distracted, but I have an idea to try."

Artur picked up his earclip and waved it at Staunton. "We're all ears..."

Boys. Be glad I don't give you a clip round yours. At least this would keep her mind off Jonathan. "Please go on."

"If you have an image of a deceased person—I mean a physical picture—you could use that as a sort of focus. It would give you something to hang on to, should your thoughts stray."

"Ah," said Artur. "Now you mention it, there was a portrait of my uncle in the room when I saw him. I'd never have thought of that."

"But how could we test your theory?" Susanna's gaze wandered around the room. "We'd need to identify a picture of someone who had passed on..." Her eye lit on a portrait, and her scalp prickled.

King Frederick.

Nauseous and gulping for air, Annetta staggered up the four flights of stairs from the Keep's basement. *Murderer.* She'd not wanted to believe Silvers about Gerald, hoping there was some innocent explanation, but Shelley's actions had left her in no doubt. Thank the Settlers she'd foiled his next attempt. She clutched her bag, glad she'd not needed her knockout powder. Shelley ought to stand trial and account for his deeds, not be drugged into unconsciousness.

Assuring herself she'd done the right thing, she thrust open the door to the residential corridor and her refuge.

The two guards inside ran towards her, lifting their truncheons.

She flinched and raised her hands. "It's only me!"

Paul's moustache bristled as he lowered his truncheon. "You should be more careful. Could have caused an accident." Shaking his head, he returned to his position further down the corridor.

Vincent lingered, his hooded eyes on her face. "Are you alright, miss?"

She clutched her bag, a hand to her chest. *Be professional.* "Sorry I startled you. Just had some problems with a patient. All sorted now. Could you let me into my room, please?"

The jangling of Vincent's keyring set her head to aching and raised visions of Shelley's imprisonment downstairs. The click of the lock and thud of the bar took on an ominous tone. Why had she thought them reassuring? Despite the spaciousness of the suite, its walls shrank in on her as she leaned against the door.

"Just call if you need anything," came Vincent's muffled voice.

"Thanks," she called back, shaking.

She straightened up. *I can't be foiling murders all the time.* Time to get back to normality, maybe have a bath and relax.

Her breathing slowed, and she almost smiled at the sight of Samuel, his papers spread out over the dining table. Pencil in hand, he sketched, his tongue protruding out of the corner of his mouth. He'd not even noticed her enter, he was concentrating so hard.

After a quick bath and change into fresh beige overalls, Annetta lay on the bed on her side of the partition. She thought over the notes she'd received from her neighbours via their ingenious rope communication system. She'd burnt the original papers, of course, so as not to get them into trouble. In the room to her left was Franka, the big cheery woman who'd been a convoy guard on the way to Maldon, all those months ago. The right-hand room housed a girl named Tabitha.

Hmm, odd. Both of them knew Shelley, but they still viewed him the way Annetta had when she first met him: capable, caring and responsible. Now she knew better, especially after today. Franka's notes about him had a tone reflecting years of loyalty, even though she'd been cursed on the same mission as Terry. Tabitha treated Shelley almost like a father figure. Both of them clung to their beliefs, despite knowing about his escape and that guard's murder. How could they both have been so fooled?

Or maybe they weren't. Maybe Shelley really had changed recently. That would make more sense, wouldn't it? He couldn't have maintained a facade of decency for years. *Maybe it really was my fault with that dratted dareth leaf.* Her lips pursed. What would they say when she told them about what happened earlier, about foiling his attack on Silvers? Well, maybe she wouldn't. It wouldn't be kind. Even though they weren't meeting face to face, it would be an awkward conversation.

"Annetta, are you back?" called Samuel. "I did another drawing."

Ugh, I just want to sleep. "Just a minute." She swung herself upright and went to admire his latest creation.

He handed her his sketch.

She reached for it, murmuring "Very goo—"

Her breath caught in her chest.

Samuel had drawn two prison cells. In one was a depiction of Shelley, chained to the wall, gagged and with a black eye. A certain squareness of his shoulder suggested a dislocation injury. The other cell held a smaller figure. A girl with long dark hair, also chained to the wall and wearing a white outfit like Samuel's. A girl Annetta had never seen before.

Clearly Samuel had had another vision, and possibly a mercy the images never seemed to perturb him. Odd how he was always seeing or drawing Shelley. But who was the girl?

"Have you seen that girl before, Samuel? She's not from Maldon, is she?" Could she be imaginary?

He wiped his hands on his trouser legs. "No, she's from here. I drew her once before, in a garden with Captain Shelley. They were on top of a building. A tall building."

A tall building? Maybe even this one, where Shelley was being held. Annetta chewed a fingernail. Despite her heated words downstairs, it wasn't right to mistreat a prisoner. Fair trial, yes. Fair punishment, yes. Even executions in extreme cases. But not chains and beatings. She'd neutralised Shelley's power with that injection, and he'd already been handcuffed. He shouldn't have presented a problem to half a dozen guards. Did Silvers have a problem with discipline? An image of the scientist's meaty fist arose in her mind, and she shivered.

Her gaze drifted to the door. Should she ask the corridor guards? Hmm, Silvers' guards downstairs also wore brown. No, Paul and Vincent weren't the right people to consult.

"Is it a good drawing?" asked Samuel.

She swallowed. "Yes, of course. It's so good I want to show someone else."

He beamed, picked up an apple from the fruit bowl and bit into it.

She rolled up the drawing and slipped it into a sock, then went to the window. After tying it to the rope, she gave two tugs in the direction of Franka's room, the signal they'd developed to indicate a message. With some trepidation, Annetta had donated a few glass vials which would clink as the rope was tugged.

A few seconds later, the rope moved in the direction of Franka's room, and Annetta relaxed. Franka would know what to do.

Only the crunch of Samuel's apple broke the silence while she waited. The rope tugged four times in the other direction, the signal for Tabitha's room. Why involve Tabitha? The picture wasn't of her, was it? There was no reason to chain up a young girl. Annetta chewed another fingernail while watching, but there was no returning tug. Well, maybe Tabitha was in the bath or something. Clever though it was, this communication method was clumsy. Why couldn't the residents just meet normally? Because it was against regulations. They were dangerous. But Samuel wasn't dangerous. Franka had been nothing but helpful and kind.

Samuel hadn't even finished his apple when three furious tugs came from Franka, and a faint tinkle of broken glass. Heart in her mouth, Annetta pulled the rope back and read Franka's reply, scrawled in soot on the back of Samuel's drawing:

That's Tabitha. She's not answering. You gotta bust us out.

Chained to the bunk in his cell, Jonathan twisted to the side, trying to ease the throbbing in his shoulder. With the painkiller wearing off, he had dared to hope, but in vain. A void lay between him and his power. He clenched his teeth on the gag, not wanting to give the guards any satisfaction. All that pain, and no way to make use of it.

Going by the shadows passing through the hatch, one guard stood outside, while a second paced up and down the corridor. Was the second one for Tabitha? If only he'd stayed away, if only he'd never visited her, she'd still be safe in her suite upstairs. *I wish I'd never met her.* That wasn't true, despite everything, but she'd be wishing she'd never met

Jonathan.

The shadows moved together. There was low muttering, and Jonathan caught a few words. "... No, keep out of her cell. You don't want to cross him..."

He closed his eyes in relief. Silvers hadn't lied—probably—about not wanting to harm Tabitha. About valuing her. That was something to cling to.

To guarantee that, he'd have to bow to Silvers' demands. Pleading guilty would be easy, but it would be a lie. Well, he'd spent so much of his life immured in lies and secrecy, what was one more lie? He had to. What was the value of a lie weighed against a young girl's life?

Monster. That's what Annetta had called him. How foolish he'd been to underestimate her. She'd hit closer to the truth than he'd imagined. If he'd been able to use his power, he'd have killed these guards without a qualm. Better that Jonathan be imprisoned—or dead—than Tabitha.

Chapter 28

You gotta bust us out.

"You're joking!" Annetta's gut clenched at Franka's demand. *Why me?* She was a herbalist, not an escapologist or rescuer. She'd no idea how to fight. But it was plain something was wrong, that someone needed rescuing. She couldn't just sit in this room and wait. "Well... we can't always use the best ingredient. Sometimes we need a substitute." Annetta, with her freedom of movement, would have a better chance than Franka to break them out.

Samuel's brow wrinkled. "Huh?"

"Just thinking." She looked him in the eye. "Samuel, we need to sort some problems, you and me and Franka. I need you to do what I say, right?"

His face brightened. "Is it a game?"

Argh! "Um, you wanted to play hide and seek downstairs, didn't you?"

He nodded.

"Well... yes, it's something like that, with a big prize if we win. I want you to sit quietly at the desk and think about where you saw the people in your drawing, but don't say anything just yet. Keep it a surprise for later. And don't move. Count to one hundred. Slowly, no cheating."

Samuel climbed on to the chair at the desk and pillowed his head on his arms, eyes closed. "One messenger bird... two messenger birds..."

Annetta rummaged in her bag for her knockout sachets from earlier. Just as well she'd been too frazzled to return them to the infirmary. After tearing them open, she put one in each pocket. She washed her hands. It wouldn't do to knock herself out. A quick glance in the mirror confirmed her flushed face and wild eyes. She certainly looked like an agitated woman. *And I feel like one too.*

Pulse racing, she rapped at the door. "Hello? Vincent? Paul?"

The hatch slid open, and a bleary eye peered through, broken veins on the cheek below. Paul, then.

"What's up?" he asked.

"Can you escort me downstairs, please? I just remembered something I need to tell Scientist Silvers, about—"

His eye narrowed. "Can't it wait until you see him tomorrow? He's a busy man."

"Um, I know." She lowered her voice. "The problem patient let something slip, and I've just realised its significance. It's to do with the, you know, trial. Information for him. Very confidential."

"Ah." He slid the hatch closed and opened the door a crack, peering inside towards Samuel.

"... twenty-seven messenger birds..."

Sweat prickled Annetta's neck. "Er... I set him to practise his numbers. Can't neglect his schooling, see?" She waved in Samuel's direction. "Keep counting, Samuel, you're doing really well."

Paul rolled his eyes and swung the door open.

She stepped into the corridor.

"Vincent," he called. "I'm just taking Annetta downstairs. Keep an eye on the prisoners for a few minutes."

"Sure." Vincent nodded from his chair just past

Tabitha's door.

Prisoners? She stiffened. Why hadn't she noticed before? What else had she been fooled about? Why had she accepted Silvers' claims and behaviour, just because he was a high-up from Ascar? She'd never have tried to explain away Mayor Sutcliff's actions, would she? *I let myself be fooled.*

Hand in her pocket, she took a step towards the stairs and waited while Paul locked and barred the door. He turned to her, his back to Vincent and obscuring her view of the seated guard.

"Right. Let's go." He stepped towards her.

She yanked her hand from her pocket and thrust it towards his face, saying, "Oh, there's an odd lesion on your nose. I hope it's not a tumour." She brushed her hand with its covering of powder over his moustache.

His hand rose to his nose. "Something harmful? What should..." He swayed and slumped against the wall by her door.

"Vincent!" Annetta grabbed Paul's arm and slung it over her shoulder. "Help! Paul's been taken ill. Come quickly!" *What am I doing?*

The guard leapt from his chair and ran towards her, helping her support his unconscious colleague and lower him to the floor. As he straightened up, Annetta tossed a second handful of powder at him, and he collapsed over Paul.

"Not *too* bad," she muttered, pulling the bunch of keys from Paul's belt. "Tabitha first, just in case she's still in her room. She might simply be unwell." Though she doubted it. And if Tabitha were inside, how would Annetta explain herself?

With trembling hands she unbarred the door and tried

each key in turn before finding the right one. She swung the door open. "Tabitha?"

Silence. And a fireplace with cold ashes.

She stepped back into the corridor. Drat, she should have let Franka out first, so she could help. *I'll do that next time, ha. At least it's easily remedied.* Keys in hand, she stepped towards Room Two.

She was just sidling past the two snoring guards outside her room when the stairwell door swung open and a man stepped through. She jumped, stifling a squeak.

Settlers' bowels, a captain! It was the big captain she'd seen on the journey with Silvers, the one who'd gone to collect Shelley. Was he in on some plot with Silvers?

He frowned as he strode towards her, his gaze vigilant. "What's going on?"

"Oh, I'm so glad you're here," cried Annetta. She clutched her chest with one hand while the other dropped the keys on top of Vincent. As they slid to the floor, she raised her voice over the jangle. "A man broke into my room." She waved her arm wildly towards Tabitha's room, its door ajar. "Must have overcome the guards. I slipped past—"

"Quiet, woman!" He gripped her wrist and dragged her away from the fallen guards towards the stairs. *Argh, I've no powder left. And he's too fast, never mind too tall.*

He stopped in the stairwell, leaving the door open a crack and peering through it. "You said someone broke into your room, but you're dressed as an infirmier. And I remember you travelling with Silvers. So why're you here?"

Drat, the man was too observant. "Um, I came here with young Samuel, one of the prisoners—"

Even though he kept his eye on the corridor, she could

feel his glare. "They're *residents*, not prisoners."

"Right, of course. Residents. Anyway, so they gave me a room here. I think one of the pris—er, residents escaped his room and overpowered the guards. He was dressed in white. Might have been coming after me because I'm a physician."

"Was he armed?"

Should he be? How could someone overpower two guards unarmed? What if this guy calls for reinforcements? Argh, what if Paul and Vincent wake up while we're talking–

"Well?" When she whimpered, his impatient expression softened. "Look, don't go to pieces on me. You're lucky I arrived and can deal with this, but you have to keep it together. Was the man armed?"

"Um, no." She gulped, sweating as her thoughts raced. "But he was big and fast. Nearly as big as you. I'm not sure you could—"

The captain straightened up, muscles flexing. "I can handle him. Stay here."

"No, I'd feel safer coming with you." She clung to his arm, but he brushed her off.

"Follow if you must, but keep out of the way." He opened the door and strode towards the room, muttering, "Why do I attract these neurotic types..."

When he paused by the two guards, her breathing shallowed. What if he spotted the keys? He'd just lock the nonexistent prisoner in, and then she'd be in trouble. But he prodded Vincent with a toe, nodded in satisfaction at the guard's grunt and walked on to Tabitha's door. Annetta could have cheered.

He drew his sabre and said, "Stay back."

She held her breath.

He stepped inside.

As soon as his foot cleared the door, she pushed it shut and slid the bar home. She wiped sweaty palms on her overalls and stood, panting, until the pounding on the door prompted her to grab the keys and lock it.

"Sorry," she called through the hatch. "Need to go rescue someone."

"You're mad! Let me out!"

Wincing at the noise, Annetta shut the hatch, muffling the captain's outraged roars. Nearly tripping over Vincent, she scurried to Room Two and released Franka. She then opened her own door to be faced with a beaming Samuel.

"Can we start searching now?" he asked.

"Er... nearly." *Argh!*

Franka grinned and slapped Annetta on the shoulder. "I wondered what you were up to. Uh, who's in Tabitha's room doing all that shouting?"

"Don't ask."

"Wow." Holding his crumpled sketch, Samuel stared at the fallen guards. "How did you do that? Can you show me next time?"

Annetta fanned her face. "I really, *really* hope there isn't a next time."

"So, where now?" Franka peered at Vincent then knelt and undid his jacket. "This one's nearer my size. Give us a hand, will ya?"

They tugged Vincent's uniform off and Samuel said, "They're in the basement. Remember the big cave with all the tunnels? Where I wanted to play hide and seek? That's where they're hiding."

"Both Tabitha and Captain Shelley?" asked Annetta. The cells might not have been adjacent.

Samuel nodded.

Franka's brows drew together. "I guess that makes things simpler, but if we need to choose... Tabitha first. Jonathan would insist on it." After disappearing briefly into her room, she returned wearing Vincent's uniform and holding a piece of string. She tied the two guards up and grabbed a truncheon. "That'll delay them. Well done."

Annetta beamed, but then she remembered the main challenge was yet to come. "Let's go."

They headed for the stairs.

Jonathan opened his eyes when multiple footsteps sounded in the corridor, and the key rattled in the lock.

Three guards approached.

"Time to go, Shelley." The first guard unlocked his chains.

He stood, swaying, and the guards grabbed his arms. He groaned through the gag, and tears filled his eyes as his shoulder crunched.

"Move, they're waiting."

They shoved him along the corridor, and he glanced into Tabitha's cell as he passed. Eyes wide, she shook her head then jabbed her hands downwards to indicate a metal box by her feet. It matched the one in Silvers' pocket. She pointed at the door. What did she mean? Did the poor child think he could help her escape? He sighed, his uninjured shoulder slumping. Their last communication ever, and he couldn't understand what she wanted to say. Nor could he tell her he was sorry.

The group of guards escorted him away from the prison corridor, and one asked, "Shouldn't one of us stay behind, to watch the girl?"

"No," came the reply. "He wants us all with Shelley." The guard spat on the floor. "This one hardly seems dangerous, all snivelling like that, but hey, we're not being paid to make decisions."

Jonathan's neck tensed at the idea of leaving a prisoner unmonitored. What if she became ill and needed help? But maybe it was for the best, with her jailers being more of a danger to her than anything else. Well, anything apart from that accursed poisoning device Silvers had planted in her cell. That was probably why he'd given the orders for all the guards to leave.

Annetta skittered down the stairs behind Franka and Samuel, her heart in her mouth. What had she landed in? What trouble lay ahead?

At Franka's upraised hand she stopped, grabbing Samuel by the shoulder. His body shook with suppressed giggles while she winced and held her breath. Footsteps climbed the stairs towards them, then a door creaked open, the footsteps passing through. She sagged with relief.

At the foot of the basement stairs—beside the room where she'd been interviewed on her arrival here—they halted again. Over the pulse rushing in her ears, Annetta heard a faint clinking and echoing footsteps. Franka flattened herself against the wall with Samuel while Annetta peered through a crack in the stairwell door.

A group of guards walked past the door, familiar from her journey with Silvers and her brief visit here earlier today. They clustered around their limping prisoner. *Shelley.* Head bowed, hands chained behind his back, a sheen of sweat on his forehead, he didn't look like a monster. He looked like a man in pain, gagged and with a bruised face.

A victim. She clenched her fists, blinking away tears. So much for Silvers' claims about humane treatment. This was all wrong.

"Shouldn't one of us stay behind, to watch the girl?" asked a guard.

"No..." The rest of the reply was lost in the scuff of feet and clink of chains.

After the guards had left, they crept into the cavernous basement.

"Which way?" whispered Franka.

Samuel pointed across the expanse. "That's where I saw them."

"Good lad." Franka's grin was visible even under the dim light. "And good timing too. Still, let's stay quiet. No point taking chances."

Jonathan made no resistance as Silvers' guards marched him through the basement and up the ramp. His eyes teared up again at the afternoon sunshine, but they were only outside for the couple of minutes it took to walk to the Council building.

Inside, they led him down a hallway to the courtroom, then up an aisle to its centre. They pushed him into a chair bolted to the floor. After chaining his wrists to the armrests, the guards left.

With his arms in front of him, Jonathan's shoulder didn't hurt so much, and he could pay more attention to his surroundings.

He'd never been here before, and he looked around, seeking anything—or anyone—that might help him. The chair to which he was chained stood in the centre of a ring-shaped table, a gap at his back. Four seats were set around it, currently empty. Calibrated stimulus generators marked each place. They'd be for the mind readers. The judges' bench in front of him was already occupied by a few Council members: Silvers and Martek on the left, Gauntlett on the right. Jonathan's jaw clenched at Silvers' brief smirk, at the complacency with which the scientist patted his jacket pocket. No help there, obviously. Behind the central position, which was currently empty, stood a second door.

A few rows of concentrically arranged seats occupied the rest of the room. A dozen or so captains were scattered around the seating, city captains to a man. The only one he had more than a passing acquaintance with was Lester. Of Susanna there was no sign. Had she been too busy to attend? Maybe it was a mercy she wouldn't witness his humiliation. *Oh, Susanna. I wish we could have had more time. I wish I had been more bold.*

Lester threw him an anxious glance. Could she really have run into trouble? Surely not. She'd always been so law-abiding, and Silvers would have made some barbed comment. Anyway, David would keep an eye out for her, after he'd checked up on—

Tabitha. Sweat trickled down Jonathan's back. If David found Tabitha missing, what would he do? He'd raise the alarm, of course, and Silvers would trigger the device. *I hope David decided to go home first, that he didn't think there was any urgency.*

The usher opened the door behind the bench, and Hastings walked in. Jonathan tensed. It was time to perform.

"All stand!" shouted the usher.

With a scrape of chairs and rustling of clothing, everyone bar Jonathan stood.

His eyes widened as the scowling Hastings moved to

stand at a seat towards one side. *That must mean–*

Queen Eleanor appeared behind Hastings and glided to the central chair. Jonathan nearly choked on his gag. Why was *she* bothering to attend? Had she run out of other amusements? She sat and nodded at the usher. A faint frown crossed Silvers' face.

"All sit!" roared the man, and they did.

The queen cleared her throat and addressed the room. "Today we have the trial of Jonathan Shelley. Mr Shelley stands accused of murdering Colin Bookman, who was found dead while on guard duty in the Keep. As all of you are aware of the existence of powers, we can dispense with the customary pretences. Other than that, usual court procedure is to be followed. Is that clear to everyone?"

Lester raised a trembling hand. "Your Majesty..."

A tinge of pink touched the queen's cheeks. "Here, captain, I am not the monarch but a judge. 'Your Honour' will suffice. I have set aside my role as queen and am just as bound by the law in this room as you are."

"Yes, ma'am." The young captain gulped. "I mean, Your Honour. If a friend of Mr Shelley's was unable to attend today, due to being, er, in custody or something, wouldn't that be a bit unfair on him, since she couldn't vouch for his character? You might take that into account?"

Jonathan blinked. Custody? *She?* Was he talking about Susanna?

Silvers barked a laugh. "What, trust a prisoner to give a character witness on the suggestion of a former rent—"

"Silence," Queen Eleanor snapped at Silvers. "The captain asked a valid question and I'm providing him an answer." She addressed Lester. "I'm sorry, that doesn't affect the proceedings. Anything else?"

"No, ma'am." Lester hunched down in his chair, his gaze on the floor.

On turning her attention to Jonathan, she half-rose, eyes flashing. "Who gagged the prisoner? And why? Remove it, immediately!"

A court guard rushed over, tried to untie the knot, then hacked the gag off with a folding knife. Jonathan worked his aching jaw and sipped from a glass of water that another guard held to his lips.

Queen Eleanor thumped the bench top. "I'm still waiting for an answer. Why was he gagged?"

Silvers stood and bowed. "Your Majesty, I had to gag him so he didn't foment trouble. I was simply concerned for security."

She glared at him. "That's ridiculous, Scientist Silvers!"

"Well," murmured Hastings, "a certain level of prudent restraint is acceptable. Especially for prisoners known to be violent."

The queen's glare turned on Hastings for a moment. "Let us proceed with the trial. The defendant shall enter his plea, following which the four mind readers will take up their positions, ready to receive his testimony. Once—That is, *if* he is found innocent, he will be free to make a counterclaim." She nodded at Jonathan. "Jonathan Shelley, how do you plead in regard to the murder of Colin Bookman?"

Jonathan's heart raced, and his hands gripped the armrests. *For Tabitha's sake.* "I plead guilty."

Silvers smiled and nodded. Gauntlett shook his head. The other captains stared, even Lester.

She paled. "What?"

He took a deep breath, and at a volume that rivalled the usher's, he repeated, "I plead guilty!"

Chapter 29

Twitching at every step, Annetta followed the others across the worn stone floor. Samuel led them through an opening in the wall. On one side of a narrow corridor lay four cell doors with a couple of benches opposite. The place was unguarded, but a metallic tapping came from one of the cells.

Franka peered through the hatch in the door and waved. "The bastard has her gagged and chained to the wall in there, just like in Samuel's drawing. These don't look like proper cells, likely converted from storage areas. But we still need keys. Samuel, you look low, under the benches. I'll look high. Annetta, check the other cells, just on the off-chance." She snorted. "Let's hope those idiot guards have left them behind."

Two of the cells were locked. The third contained only the odour of sweat and despair. Annetta's shoulders straightened. She was doing the right thing.

"I found something on the floor." Samuel held up a palm-sized metal box with two buttons on one surface. He shook it then handed it to Franka. "Do you think there's a key inside?"

"Mmm..." came from the cell.

"Seems odd, but let's open it up." Franka turned it over in her hands, pressing the buttons one by one and then together. She prodded and pressed the other plain sides before shaking her head.

There was a rattle of chains and a louder "Mmmmf..."

"Just a second," called Franka. "We're working on it. Ah, bugger it, let's not be delicate." She threw the box down on the stone floor then stamped on it. The metal cracked. Picking it up, she peeled it open like a boiled egg and peered at the fragments.

"Anything?" asked Annetta.

"Nah." Franka scowled. "Why would someone leave an empty box lying around? As a joke? A distraction? Any more ideas?"

Creaking and jangling from the cell prompted Annetta to look through the hatch. Tabitha, gagged, wrists chained to the wall, bounced on the bunk and pointed at the door.

"We're still looking." She tried to smile.

Tabitha frowned and shook her fists at the door.

"We just have to find the key. Be patient."

"Mmmm!"

"Look, Tabitha." She gripped the bars of the hatch. "We can't just pull the door—"

The door swung open. Annetta gawped.

Franka trotted over. "Well done."

"But I didn't—"

"I meant Tabitha." Franka grinned. "Looks like she's been practising her power. Picked the lock. I should have expected that after she strung that rope between our windows. Let's help her get these chains off."

While Annetta untied Tabitha's gag and Samuel chattered to her, Franka disappeared in search of some tools.

As soon as the gag was off, Tabitha gasped, "I can't believe you survived that poison box! I'd just managed to move it out of the cell when you arrived."

Knuckles whitening, Annetta twisted the cloth of the gag while Samuel said, "The box I found? Franka broke it.

It was empty."

Tabitha's fists clenched. "Empty? It was a trick!" She yanked on the chain attaching her manacles to the wall. "We need to help Jonathan. Jed's blackmailing him into pleading guilty."

I plead guilty.

There, Jonathan had said it, cast the dice to roll as they would. Things were out of his hands now, and others would decide his fate.

Lester gaped at him. The lad might never learn the truth of it, and neither would Susanna. It was some small consolation that Tabitha knew Jonathan's reasons. However, she'd have to take care whom she told. Maybe one day...

A buzz of voices grew, settling only when the usher shouted, "Silence!"

Queen Eleanor leaned on the bench, a loose tendril of hair sticking damply to her face. "Let me be clear about this. You, Jonathan Shelley, are pleading guilty to the murder of Colin Bookman."

"Er, yes. Your Honour." Hadn't he just said that?

"Are you sure?"

"Yes, I am." Jonathan's brow wrinkled. Why was she questioning it? It wasn't as if he'd claimed innocence. Wouldn't she be pleased at the short trial, so she could go off and play with her blimps?

She clenched her fists, closed her eyes.

"Your Honour," murmured Hastings. "Since Shelley has pled guilty, we should proceed to the sentence."

"Do you wish to appeal for clemency?" Her voice was plaintive as she regarded Jonathan.

He swallowed. "No."

She frowned. "I think we need to know more about your reasons, before deciding on the sentence."

Hastings coughed. "As the defendant has pled guilty and is not appealing for clemency, his reasons are irrelevant." At the queen's glare, he added, "You did state that you are bound by the law in this court. No Queen's Discretion. The only exception would be if he were suspected of a worse—"

Her hand sliced through the air, cutting off Hastings' words. "Quite right, Councillor Hastings. Thank you for reminding me of the law. I shall proceed."

The councillor relaxed into his chair, a faint smile on his lips.

The queen straightened. "Jonathan Shelley, I accuse you of the murder of Frederick Samson. How do you plead?"

Jonathan gaped. Who—"King Frederick? You think I murdered *King Frederick?* What idiocy is this? Of course not! Uh, Your Honour."

Silvers scowled, placing a finger over his jacket pocket. Jonathan glared back, although sweat broke out on his forehead. *Don't take this out on Tabitha.*

"Very well," said the queen. "Since you have entered a plea of innocence in regard to this charge, I call upon the mind readers to take their places." She nodded at the usher. "Summon the Royal Chief Guard."

The usher slipped out, and four captains filed forwards to take their seats around Jonathan. Silvers' scowl deepened. *Shit!* Tabitha was unprotected and alone. If Silvers' blackmail were exposed, he'd kill her out of spite.

Annetta was relieved to find Tabitha's wrists uninjured. "Who put these on you?"

"Jed. Said he was taking me to see Jonathan, then his guards jumped me when we got here." She chewed her lip. "Though he did check the cuffs weren't too tight."

"Found something!" Franka returned, grinning, with a chisel and hammer. "Plenty of these lying around, what with all the junk down here." She inspected Tabitha's handcuffs, shook her head and instead picked a spot on the chain near the wall, setting the chisel to one of the links. "It's weaker here."

"Hurry!" Tabitha hauled on the chain once more as Franka hammered the chisel. "We need to get to the Council building." The chain broke, and she staggered back, detached pieces cascading to the floor.

"Better get there then." Franka frowned. "Kids, just give me a moment while I speak with Annetta."

Tabitha and Samuel left the cell.

What did Franka want now? "Um, you need me for something?"

"Yeah. This power I have, of scaring people. Might help us get to the court without a fight. But..."

Annetta's palms grew clammy. "You need a trigger. Pain."

Franka nodded and rolled up her trouser leg. "You being a physician and all... See, I have a recent scar on my leg. If I squeeze it—or someone else does—it can trigger my power. But I can't reach it and remain prepared for a scrap. So you'll need to."

"Alright. We're out of options." Her brow wrinkled. But how had Tabitha managed?

The four of them jogged back through the cavern and

up the ramp that Franka said led to the Royal Compound. Annetta's slippers scuffed on the paving stones, and she blinked at the spray from a fountain. Her back prickled as they approached the square stone Council building. Nobody stood on guard outside.

She clenched her jaw to keep her teeth from chattering when they entered the foyer. Its peaceful coolness echoed with soft footsteps and the rustle of papers while clerks carried documents back and forth.

Franka approached the reception desk manned by a sleepy girl sorting papers. "Where's today's trial taking place? The Bookman murder."

The girl consulted a notebook and pointed. "Main courtroom, last room on the left. Er, should you be here?"

"I'm escorting special witnesses." Franka's voice was firm.

"That's fine then." The receptionist returned to her filing.

"You've got the right tone to be a captain," muttered Annetta as they moved along the corridor.

"Bureaucrats!" Franka snorted. "They never really pay attention."

Heart hammering, Jonathan wriggled his arms in their chains. But he couldn't avoid contact with the mind readers as they switched on their boxes and gripped his hands. ... *thinkaboutsomethingelse...* Sweat streamed down his face at the assault on his mind, at the army of captains trampling through his thoughts.

With a groan, he squeezed his eyes shut, focussing on one idea. *I killed Bookman. I killed Bookman.*

One by one, the intruders withdrew from his mind. He

sagged, breath rasping.

"I apologise, Your Honour," said the spokesman for the mind readers. "None of us has been able to make out any of his thoughts."

Ha, I withstood you. He glanced at Silvers. The smile had returned to the scientist's face. He met Jonathan's eye. Extending a fist, thumb pointing down, he mouthed, *Plead guilty.* Jonathan's jaw tightened, and he nodded.

Queen Eleanor's eyebrows rose. "Why not? Does he have some kind of natural resistance?"

"No, we've all mind-read him before. I can't explain it."

Silvers' voice slid into the debate. "I apologise once again, Your Majesty. Because Shelley's power is so dangerous, I gave him a drug before the trial. One that would suppress his power so everyone here would be kept safe. Looks like it had a secondary effect of preventing mind reading. I don't regret my actions though—he tried to kill me earlier and only failed because of the drug. Isn't that right, Shelley?"

"Yeah, Silvers." He bared his teeth. "A shame I failed. I plead guilty to that one too, if you want to make a charge. Oh, and I've changed my mind about that other charge, about killing King Frederick. I'm guilty."

The queen scowled at him. "Do you appreciate the gravity of what you're saying? This isn't all a big joke. Regicide is a capital offence."

"I'm aware of that." His heart raced, and his hands trembled. A capital offence was good, wasn't it? Immediate execution. No need to cave in to more of Silvers' demands, and it would leave Silvers no reason to harm Tabitha. Why had this become so difficult? They'd both gone too far to back out now. He pushed through the fear and said through dry lips, "I'm just... making things easier for everyone. Getting this over with."

"Very well. You've rejected every opportunity I've offered." Her lips tightened. "Let's do this formally. Jonathan Shelley, how do you plead in regard to the murder of Frederick Samson?"

Jonathan's shirt stuck to his back with sweat. *Getting this over with.* "I..." His gut churned, and the words caught in his throat. "I... plead..."

Annetta's pulse quickened when they reached the end of the corridor. Two city guards stood outside a wooden door larger than the others. Hands gripping their truncheons, they straightened as Franka approached.

"Last minute witnesses for the trial," said Franka, eyeing the truncheons. "Let us through."

The guard on the left frowned. "We received no communication."

The other said, "Court's in session already. No interruptions unless the judge orders it." His gaze lit on Tabitha and her chains, and his eyes widened. "Hang on, you shouldn't be—"

"Now, Annetta!" snapped Franka.

Annetta crouched and grasped Franka's calf, squeezing as hard as she could. "Sorry, sorry, sorry..." Though whether she was sorry for Franka, or the guards, or herself even, she couldn't have said.

"Ah, no!" The first guard's truncheon fell from his hand and he fled up the corridor.

The other guard paled but stood his ground, lifting his weapon in a shaking hand. "N-n-no... entry..."

Franka smiled at him. "Wanna bet on it? Though with

your baton drooping like that..."

He swung his truncheon, and she skipped backwards away from the still-crouching Annetta. The guard staggered forwards a few steps, leaving the door at his back exposed.

What are you waiting for, silly! Grabbing Samuel and Tabitha's hands, Annetta slipped behind the combatants towards the door. She set her teeth and shoved it open. Her momentum drove her in a few steps, just in time to hear, "I... plead..."

There was no time to find an official. She'd have to act *now*. She gulped in a breath.

"Stop the trial!" Her shout echoed off the walls, partly masking the scuffle outside.

All heads turned towards her, apart from Shelley's. He was chained to a chair in the centre with his back to her.

Face flaming, she shrank under the attention. "Um..."

With a scrape of chairs, a dozen captains leapt up, hands on sabre hilts. The floor thudded with their footsteps while Annetta stepped back, dry-mouthed and shaking. But instead of approaching her to drag her away, they lined up between Shelley and a table at the room's far end.

Tabitha pushed past and ran to Shelley's chair, manacles jangling. "Jonathan!" She draped her arms over his head and hugged him to her chest.

"Ungh... Tabitha... My dear girl..." His voice shook.

"What is the meaning of this interruption?" The demand came from a black-clad young woman seated behind the table.

Tabitha jerked her chin at Silvers. "*He* kidnapped me and put me in a cell! So Jonathan would do what he said!"

"And I'm sure he killed Bookman," added Shelley in a muffled voice. "I certainly didn't. I'd like to withdraw my plea."

Red-faced and sweating, Silvers surged to his feet. Mouth open, Annetta waited for him to explain. Surely there had been some miscommunication or mistake that would make sense. Instead, he pushed over the white-haired man beside him, knocking him into the woman. As they crashed to the floor, Silvers leapt for the door behind them.

He pulled the door open. A large man wearing red stood outside, hand raised as if to knock. Both men jerked back a step.

"Take him down, Paton!" shouted the woman.

Paton's fist drove forwards, and Annetta could have sworn she felt the impact in her bones. Silvers slammed back against the table and collapsed.

Flexing his hand, Paton stepped into the room. He dropped a coil of rope on the table and offered the woman his arm. "What now?"

She clambered to her feet and pointed at Silvers. "Never mind me. Tie this one up. The rope isn't needed for Captain Shelley."

At the reminder that Shelley was injured, Annetta winced. *Be professional.* "Samuel, let's sit you down and I'll get to work. Tabitha, I need to see to, er, Jonathan's shoulder." She walked towards the prisoner's chair. "He's hurt. Can you move away, please?"

"Unchain him," ordered the woman. "And remove the girl's handcuffs. Tabitha, is it? I saw you in the rooftop garden once."

"You did?" Tabitha kissed Shelley's unbruised cheek, which reddened. "We went there for a picnic."

Annetta blinked. Was that when Samuel had drawn them?

One of the captains, a dark-haired young man, came forwards. "I'll look after the children."

He's very *good looking.* "Thank you."

A couple of guards removed Tabitha's manacles and Shelley's restraints. She clung to his hand until the captain led her away to a nearby row of seats, Samuel following them.

Annetta nodded at the woman in black. Best to be polite. "Thanks, miss. Could I have scissors and bandages, please?"

The handsome captain leaned forwards and murmured, "You should call her 'Your Honour'."

"What? Oh." The woman was the judge? *Gah, I wish I'd known that sooner.* Annetta fanned her face. "Sorry, you look so young. Um, Your Honour."

"Fetch the medical kit." The judge turned to Paton. "Your timing is impeccable."

He shook his head and snorted. "Your Majesty, how do you do it? I can't leave you for even an hour and you run into problems."

Your Majesty? Heat flooding through her, Annetta focussed on her patient. "Captain Shelley, let's see to your shoulder. And, um, sorry about earlier."

"I never thought I'd be jealous of a royal guard." His voice slurred. "That punch was beautiful..."

Chapter 30

Jonathan's shoulder itched under its strapping, but he was too ensconced in the plush armchair to move. Besides, he didn't want to dislodge Susanna from her perch on the arm of his chair.

He blinked at the swirling patterns on her chiffon blouse: purple, lilac and red. Glorious royal colours. And nearly transparent too!

Her cheek dimpled as she glanced at him, and she squeezed his good hand. *Did I say that out loud?* He let his head drop back against the cushion, closing his eyes. "Where am I?"

"Royal library. It's a bit of a squeeze with all of us."

"Squeeze? I like that." He rubbed her knuckle with his thumb.

"Captain Shelley, *please* concentrate," said a man.

Opening his eyes, Jonathan focussed on the red blur in front of him, which resolved itself into Paton: eyepatch, bandaged hand and all. "Wonderful punch."

"Thank you." Paton spoke over his shoulder. "Will he be like this much longer?"

"Sorry. I, um, overdid the dosage. He'll be fine after a night's sleep."

"Annetta?" He peered in her direction. "You drugged me *again?*"

"Yeah, had to manipulate your shoulder. And sorry again about the other thing."

His forehead creased. "What other thing?"

"You know, the... other drug, with Silvers."

Silvers! Susanna hopped out of the way as Jonathan lurched forwards, sliding out of the chair and ending up on his knees.

Paton, shaking his head, propped him back in the chair. "It's fine, Shelley, he's safely in the Council's prison. A proper one, not like that makeshift dungeon where you were held."

"Good. Bastard." Jonathan's eyelids drooped.

"I think we'd better start," said a woman off to one side. "I want to go over the evidence quickly, while it's still fresh in our minds. Susanna, can I rely on you to inform Captain Shelley of anything he might be too, er, preoccupied to remember?"

"That's fine, Eleanor."

Queen Eleanor? Only Susanna's hand on his shoulder stopped Jonathan from trying to stand. He opened his eyes a crack.

"The mind readers examined Silvers." Eleanor's lips turned down. "He was quite open about his actions and even took pride in them. Susanna and Lester, you were on the right track. He schemed to curse people deliberately, claiming we should have more people with powers. He impounded Captain Shelley's assets—legitimately—but then used them to fund his pursuit, including bribery of several guards." Her voice grew hard. "They have been dealt with. And yes, it was Silvers who poisoned poor Bookman, in order to frame Captain Shelley and keep him in captivity permanently for experiments."

"Just call me Jonathan," mumbled Jonathan. "Otherwise I can't call you Eleanor."

A girl giggled. *Tabitha.* He smiled.

Paper rustled as Eleanor consulted some notes. "Then there was his kidnapping of Tabitha, although his threat to Jonathan of a remote control poison box was a bluff. At least he didn't stoop that low, but maybe only because there's no *techne* for that. Going further back, Silvers had previously blackmailed Kenneth Staunton into retirement. Kenneth has something to say about that."

"That's right." Staunton's voice was firm, not the quavering tones Jonathan remembered from their last encounter. "I must apologise to Captain Shelley for misleading him when he visited, but the situation required it."

"That's me, fall guy for everything, blundering around like an idiot," Jonathan grumbled.

"I'll start with King Frederick," said Staunton. "He and I discussed the curse several times, regarding the mechanisms of transmission and also the powers gained by the afflicted. He was convinced the realm was approaching a crisis and that more people with powers would be part of the solution. He asked for my help."

"Hang on." Jonathan squinted at Staunton, who was sitting opposite him. "King Frederick asked *you* to curse more people? It was Silvers doing that, not you."

Eleanor, seated to Staunton's left, winced.

Staunton's lips tightened. "You know how the curse is viewed, and the reaction of ordinary citizens. How would you feel if I told you I was deliberately cursing people?"

"I'd kill—Oh." Jonathan pushed himself forwards with his good arm, thankful for Susanna's hand on his back. "You weren't a drunkard at all! You set Silvers up to do your dirty work, letting him think he had a hold over you, and all the time you were directing his movements. I bet it was on your advice he got Lester to make that clumsy brainwashing attempt on the guards." He ignored Lester's offended yelp. "The brainwashing would fail, and it would draw attention to his crimes. Silvers was more of a fall guy than I was. And you dropped enough clues that he'd be found out eventually. I *knew* there was something odd about you!"

"Now you begin to understand. King Frederick and I argued for months, and it was purely because he had such a strong belief that I yielded and started such a project. In fairness to your father, Eleanor, he didn't suggest the setup with Silvers. That was my scheme. Silvers has a callousness that was, er, necessary for the research. I deeply regret that the situation got away from me so badly, beyond laboratory experiments. I'd thought that after a certain time period I, or Lady Nelson, could request his dismissal. Nobody would regret losing Silvers."

Jonathan clenched his fists. "Or he might have been murdered by someone like me. I don't like you, Staunton."

"Sometimes I don't like myself. I really hadn't imagined that Silvers would stoop to theft, blackmail and murder." Staunton coughed. "Ah, Eleanor. Did you happen to find your father's notes?"

"No." Eleanor screwed up her face. "I had gone through his desk and his files after his passing. They were empty. Suspiciously empty, come to think of it, given how often I saw him writing. And Kenneth, I appreciate your tact, but I want to be fair to *you*. You told me my father intended to keep the current system of training with pain. The novel methods were something you supported."

Staunton sat back. "That's a damn shame about the notes. I know what he told me, what he believed." He winced slightly. "Your mind readers couldn't find any spots where I might have forgotten something. So you don't have any information about what drove him to have such a strong conviction."

Susanna leaned forwards. "I may have an idea about that, if we could call on someone else's help. We're meeting again tomorrow, aren't we?"

Eleanor nodded. "This is a right mess."

"Indeed," said Staunton. "Silvers is in custody. You can put a stop to his experiments, pretend they never existed. Will you?"

She rubbed her temples. "I need to think about this. My immediate instinct is to stop it, but my father must have had a reason." She straightened. "Of course, he may have been mistaken. However, I wholeheartedly support a shift in the training of the afflicted, away from this obsession with pain. Kenneth, the mind readers tell me you're sincere in this desire. Will you rejoin the scientists in the Keep?"

"Delighted," he murmured.

Jonathan glared at him. "I'll be watching you."

Eleanor drummed her fingers on the table. "Fellows is there already, but to make up three we need to replace not just Lady Nelson, but Silvers."

Jonathan's scowl deepened. "And not with an evil bastard this time. Uh, Your Majesty. Eleanor."

She smiled. "No fear of that. I want someone who treats the afflicted humanely and understands what they're going through with their training."

He stared. Where would she find someone like that?

"There's never been a scientist with powers," she said. "A grave mistake, in my opinion. Susanna, you've done amazing work with Tabitha, helping her to control her power. Are you willing to take on the post?"

"I would be honoured," said Susanna.

Scientist Susanna? It has a ring to it.

Staunton stroked his beard. "And who is to be Chief Scientist? It's a challenging position, requiring not just scientific knowledge but political experience..." He eyed Eleanor's frown.

"Thank you for your comments, Kenneth, but I don't think you would be suitable. I'm sure your intentions were noble, but your plan led to a lot of suffering, even if that was directly caused by Silvers." She raised her chin. "No doubt you'll understand that the, ah, *political* consequences of your actions becoming widely known could be significant."

"So... Fellows?"

Nice chap, but a bit soft. Jonathan could almost see the cogwheels turning in Staunton's mind.

"No." Eleanor's lips firmed. "I shall appoint Susanna. With her direct practical experience—and of course her *special* ability—she's the best person for the post. I hope you understand."

Chief *Scientist Susanna? I hope she's not too elevated for me now.*

Staunton's jaw clenched. "Perfectly, Your Majesty."

"Good. Now, all this talk hasn't shed light about my father's death, although that wasn't the purpose of this meeting. Today's incidents had to be dealt with first. It's getting late, so I suggest we resume tomorrow morning. Artur will be able to join us then, after his odd turn earlier while I was at the trial. Martha tells me he's still asleep." Eleanor regarded her hands. "He's had... health problems recently, and I don't want to push him. And I think we all have enough to reflect on overnight. Kenneth, could you please make sure Lester finds his way out?"

Lester stood and tugged at his collar. "Thanks. I've never been in the palace before—I'd hate to get lost. Do you need me to come back tomorrow, Your Honour?" He slapped his forehead. "I mean, Eleanor."

She laughed. "No, that's fine. I don't want to take you away from your regular duties. Right... Annetta, Franka, Samuel and Tabitha, Paton will escort you back to your quarters in the Keep. You'll be provided with keys to your rooms."

"I'll make sure of it," growled Paton.

"Oh!" said Annetta. "I, um, locked someone in Tabitha's room earlier. A captain. I hope he's not too mad. I mean, I hope he's alright."

With an eyeroll, Paton stood. "I'll sort that too."

Jonathan's eyes drifted closed again as Paton led the others out.

"Come along, Jonathan." It was Susanna's voice.

He groaned. "Can't I sleep in this chair?"

"No, you won't be able to move in the morning." She took his hand and tugged gently. "It's not far."

Enjoying the touch of her hand on his elbow, he struggled to his feet. He followed her down a corridor, up a flight of stairs and along another corridor. "Are we nearly there yet?" *I could even sleep on this carpet.*

She laughed and opened a door. "We're here."

After allowing her to pull him inside, he gazed around at the carved walnut writing desk, the chairs and brocade-upholstered chaise longue. *Damn, it's too short for me. But I won't complain. Not if it means I'm close to her.* "Where are we?"

"The suite Eleanor's provided for my use. For *our* use, now. And no, I don't plan for you to sleep on the chaise longue. Doesn't take a mind reader to tell what you're thinking."

His breath caught as he gazed into her eyes. "You're alright with sharing a, uh, room?"

She dimpled. "Of course. Otherwise I'd have requested another suite."

"I mean, I'm not in a great state." He waved at the strapping. "I've been imprisoned, drugged, beaten up... I can't even dress without help."

Still smiling, she reached towards him, stroked his cheek with her thumb, and undid the top button of his shirt. "That, my dear Jonathan, is rather the point. What would you do without me? Come on, let's get you into a bath."

Safely back in her suite, Annetta sat with Tabitha and Franka at the dining table. They traded stories while Samuel demolished the last of the strawberry cake. What a difference it made, to be able to come and go freely. Paton was a marvel. When she'd asked him about the other residents on the floor, he'd frowned and said safety had to remain a priority. However, with a combination of Susanna's training and Annetta's remedies—*I must get cracking on batch production*—it should be possible to release most of the residents, eventually.

Tabitha nibbled a piece of flapjack. "I was lucky, though, and Jonathan prevented Jed from visiting me." She pulled a face. "Well, until Lady Nelson passed on."

Samuel wandered over to the desk, wiping sticky fingers on his overalls.

Jed. Annetta squirmed. What an idiot she'd been, falling for his words and false manner, blinded by his position. She'd overlooked so many things that didn't add up: the money he was throwing around, the guards he'd hired personally and his insistence that Captain Shelley had really tried to murder her, for a start. And someone else had borne the brunt of the damage. Poor Captain Shelley, and poor Tabitha... and poor lots of other people too, by the sounds of things. She'd have to make things as right as she could. Still, even though Silvers' motivations for bringing her to Ascar were wrong, her knowledge could be of use. She sighed. A return to Maldon wasn't on the cards just yet. But she could send a message and let them know she was thinking of them.

"One day soon, I'm going to punch that man." Franka flexed her wrists. "He won't know what's hit him. Actually, I want him to know that *I* hit him. I guess I'll need to make captain first, so I can visit prisoners officially. And after that, I want to get back to work. I've spent enough time in this heap. Tabitha, do you want to tag along when I go out on convoy?"

"Maybe." Tabitha tapped her chin. "But... I'll ask Jonathan first. He'll know what's best for me."

Franka grinned. "Of course he does. Captain Shelley's the best."

"Captain Shelley?" Samuel returned to the table, clutching a sheet of paper. "He's nice."

Everyone believed in him apart from me. Annetta glanced at the paper and blinked. Cheeks flaming, she snatched it from Samuel. What if Tabitha saw it? "Did you have to—"

"What's up?" Franka leaned over to peer at it, threw her head back and roared with laughter. "Well, someone's having fun."

"Can I have a look?" asked Tabitha.

Annetta gulped. Franka wouldn't see any harm in it, but—

Franka shook her head. "Sorry, kiddo. He'd be dreadfully embarrassed."

"Oh." Tabitha sighed. "I suppose he's in the bath, or something like that."

Franka's lips quivered. "Yeah. Something like that."

Lying in a soft bed for the first time in weeks, Jonathan opened his eyes and stared up at the moonlight glinting off a light fitting. He frowned and slid his good hand to the side, his fingers drifting over cool bed linen.

He turned his head towards the window. Silhouetted in the frame, Susanna faced outwards over the city.

"Problems sleeping?" he asked, slipping from the bed and joining her at the window. He stood behind her, wrapping his arm around her waist.

She leaned back against him. "Yes, too many things to think about."

He kissed her ear, nibbled his way down her neck, tasting salt. "Have I upset you?"

She shook her head. "No, not you. It's something else."

"I don't want to pry, but would it help to talk?"

Her voice trembled. "We'll need to discuss it in the morning. Meanwhile... let's go back to bed."

Chapter 31

The following morning, Jonathan scowled in the mirror while Susanna helped him into an indigo velvet robe. He looked like a right fop!

Eyes crinkling, she smiled and patted his chest. "You cut a fine figure."

"I do?" He couldn't see it himself, but if she liked it, he'd put up with a lot worse.

Hand in hand, they strolled back to the library.

Paton, standing behind Eleanor, smirked as they entered the room. "Looks like you're a bit more with us today, Shelley. Nothing like a"—he glanced at Eleanor—"good night's sleep to aid recovery."

"Good morning," said Artur from behind them, his voice tremulous.

The young engineer leaned against the doorframe, blinking with reddened eyes. Jonathan remembered the last time they'd met, over a leisurely dinner. Obviously Artur hadn't slept well either.

"I'm glad you're here, Artur," said Staunton from his seat beside Eleanor. "How did you get on after I left you to your practice?"

Susanna's hand tightened on Jonathan's. She said, "Can we discuss it later? It's... tricky."

Eleanor glanced up from her notes and frowned, then she stood as her gaze landed on Artur. "Do you want to recline on the sofa?"

"Thanks." Artur sank on to the sofa while the others arranged themselves around the table, leaving one space free.

A footman tapped on the door and announced, "Captain Honeyman."

Jonathan stroked Susanna's hand as he studied the newcomer, a young city captain whom he vaguely recognised from his rare forays to the captains' lounge. *I've certainly not seen him in the gymnasium. He doesn't look very robust.*

Honeyman bowed then pulled a monogrammed handkerchief from his pocket and dabbed his brow. "Sorry I'm late. They're a bit slow in the Checkpoint Building today. Seems they've lost some staff."

"Thank you for attending, Captain Honeyman," said Eleanor. "We're all on first-name terms here. Do you mind if I call you Richard?"

"What?" The man's eyebrows shot up. "Oh, if you wish, Your Majesty." With a pained expression, he sat down. "Ah, Eleanor. How may I be of assistance?"

Susanna spoke. "Eleanor's trying to locate documents that King Frederick may have written."

"*May* have written? You're not even sure they exist?"

Eleanor shook her head. "I'm fairly sure they did, although they may have been destroyed. This is a long shot, but it's important."

He pursed his lips. "What can you tell me about these hypothetical documents that may already have been destroyed?"

"They'd be on royal embossed notepaper and in my father's handwriting. Here are some samples." She slid a few sheets across the table to him.

"Right. My power works best with precisely described items, and this general search may be tricky. His handwriting's quite distinctive, fortunately, with those bold flourishes and strong underlines. I'll need, ah—" He blinked as Paton placed a calibrated stimulus generator before him and a second box in front of Susanna.

"Susanna's just going to hold your hand while you're working," said Eleanor. "She's got some ideas."

"She has? But she must know I'm not inter—" Richard looked at Jonathan and Susanna's entwined fingers and blushed. "Oh, not that. Right."

While Susanna and Richard prepared, Jonathan squinted at the Ascar street map laid out before them, blinking at his ignorance of the city. Maybe he could spend more time here. Just to get to know the place better.

With the boxes activated, Richard studied the notepaper and handwriting then closed his eyes. "Royal notepaper... handwriting..." He wriggled the fingers of his free hand. "Plenty in the palace, no surprise there. Council building has a fair amount. Smaller pieces scattered around." He opened his eyes. "Your Majesty, did your father often write to ordinary citizens?"

Eleanor pondered, tracing circles on the tabletop. "Damn. He did, as I do. Letters of thanks for public services, statements of support for good causes. That sort of thing."

"No way to narrow it down? I'm sensing a lot of locations here."

A memory niggled at Jonathan. "You can sense specific writing, can't you?"

Richard waggled a hand. "In a way. It's precision of description that I need. Such as a letter addressed to so-and-so, filling half the page, in such a colour ink..."

Jonathan persisted. "You could look for certain words,

maybe? Even certain letters? Perhaps 'JS' engraved on a gold disc?" He didn't bother hiding his snarl.

"Ah, yes." Richard flushed then paled. "Sorry. I really didn't know how he was doing it."

After Jonathan and Richard explained about the device Silvers had implanted in Jonathan, Eleanor's jaw firmed. "I guess it's coincidence you and Silvers have the same initials, but it sounds like he planned to use the discs more widely. Paton, add that to his record sheet and arrange to question him again. Returning to the business of the notes, Jonathan's suggestion could be useful. We're looking for references to danger to the realm, so related words..."

After some discussion, with heavy input from Staunton, they drew up a short list of terms King Frederick might have used such as "increasing danger", "crisis", and "invasion", none of which he would have used in regular correspondence. Jonathan snorted at this last one. Where was there to invade from? The realm was nearly surrounded by sea and rocky coastlines, its final border an expanse of barren wasteland. Supposedly the Settlers had crossed that wasteland—before it became a wasteland—and that was as good a story as any. But no further travellers had arrived in living memory.

A crease on Richard's forehead deepened as he searched. "I'm getting something. It's difficult, feels fragmented. But I've found a concentration of these words—" He grabbed a pen and stabbed the map. "Here!"

Richard slumped back in his chair while Susanna flicked off the boxes and removed her earclip.

Eleanor picked up the map. "I know that location! The house belongs to Isabel. But why would she collect my father's papers? I could understand *how*..."

Paton grimaced. "I warned you it would cause problems, but you insisted."

"Yes. I was foolish." She glanced around everyone. "Isabel suggested that since her house backed onto the Royal Compound, she build a back door, so she could come and go secretly. I approved it, and it *was* useful for some of our projects. But maybe she wasn't using it just for my benefit."

Jonathan's eyebrows rose. He'd wondered why she kept no servants. That must have been why Isabel remained in the family home by herself.

Eleanor frowned at the handwriting samples. "Why didn't she just request copies rather than stealing them? I'm sure he discussed his ideas with her more than he did with me. I admit, I... wasn't that interested." She chewed her lip. "I should have paid more attention."

Massaging her temples, Susanna nodded at Artur. "It's time to tell everyone."

Artur swung himself upright and addressed Eleanor. "After you left for Captain Shelley's trial, Kenneth suggested I try concentrating on an actual picture of someone we knew was passed on. To see if I could find out how they died. There was a painting of your father in the suite. So we tried it. I hope you don't mind." His shoulders hunched.

Eleanor shook her head. "Go on."

"I mean, it was a stroke of luck that... Well, Susanna helped."

Staunton tugged his beard. "And it worked? I saw you starting to get the idea, but I didn't want to distract you."

"Yes, we kept trying after you left. Finally King Frederick, er, spoke."

"About how he died?" The scientist's eyes widened.

"Not quite in those terms. I mean, it feels like I'm observing someone, not having a two-way chat. He had company. I can't tell who, but they'd had a bottle of wine together."

Eleanor stared at them. "He never drank when holding audiences. He always wanted to keep a clear head with visitors. We might have a glass with dinner, if it was only us, but that was all."

"It seemed like a regular conversation, but they started arguing. He was furious. Said something about duty and obeying orders." Artur winced and pressed a hand to his chest. "Then he complained of pain in his chest. Heat and sharpness. Burning." He sagged back on the couch. "He... didn't say anything after that."

"But his heart was fine. No reason for—" Eleanor's hand flew to her mouth. "Burning? *Isabel* killed him? You're lying!" She took a shaky breath. "Anyway, they did an autopsy. He wasn't... burnt up inside. So it couldn't have been her."

Poor Eleanor. Pushing away the image of Gerald's last smile, Jonathan cleared his throat. "I know *I* could kill someone by squeezing or blocking a blood vessel in his heart. Targeting it. Assuming Isabel's control is at least as good as mine, she might achieve a similar effect using, uh, heat sealing?"

"Fulguration?" suggested Staunton.

"I know what I sensed." Artur closed his eyes. "Don't know if it's true or not."

"At least we can try to get the notes back," said Paton. "Artur, you wait here."

The rest of them left the palace, and Paton led them to the Royal Compound's wall. Behind one of the patches of ivy stood a doorway barely two hand spans wide, and painted to match the adjacent stone.

As they approached it, Susanna held up a hand. "If she happens to be there, we'd better not confront her." She closed her eyes. "I sense... nobody inside. On you go, Jonathan."

The drug would last a full day, Annetta had said. Might as well find out. Placing his hand on the door, he called his power and directed it at the lock. *Ha!* It clicked, and he pushed the door open.

"I'll go first," said Eleanor. "If Susanna was mistaken and Isabel's inside, I think she would talk to me."

Paton scowled, eyeing the narrow passage and then his own bulk. "I suppose you won't allow me to enter ahead of you?"

She raised her chin. "No. This is my responsibility."

One by one, they filed in, to search Captain Isabel Hanlon's home.

My dear Eleanor,
If you're reading this, it means I messed up somewhere and won't be coming back. I don't want to leave you wondering, so this is, I guess, a confession.
You see, I killed your father. Not on a whim, but because, in my judgement as a human being, he was a danger. As king, he was in a position to do a lot of damage.
You'll see from the notes I've hidden with this letter that he believed we will be invaded, sometime over the next several years. I can't speak to the truth of that. His proposed solution was to manufacture more afflicted, more people like me. I could just about understand that idea though it sticks in my craw. What I couldn't countenance was his plan that curse victims be forced to undergo training, using blackmail and threats to their families,

and that the current training based around pain should continue as it's supposedly proven to be effective. I could be charitable and suggest your father's beliefs may have been born of desperation. But he would have transformed society, and not for the better.

Susanna tells me she has ideas for training powers that don't involve pain. I wish her luck with those. As to your father's claims, you can consult these notes and make your own decisions.

Rest assured, even if I am alive, I won't come after you if you conclude that the realm needs more people with powers. However, if you follow your father into cruelty, I shall not rest until you follow him into death.

Your affectionate cousin,
Isabel xx

The words blurred. Eleanor pulled out a handkerchief and wiped her eyes. "How did I not spot it? How could I have been so fooled?" First by her father. Then by her only remaining relative. *Oh, Isabel.*

Susanna touched her shoulder. "You weren't to know. And... she cared for you."

She even refused the throne when I offered it to her. Eleanor's grip tightened on the papers. Her father's notes lay under Isabel's letter, but she couldn't face reading them right now. Had the regal figure she'd looked up to all her life been just a false persona? Had she never really known him? Later, she would need to consider his words and the evidence, and to make her own decisions. Not just for herself, but for the realm. And if she decided wrongly, what would be the consequences?

"Your Majesty," said Paton, "we've not found anything else. I've suggested Staunton return home, and perhaps the rest of us could return to the palace? I'll ensure the back door is sealed after we pass through it."

Eleanor straightened. "She's been good at tidying up after herself, hasn't she? I wonder if she's still alive, out there in the wilderness."

"If I could manage, I'm sure she could too," said Jonathan.

But would that be a good thing or not? *I can't help wishing she's alive, but still...*

They walked back to the palace. Susanna and Jonathan disappeared to their suite, and Paton went to make his arrangements.

Artur lay snoring on the couch in the library, a rumpled blanket slipping towards the floor. She knelt and gently tucked it around him, almost smiling. He looked so young. She'd make things up to him, somehow.

Approaching footsteps echoed along the corridor: Paton's measured tread and another, lighter set. Eleanor stood.

"... You need to inform Her Majesty yourself," said Paton as he rapped on the doorframe.

Eleanor glanced at his companion, an unfamiliar city guard. "What is it?"

The man saluted. "Your Majesty, I work in the Council detention cells. Earlier today we found a deceased prisoner."

A sense of foreboding crept over her. "Who?"

"Jed Silvers. I can't understand it. He seemed perfectly fine on arrival. Nothing untoward in his cell. And when we examined the, uh, body, there wasn't a mark on him..."

Eleanor's pulse rushed in her ears.

... there wasn't a mark on him...

Acknowledgements

I'd like to thank everyone who contributed along the way while I have been writing, particularly all the good folks at Scribophile. Special mention must go to Philip Folk, who has been unstintingly encouraging, supportive and inspiring throughout the whole process.

Mistakes and inaccuracies are, of course, my own.

If you enjoyed reading this, maybe you'd like to take a few minutes to leave a review on your favourite book website. I'd also really appreciate word-of-mouth recommendations to any friends who might enjoy the world of Numoeath.

About the author

M.H. Thaung works in a pathology laboratory in London, England. When not supporting patient care or biomedical research, she enjoys putting characters in odd situations and seeing how they react.

If you're interested in exploring the world of *A Quiet Rebellion* further, feel free to drop by:

Website: **mhthaung.com**

Twitter: **@mhthaung**

Other books

*A **Quiet Rebellion: Guilt*** (Book 1) is available in ebook and print formats.

*A **Quiet Rebellion: Posterity*** (Book 3) is available in ebook and print formats.

*A **Quiet Rebellion: Short Tales*** is an ebook-only collection of flash fiction set in the same world.

*The **Diamond Device*** is a light-hearted steampunk adventure where an unemployed labourer and a thieving noble race to foil a bomb plot and avert a war.

Printed in Great Britain
by Amazon

80739187R00181